Printed in the United States of America
Second Chapter Publishing
First Printing, 2016

ISBN 978-0-9976677-07

Cover art Courtesy National Gallery of Art, Washington

Angelique's Storm

TABLE OF CONTENTS

Chapter One

It was early morning and the post-dawn sky still wore its cloak of red and gold as the black-curtained carriage slowly meandered along the cobblestone streets. The driver avoided cracking his whip, having found that a simple "yaw," was sufficient to guide the magnificent animals, who bore the weight of the buggy. They were stealthy and strong, these steeds, and seemed to avoid water-filled holes and other hazards by instinct. He often thought of the term "horse sense" as he drove the wealthy to their destinations. Sometimes it seemed that the stallions and mares had more intellect than those who held the money and power in this city. Guiding the horses off of the main road and onto the dirt path of the cemetery, he silently counted the rows until he reached the familiar spot. And they too, seemed to know that they had reached the right place, having taken this trip on so many a morning. They stopped short before the driver could even whisper "whoa." He slid from the high leather seat and paused to pet his equine colleagues before opening the door for his employer. He knew where his loyalties lay.

Angelique Chauvin Latour extended her gloved hand as she carefully descended from the carriage.

"Madame," the driver said, tipping his hat in a gesture of courtesy.

Without uttering a word, the woman slowly began the short walk to the large white tomb inscribed with the birth and death dates of her husband. "January 6, 1856," she whispered, kissing her fingertips and placing her hand on the engraved marble, "that's most certainly the day that I died, too."

"Jean Paul," she spoke his name, tears forming in her eyes, "how could you leave me so utterly alone?" It was a rhetorical question, and she knew it. Like so many of the details surrounding his death, she was only left to wonder. And perhaps that was why she made this regular morning pilgrimage. Although it defied all logic, she somehow expected to find the answers here, where the remains of her beloved rested. She prayed that he was at peace, although she had her doubts. The old ones say that an untimely death makes the soul restless, and it often prowls its earthly home in search of the door that will take it to the light of what lies beyond. That thought was more unsettling than losing him.

"Rest in peace, mon chèr," Angelique whispered, as she raised the black veil which covered her face to wipe the tears away with her linen handkerchief. "Je t'aime."

She paused to lovingly touch the tiny angel that denoted the other inhabitant of this ghostly home, her child. "Ma petite fille," she said in a barely audible voice. Her beloved daughter had perished only thirteen months earlier in the horror which was the yellow fever epidemic and yet, the grief was still so raw that she felt as though it had happened only yesterday.

Angelique thought back to that terrible time when she had stood watch over the child's sick bed, praying to the Blessed Mother to have pity on her and intercede to save her baby's life. The cold compresses she had placed without fail on sweet Josephina's forehead became hot almost immediately, and she knew that only Divine Intervention could change the inevitable outcome. And yet, on the seventh day of her illness, she managed to find a glimmer of hope when the child opened her eyes and smiled. "Mama," she had said, and Angelique had managed to get her to take a few sips of the dark tea that the old slave, Hannah had made that morning. It was a sure cure, the woman had claimed of the recipe, given to her by her mother and grandmother. And Angelique, although afraid to ask what was in the concoction, would have believed in anything, if it meant the possibility of curing her baby girl.

For a moment, Angelique thought that there was some improvement, and she found herself dozing in the slipper chair that she had pulled by Josephina's bed as she held her vigil. She awoke with a start at twilight and hastily moved around the nursery to light the oil lamps. She looked over at her child, so beautiful and calm in sweet slumber. Her heart swelled with love. Reaching over to touch the child's forehead, she knew immediately that the life had left her baby. She was cold. Angelique opened her mouth to scream, but it came out as an inhuman cry, much like that of a wounded animal. Jean Paul and the rest of the household ran into the room to find her holding Josephina in her arms, rocking her back and forth as she screamed "no, no, no," over and over again.

For three days, Angelique refused to let anyone near her baby, anger and sorrow overtaking reason. "You will not put my child in a darkened tomb," she wailed. "She will be afraid and all alone." And she threatened to kill anyone who dared try. In the end, Jean Paul had enlisted Hannah's help once more, knowing that Angelique trusted the old woman who had been with her since she had been a child herself.

"Drink this, honey," Hannah said, offering Angelique a powerful sleeping potion.

"No," Angelique replied, steadfastly refusing to take even a sip.

But Hannah was a shrewd one and used a bit of logic. "Baby, you can hold Josephina for a month if you want, but how long you think you gonna hold up with no food or water in your body?"

"Until I die," she replied. And at that moment, she would have chosen death just to be with her precious daughter.

"Well, you think that beautiful chile would want her momma to die?" Hannah asked. "She up there with the angels having a good old time. Shoot, she sitting on the lap of Our Lord Jesus right now. Sugar, she done left that body three days ago."

"Stop it," Angelique snapped. "I don't care."

"Well, you should ought to care, Miss Angelique, because you got some more babies up there in that same heaven waiting to be born to you and Mr. Jean Paul. What ya gonna tell dem?"

Angelique stopped for a moment and considered what the old woman had said. Was it possible that she could have other babies? Josephina was irreplaceable, of course, and losing her would leave an empty place in her motherly heart forever, but to fill her home with the laughter of children was all that she had ever hoped for in this world.

She turned to Hannah and wiping the tears from her cheeks, she took the cup from her, gingerly sipping from it. Within minutes, her eyes became heavy, and she loosened the grip on the body of her dead daughter. Jean Paul and the undertaker moved in quickly to take Josephina from her, placing her in the tiny casket that had been procured for her internment.

When Angelique woke the next morning, Jean Paul sat beside her on the bed, patting her hand in an effort to console her. "Our baby is at rest," he said. But it brought her no comfort

"How could this be God's will?" she questioned.

But Jean Paul had no answers for her, no Biblical verse or whispered prayer to ease her pain. And it wasn't until a full week later that she was able to make the short journey to the cemetery to visit her daughter's marble grave. But doing so brought her a strange peace, and she found herself making the trip on most mornings.

Angelique, numb with the pain of her loss, had gone through those days of sorrow out of habit as she simply went through the motions of her daily life. Unable to sleep, she took to walking the house like a phantom in the night, reliving the moment of Josephina's passing over and over in her mind, torturing herself with thoughts of how she might have altered the tragic outcome.

No friends had come to call, fearful of the house of death. The fever aroused terror in the hearts of everyone in the city and they avoided any place where the contamination might linger. But letters of condolence came, and Angelique read each, written with care, hoping to find some solace and comfort there. But none came.

She ate meals alone in her bedroom and refused to dress, preferring instead the silk dressing gown until Hannah insisted that she change clothes lest the neighbors begin to complain of the smell. Angelique spent so little time with Jean Paul that she didn't notice his long absences from home. She had detached herself from him so completely in her grief, a reality that she would come to regret a year later. Perhaps if she had been more aware of his pain; perhaps if she had acknowledged his sadness; perhaps if she had been a better wife, she might have saved him. But perhaps there was nothing that she could have done. Nothing at all.

Chapter Two

Angelique had lost her entire family in such a short span, a cruelty that was hard for her to fathom. Her life, once filled with such promise, felt empty and the sadness was overwhelming, but so was the anger rising in her heart, which she battled with regularity.

"Take me to the French Market," she ordered the driver.

"Of course, Madame," he answered as he helped her back into her cloaked carriage.

The horses proudly pranced along the streets of New Orleans. Angelique peeked through the drawn curtains at the pedestrians scurrying to and fro as they attended to their daily business. Their normalcy seemed an affront to her pain, an attack on her sensibilities. She could feel her hands clinch into a fist.

If I were a man I could punch something or someone, she thought. *The release would be so sweet.*

The driver signaled the horses to pull into the designated spot near the market stalls. They haughtily moved their heads from side to side in anticipation. They knew that they would be watered here. Once again, the driver moved to open the carriage door as Angelique gracefully exited.

"One hour," she said.

"As you wish, Madame." He removed the watch from his breast pocket to check the time. 9:32.

Angelique weaved her way through the busy market, stopping to examine the wares on display by the various vendors. She stared longingly at the numerous pastries, selecting two of most tempting ones for an afternoon treat. She bought sausages for supper because they were on sale, "un bon marche, a bargain!" the butcher had exclaimed. And she found two spools of delicate thread for her petit point. The creole tomatoes looked particularly enticing, and she asked the merchant to choose two for her. "Pour aujourd'hui, to be eaten today," she said with a sad smile. On most mornings, she would have sent Hannah with the other servants to purchase provisions for the house, but on this particular day, when her grief was palpable, she needed the diversion. And yes, while it was unusual for an unaccompanied women to do such a thing, especially given her station, Angelique was accustomed to living life on her own terms. At least she had been before Jean Paul entered her life.

She entered the small café and ordered a café au lait. The waiter gave a slight bow, in deference, no doubt, to her mourning attire. She was bound by custom to wear it for a full year following the death of her husband, but having donned the somber apparel four years earlier after losing her parents and then once again after sweet Josephina left this earth, she felt that she had lived much of her adult life dressed in sorrow. She carefully lifted the black veil as she took a sip of the rich, creamy coffee.

Angelique recalled her youth on the plantation. She had been a willful child, a free spirit, refusing to follow the rules of "ladylike behavior" that her mother and Hannah had tried to instill in her. Life was a fun adventure in her mind as she embraced each day with delight. And during the summer, months, which were among her happiest, Cousin Lily, her partner in crime visited from Charleston. The duo spent hours planning mischievous deeds, whispering well into the night under the mosquito net of her canopy bed, until her mother came in to scold them.

On most sunny days, she could be found climbing trees and catching frogs, exploring with wild abandon, as she reluctantly returned home with her jet black hair a tangled mess, her steel blue eyes ringed in grime. Her dress, covered with the black muck of the Mississippi Delta, was often beyond saving. Hannah would shake her head in exasperation when Angelique appeared at the kitchen door.

"Chile, you is a dirty mess," she would say, "Let's get you into a bath before Miss Emma sees you and whips your butt." And she'd fill the copper tub with water poured from the large iron kettle she kept on the woodstove. Angelique had complained loudly as Hannah scrubbed her skin raw, but she was grateful to the old Negro woman who kept her secrets. That loyalty and affection continued well into adulthood.

At twelve, Angelique was sent to a French-speaking convent school in New Orleans in order to receive the best education possible. Her mother, aware of the need to turn her strong-minded daughter into a proper Creole lady, prayed that the nuns would work their magic with her.

"Pourquoi?" Angelique questioned. "Why must I go away?" she had asked when she saw that her trunk was being packed for the trip.

"Because I love you, chèr," her mother said. "I want the very best for your future and an education with ensure that. You must learn to become a refined lady. Someday, you will be married and the mistress of a fine house."

Angelique cried in protest, folding her arms in defiance, but in the end, she accepted her fate. To do otherwise would have been an exercise in futility.

And indeed, sheltered from the realities of life beyond the cloistered walls, Angelique grew into a poised and polished beauty, who could handle the amenities of any social situation. And the wild streak, the adventurous spirit that had become her trademark, had been contained, at least while in public.

At seventeen, she was ushered into white Creole society, presented at an elaborate party hosted by her parents at their plantation home. She had no shortage for suitors: her legendary wit and fetching appearance made her popular among the eligible young men in the parish, and her dance card was always full when she attended soirées at neighboring estates.

It was on one such occasion that she met the dashing Jean Paul. She had been dancing a waltz with Benjamin Lebouef, a young man who had shown a keen interest in her as he managed to monopolize her every free moment with his enthusiastic talk of cotton planting and squirrel hunting. She did her best to feign attention, but in reality, he bored her to tears. She had hoped that her parents wouldn't push for a marriage with him just because of his family's adjacent plantation. She understood all too well that women were merely bargaining tools in the acquisition of land, and she was determined not to be a pawn. She wanted a love match and by golly, she would hold on to her virtue steadfastly until she got one.

As the young Monsieur Lebouef twirled her around the dance floor, she could feel Jean Paul's eyes on her. She politely ignored him, keeping her gaze fixed on her partner, but in one moment of weakness, she managed to lock eyes with him, and he smiled in return, bowing in recognition. She blushed in response and wondered if she could feign a dizzy spell in order to leave early. But before she could set that plan in motion, the swarthy Jean Paul had tapped her partner on the shoulder and swept her away in a tight embrace.

"Monsieur?" she had asked, implying dozens of questions in that one word.

"Pardon, Mademoiselle," he said, which sounded more like a statement than an apology. "But you are the most beautiful woman in the room, and I was afraid that I would hate myself tomorrow if I didn't take the opportunity to hold you in my arms."

Angelique blushed once more as she caught her breath. "You are very forward, Monsieur."

He laughed loudly. "I am simply a man who is accustomed to getting what he wants, chèr."

"Je regrette, Monsieur," Angelique said, "but you can't have me."

"That remains to be seen," he said focusing his dark eyes on her.

Angelique was grateful when the music ended, and she quickly parted company with the stranger. But there was something quite mysterious and seductive about the older man. He was, no doubt, a little dangerous as well, a thought that intrigued her, in spite of her instincts, which told her to stay far away from him.

Three days later, when she came downstairs to join her mother in the library, she was surprised to hear his voice coming from her father's study. She tiptoed to the door to listen to their conversation.

"Monsieur Chauvin," he began, "I was fortunate enough to make your daughter's acquaintance last Saturday night at Belle Reeve."

"Yes," her father replied, "and?"

Angelique tried not to giggle. Her father was a no-nonsense Frenchman. He was going to make this man squirm.

Jean Paul cleared his throat. "I have come to ask your permission to court her."

Her father laughed, a deep belly laugh. Angelique was his prize, and he would not give her away so willingly. "You are aware, Monsieur, of the age difference, no? My daughter is a beautiful young girl, and if you will pardon me, you are an old man."

It was an obvious observation. Jean Paul was thirteen years older than she, but he had not considered that to be a stumbling block. "C'est vrai, Monsieur. It is true. But I am also well-settled, a landowner myself, having inherited my family's plantation and certainly capable of taking care of your daughter in the way in which she has become accustomed. My intention is marriage."

"Marriage, you say?" her father asked.

"Indeed, Monsieur," he boldly replied.

"Ah, yes. My Angelique is a bit of a spoiled pampered beauty, although she has a willful streak that you have not yet uncovered, of course," her father said with a chuckle.

"I look forward to learning more about her," Jean Paul said, "with your consent, of course."

Monsieur Chauvin paused to consider the implications and quietly rose from behind his massive desk, extending his hand to Jean Paul. "You may see my daughter if she is in agreement. But mark my words, Angelique is my only child, my treasure. If you hurt her, it will cost you dearly. And I will not hesitate to exact my revenge." He focused his stare on the suitor, just to reinforce his seriousness.

"Merci, Monsieur," he replied, grinning in response. "I am most grateful. Rest assured, I will guard and protect her with my own life, if need be."

Angelique bounded from the hall into the kitchen, petticoats fluttering in her wake.

"Hannah," she whispered. "I am to be courted!"

"Is that so?" Hannah asked, wiping her hands on her stained apron. "And who is dis lucky man wantin' for to steal my baby?"

Angelique sat on the stool and began to laugh. "I have no idea. Why, I don't even know his name."

***

The clock on the wall of the café began to chime. "Eleven o'clock," Angelique said out loud. To no one in particular. "I have sat here far too long, lost in my memories." She opened her black velvet pouch and placed a coin next to her half empty coffee cup. Gathering her purchases, she made her way back through the market to her waiting carriage.

"Madame," the driver said rushing to meet her when he spotted her in the crowd. He took her packages and gently escorted her to the waiting carriage. "I was afraid that you had gotten lost." He cared for her more than he would readily admit, even to himself.

"Lost," she repeated absentmindedly. *What a sad, dismal word,* she thought, *and how perfect it is to describe me.*

Chapter Three

Safely back in the carriage, Angelique continued her reverie to that time long ago when her life with Jean Paul had not yet begun.

He had arrived at the Chauvin family plantation the following afternoon, clutching a bouquet of lavender and violets.

"The old fella doesn't waste a minute, does he?" her father had observed with a chuckle as he sent a servant to retrieve his daughter.

Angelique, who had been horseback riding only moments earlier, appeared in the parlor, her long braids coming undone, her oldest skirt torn from an encounter with a blackberry patch. When she saw Jean Paul, she stopped short.

"Oh," she said with a gasp, "it is you."

"Mademoiselle," he said, moving forward to kiss her gloved hand. "Let me formally introduce myself. My name is Jean Paul Latour. And with your permission, I am here to court you."

She smiled. At least now she knew his name. "Monsieur Latour," she said, quickly removing her hand from his grasp. "What makes you think I would be interested in such a thing?"

"It is my greatest wish," he said.

Angelique carefully examined his face, looking for a hint as to his sincerity. She saw none and wondered if perhaps he was a good card player, since he seemed to hide his emotions so well. She was momentarily distracted by the half circle scar on his right cheek, and she wondered when she would feel comfortable enough with him to ask how he got it. She had heard him invite her father to call him Belafre, which is scarface in French, but she hadn't understood why until she saw the distinguishing mark. In any case, she thought it made him interesting. Yes, there was something quite attractive about this dark Frenchman, and she considered the possibilities. "Perhaps you might want to join me on a ride, since your visit interrupted mine," she suggested.

"Gladly," he said, flashing his dangerous smile.

"Take one of the servants," her father admonished. "Your reputation is at stake, chèr. You cannot leave this house without a chaperone."

Angelique started to protest and then thought better of it. There would be no winning of such arguments with her father, who above all else, had her best interest at heart.

She and Jean Paul galloped through the fields, the servant trying hard to keep up on the old mare he had been assigned. They laughed as they looked back at him waving his arms in a frantic series of gestures. And finally, they stopped to rest their horses near the pond on the outer section of the plantation.

The conversation flowed between them freely, and Angelique listened intently as he told stories of his adventurous trips to Atlanta and Charleston, promising to take her there someday. He spoke of his parents' untimely death, the result of the influenza epidemic, lamenting that he had been away at the time. He told her of his New Orleans house, a Creole townhouse that he used for weekends, often after attending the opera. And he described his own plantation, which, as the eldest son, he had inherited. Of course, he failed to mention his lazy streak, which kept him from attending to much of the daily grind that running such an enterprise involved. Nor did he brag about his mounting debts, a detail that jeopardized his land like a coyote eyeing a fawn for dinner. No, Jean Paul was on his best behavior, charming Angelique with every word and gesture. She was a good catch in his mind and the fact that her family was so well-heeled meant that if he could make her his wife, her future inheritance would be available to him to shore his holdings and keep the creditors at bay. Angelique was the key to his future: that much he knew.

As they slowly walked the horses back to the stable, Angelique felt her heart soften toward this man. She began to imagine falling in love with him, picturing a future filled with excitement and adventure. They would travel, allowing her to experience the world outside of the confines of South Louisiana. He would introduce her to passion, a thought that made her blush, but also filled her with breathless anticipation. *Yes*, she thought, *I could give this man my heart.*

And so, when he proposed six months later, presenting her with his mother's ruby and diamond ring, she gladly accepted. In 1850, on a hot July afternoon, exactly two months before her eighteenth birthday, Angelique became Madame Latour, and she began her life with Jean Paul, one built on illusions and falsehoods.

Chapter Four

Returning from the market, the day passed quickly as Angelique filled her afternoon with mindless pursuits. She worked on her petit point, using the newly purchased thread, as stitch by stitch the delicate tapestry began to take form. Growing tired of that, she read a little from a volume of poetry her father had bought her for her sixteenth birthday. When the sun went down, she ate dinner with Hannah in the kitchen, a practice she had begun after Jean Paul's death. It was inappropriate by the standards of the day for master and slave to dine together and Hannah said as much, but Angelique would not be swayed. She was never one to do what society dictated, breaking whatever rule of propriety that suited her.

"Would you rather me eat all alone in the big dining room?" she asked. "Am I to talk to myself?"

"Not fittin', missy, no, it ain't," was Hannah's reply. But Angelique knew that the old woman was secretly pleased to have the company as well, and they were careful to keep it secret from the rest of the house servants. During those moments, they talked about the old days, when Chauvin Plantation was the toast of the Mississippi Delta and eighty-five slaves lived and worked there. And Hannah would weave vivid tales of life among them, which never failed to mesmerize her, even as a child.

On those quiet evenings, Angelique spoke longingly of her parents. Oh, how she missed them. The cholera had spread quickly through the plantations in the lowlands, and Jean Paul had moved them to their city home in New Orleans until the threat was over. Thankfully, they had been spared. But when the messenger arrived with the devastating news of her family's demise, Angelique took to her sick bed, racked with guilt and despair. She somehow thought that if she had been there she could have saved them, nursed them back to health, an idea that both Hannah and Jean Paul had readily dismissed.

"When da Lawd wants to call you home, you ain't gotta choice," Hannah said in her practical way of explaining something as complicated as death.

"Dey is in heaven, chile," she had said, "if you is wantin' to cry for somebody, cry for us who still have to walk this earth, eaten up with the grief."

Angelique had agreed with that bit of wisdom. Sometimes, the pain and sorrow of being left behind to miss those you love had to be worse than dying yourself.

Thinking back, she saw the folly of her lapse in judgment, her sadness distracting her from making sound decisions. With her immediate family gone, Angelique had grown more and more dependent on Jean Paul and was grateful when he took over the task of liquidating the assets from her inheritance. He had assured her that he had her best interest at heart, that her money was secure, telling her that he had placed it in a reputable bank for safekeeping. And six months later, when he advised her that he had borrowed a tiny amount to pay for cotton seed, he had guaranteed her that he would pay it back in full soon after the crop went to market. She believed him because she had no reason not to, and as her husband, he had that right afforded to him, one she could not easily challenge, even if she had a mind to do so. Preoccupied by grief, she absentmindedly signed whatever document he presented to her without even glancing at it, a choice she would later come to regret. But at the time, nothing much mattered to her. Her heart was woefully empty.

Only when Angelique discovered that she was pregnant with Josephina did the light return to her eyes. She admired her swollen belly in the mirror each morning and delighted in trips to the shops along Royal Street to shop for the baby's layette. The pregnancy was uneventful, and she glowed, growing more radiant and contented with each passing month. Jean Paul had hinted on more than one occasion that he hoped for a son, but when the baby girl emerged from Angelique's womb, he cheered and said she was exactly what he had wanted. The fact that the precious infant had been born beautiful and healthy was enough for Angelique, who rejoiced and thanked God for the blessing.

The event of Josephina's christening at St. Louis Cathedral was a cause for celebration. The rosy-cheeked infant, smiling her toothless grin, looked like a cherub in her long white batiste gown as the parents proudly cradled her in their arms. For the party afterwards, Angelique and Jean Paul spared no expense, hiring a group of fiddle players to provide music as the guests gaily danced around the courtyard, sipping cognac and wine. The elaborate white cake, from the best bakery in town, was a huge confection, befitting a princess, and the servants worked overtime to prepare the impressive feast of oysters and venison with a various array of accompaniments. More than one party goer had deemed it the best party and finest meal ever, much to the delight of their hostess. The merriment lasted well into the night, and Hannah eagerly offered to put the baby to bed so that Angelique could remain with her guests.

"Have some fun, chile," she whispered as she left with Josephina. And Angelique reluctantly let her go, wanting nothing more than to keep the sweet baby nestled in her arms.

Those three years of Josephina's short life were among the most joyous for Angelique. Her beautiful baby was even-tempered, smiling and cooing for hours on end, enchanting family and strangers alike. In the quiet moments, Angelique would rock her to sleep, taking in the intoxicatingly sweet infant smell as she sang the French lullabies that she herself had heard as a child. There were days when they strolled along the levees, watching the boats navigating along the river or visited the markets, choosing sweet treats. And on sunny afternoons, they had picnics in the park as they watched their darling girl chase a ball in the green grass, her laughter echoing in the wind. It was the best of times, and Angelique basked in the contentment.

But such moments can be deceiving. Happiness is fleeting. And sadly, Angelique had no idea of the secrets that Jean Paul concealed from her, the treachery that lurked around the corner which would inevitably destroy her joy.

Chapter Five

As Angelique writhed in her massive canopy bed, she moaned with pleasure, the mosquito netting rippling like puffy cumulus clouds in a summer sky. She was dreaming of Jean Paul, experiencing a moment of passion between them that felt so real that she sat up in bed as she said his name out loud. But she didn't need to reach over to the place where he had once slept to know that it was vacant and empty, much like her heavy heart.

With sleep impossible, she rose and walked over to the window, gazing out into the moonlit night. The city was quiet, gaslights casting eerie shadows on the cobblestone streets. Jean Paul's death was still a mystery to her, the unanswered questions haunting her, hanging in the air like a dense fog. Perhaps the peace that eluded her, the harmony that she so desperately needed for emotionally healing was linked to unlocking those secrets. But so much of it defied explanation.

Angelique remembered that terrible January day. It had been bleak out, with a nip in the air; the kind of damp Louisiana dawn that chills to the bone. But Jean Paul had insisted on going on a hunting trip that had been planned weeks in advance. He claimed to be meeting up with some of his friends, although she didn't think to ask who they were. It seemed an unimportant detail at the time. She stood shivering in the kitchen of the plantation, wrapped in her wool shawl, praying that the warmth of the fireplace would take away the early morning cold.

"Do you have to go, chèr?" she asked him.

"Oui, my love. When I bring home a lovely rack of venison for Hannah to cook, you will be glad that you sent me out," he said pulling on his leather boots.

But Angelique was unmoved. "Why won't you stay with me?" She asked as she hung her lip like a petulant child.

Jean Paul laughed at her and gathered her in his arms. He kissed her lightly on the lips and smoothed her hair. "Je t'aime," he whispered, "don't ever forget."

And as she stood at the back door, watching him ride out of sight; a feeling of unease, an inexplicable melancholy, washed over her.

Six hours later, his horse returned home, but Jean Paul was not on its back. Angelique tried not to panic, as she rallied the overseer to go out with a search party to find him.

At sunset, they returned, bearing a lifeless body, which Angelique knew was her husband before anyone had even uttered a word to her. She ran to him, but was stopped by one of the men, a stranger who had joined in the hunt.

"No, Madame, you can't," he said.

"Why? I must," she wailed. "He is my husband!"

The men tried to block the view, having done their best to shroud the body in a horse blanket. But the blood seeped from the wound, forming a crimson pool at their feet.

"Please. I don't understand. What happened?" Angelique cried. "How?"

"We don't know. He was already gone when we found his lifeless body. An unfortunate accident, no doubt. Shot in the face, I am afraid. Poor Monsieur Balafré. Such a tragedy."

It seemed odd that to her that they would have called him that name, his nickname, used only by those who knew him well. These men were unfamiliar to her. But none of the words made sense in Angèlique's mind and all she could do was scream in terror until she had no voice left, and Hannah came to take her away.

The devastating injury meant that there would be no way to identify her beloved spouse, a condition she found most distressing. The half circle scar, the result of a childhood fall, had been obliterated, along with his handsome face. Although having been assured that it was not possible, Angelique held onto the hope that it had all been a simple mistake that Jean Paul would return home with some tall tale about having been thrown from his horse, walking the long distance back and wondering what all the fuss was about. But when we failed to reappear, she had no choice but to accept the cruel reality of her loss.

And two days later, she sat the widow's vigil over her husband's body. The casket had been nailed shut at the insistence of the undertaker. "For your own good, Madame, to spare you the pain," he had said. And she wept uncontrollably, for she had not been able to touch him or kiss him goodbye.

On the third day, when the hearse bore the body of Jean Paul to the cemetery in New Orleans to be laid to rest next to their baby girl, Angelique donned the black veil once more and knew with certainty that she had seen more sorrow in her twenty-three years than many would over an entire lifetime.

There is no time limit on grief, she thought, as she returned to her bed, but she had to dig deep to find something to cling to in the dark days, to pull herself out of the utter despair she felt. Could she dare hope that someday she would experience joy once again? She searched for the word. *Optimism. Was that it?* The concept seemed so foreign to her, so utterly impossible to imagine considering all that had transpired. The pain was too real, too new.

But before she could begin to hope for the future, Angelique knew that she would have to fight her way through the labyrinth of emotions she was feeling. She would battle the monsters of sorrow that were ever-present. She had no choice. Life goes on, irrespective of grief. And there would be pressing business details to handle, the estate to settle. She could not postpone this forever since it was necessary before she could even consider moving on with her life. With her father gone, she worried about her ability to navigate the legalities, especially with the power-hungry old men, who could determine her fate with a simple signature. She would have no champion, no hero. No, she knew with utter certainty that she would have to fulfill that role herself. As Angelique drifted off to sleep, she prayed for the courage and strength she would most definitely need in the days ahead.

Chapter Six

"1500 Gravier Street," Angelique told the driver, "It is the Citizen's National Bank."

"Of course, Madame," he replied as he mounted the high seat and coaxed the horses into action.

Angelique concentrated on the speech she had carefully penned and then memorized by the light of the oil lantern. She knew that she would be perceived as a helpless female, schooled only in womanly arts, and she intended to play that role for all it was worth. She said a silent prayer of thanksgiving for her mother's foresight. Her education would be priceless at this point in her life, giving her the only defense against those who might take advantage of her gender.

Carefully reciting the list of holdings from her inheritance, she figured that she would have enough in liquid assets to get the cotton sowed next month and pay the small staff. She would order a slave count and see to it that all were healthy and well-fed before planting time. The taxes on Jean Paul's plantation, Terrebonne, would be due as well as that on their New Orleans home. But she had the proceeds from the sale of Chauvin Plantation safely in the bank. She hoped she would only have to touch a portion of her nest egg. And besides, she reasoned, a good cotton yield would repay any cash she might have to outlay, and she should have the place operating at a profit by the end of harvest time.

Angelique found the idea of being thrust into the role of plantation owner a bit unsettling. She was no businesswoman, by any stretch of the imagination, but she was her father's daughter, and she had seen him negotiate the price of his crop from the time she was a little girl. She had often ridden out with him in the fields and delighted as he pointed to the tiny plants emerging from the rich Louisiana soil. She listened as he had cursed the wretched insects that attacked the tender vegetation, celebrating with him when they had been brought under control, often in the most unorthodox of ways. She saw him worry about breeches in the levee and the incessant spring rain, which could flood the fields, rendering everything in its path, useless. And she giggled as he would tickle her face with the soft puffs of snow white at picking time. She smiled at the memory. Her mother may have made her into a lady, but her father gave her the determination and skills she would need in the years ahead. She adjusted the hat and veil she wore, forcing herself to sit erect in the seat. Yes, she was Angelique Chauvin Latour, and she was nobody's fool.

Moments later, the carriage pulled up to the front of the bank and Angelique took a deep breath as she made her way into the impressive marble-floored lobby. She was quickly ushered into Monsieur Devereaux's walnut-paneled office. He rose to greet her.

"Madame Latour," he said, extending his hand. "It is so wonderful to see you again, although I wish it were under happier circumstances."

"Monsieur," she said, carefully removing her glove so that her skin touched his.

"Please accept my condolences on behalf of myself and all of us here at the bank. The loss of Jean Paul is both shocking and tragic."

"Thank you, Monsieur. I think that I am still a bit numb over the events that took him from me."

"Of course, of course. Such a terrible accident."

"Yes, it was," Angelique replied. She used that as a cue to slowly lift the black veil covering her face as she wiped away a tear, carefully folding it up and over her bonnet. She would not be hiding behind a piece of cloth today; no, she intended to stand eye-to-eye with this man who held her financial well-being in his hands.

"How may I help you?" he asked in that condescending way of men in power.

"Well, as you know, with Jean Paul's death comes many decisions that need to be made. I am afraid that in my grief, I have been unable to attend to these matters in a judicious manner, which I am sure you can appreciate."

"Certainly, my dear," he said. "Please, have a seat."

Angelique positioned herself on the stuffed velvet chair and leaned forward slightly. She looked the man directly in the eye and began. "Now, I most certainly have no choice. Although I have searched the house for the proper paperwork to present to you, I have been unable to locate it. My husband, it appears, was not very good at such things. And so, I need your assistance."

"Yes, yes… I understand that. May I say, Madame, your visit today is timely. We were in the process of arranging such a meeting with you, while still trying to be respectful of your bereavement, of course," he said nodding slightly.

"And for that I am most grateful, Monsieur." She took a deep breath. "If I may explain," Angelique began.

"Yes, yes, please do," he said.

"I am aware of the fact that Jean Paul deposited the proceeds from my inheritance, particularly the money from the sale of Chauvin Planation, here with you. I most certainly have taxes to pay. But it is also my intention to draw upon those funds as need be in order to plant this year's cotton crop at Terrebonne."

The banker raised an eyebrow. "I see. And were you planning to take over those duties, my dear? All by yourself?"

She knew that he was mocking her. The thought of a woman running an entire planation was unheard of; he was about to put her in her place, but she was one step ahead of him.

"Monsieur, I know that it is unconventional, but I assure you that I am quite capable. I have a loyal staff in place, well-trained slaves, and the motivation to do well. This was Jean Paul's legacy. I must do what I can to preserve it."

Monsieur Devereaux cleared his throat. Angelique thought that he was trying to stifle a laugh as well, and she did her best to control her anger. "My dear Madame Latour, this will not be possible, given the circumstances."

Angelique raised her chin, looking the banker directly. "What do you mean, Monsieur?"

"I am not quite sure how to explain this to you, Madame, so you must forgive my candor. I am afraid that you have no idea of the legacy that Jean Paul left you, do you?"

"Pardon moi?" she asked, trying to control the rising anxiety. "What do you mean?"

He leaned back in his chair. Angelique suddenly had an uneasy feeling in the pit of her stomach. She braced herself for what was to come, but she felt with certainty that it wasn't good news.

"Soon after your husband opened the account with the capital from your inheritance, he began to withdraw from it. Quite regularly, I might add. He managed to deplete that entire amount within a two year period of time. I regret to inform you that it is all gone."

"What?" Angelique asked in disbelief. "That is not possible, Monsieur. Are you sure?"

"I am, Madame."

Angelique stifled the urge to cry, pinching her hand as a diversion. She would not show weakness here and frantically began to search her mind for a solution; certainly this wasn't a dead end. There had to be a way!

Taking a deep breath, she responded, "Perhaps then, you will consider a loan, with repayment due when the crop is sold at market? I do have the plantation, with all of its assets, as well as the New Orleans home. That is a sizeable bit of collateral, I would think," she said. She was careful about the terms she used. Of course, it was a risky proposition, but she knew that she had no choice.

There was a stillness in the room, a silence that was deafening. Monsieur Devereaux rose from his chair and moved toward Angelique.

"My dear Madame Latour. It appears that there is much you have yet to learn about your husband, Jean Paul."

Angelique swallowed hard. "Enlighten me," she replied, gathering all of the courage she could muster.

The banker looked at her with pity. It felt like a stab in her already broken heart.

"Monsieur Latour had been borrowing against those properties for a number of years. We extended him a line of credit, based on his good name and the potential for repayment, but when that was not forthcoming, we had to desist. I am afraid that we began foreclosure proceedings two months before his untimely death. It is why we wished to speak with you."

"I don't understand," Angelique said. "The bank owns everything?"

"Unfortunately, yes," he replied.

"But why? What was his reasoning? I understand the need for an advance for planting, but surely he was able to repay that amount."

"One would think so, Madame, but I am afraid that we were misled as well."

"What do you mean?" Angelique asked, the panic rising in her voice.

"Madame Latour, did you not know that your husband was a gambling man?"

"A what?" she asked. "Surely you are mistaken. I have never known my husband to engage in such activity."

"I wish that were that case, but we have learned that we were not the only creditors to whom he owned money. There are some rather unsavory types, who have been here to inquire about his assets as well."

Angèlique's head was spinning, and she thought she was going to faint. Jean Paul had never shown any signs of engaging in games of chance. Was there something she had missed? She wondered if she had ever truly known the man to whom she had given her heart so completely.

"Je regret, Madame. I am so sorry to be the bearer of such terrible news. And I do hope you know that I wish I could help, but I am sure you understand our position here at the bank. Unfortunately, our hands are tied."

Angelique sat in silence, unable to speak. She realized that she had been holding her breath as she slowly exhaled.

"Please, Madame, give yourself a moment. You have had quite a shock, most certainly. Can I get you anything?"

"A sip of water, s'il vous plait," Angelique answered.

Monsieur Devereaux left the office as she sat, her hands folded in her lap. She stared straight ahead at the massive oil portrait hanging on the wall, mesmerized by the way the afternoon light illuminated it, casting fragmented shadows upon it. Angelique felt like a stranger in her own body as she sat transfixed by the orderly furnishings in the stuffy office. Numb with emotional pain, she could not force her brain to produce a coherent thought, nor could she will herself to move. He returned with the water, but Angelique was unable to drink. She carefully placed the glass on the adjacent table and rose to leave.

Having no parting words for the banker, Angelique walked to her carriage, her head hung in shame and disgrace.

Safely back home, a place she no longer owned, she walked straight up to her room and locked the door. And no amount of sweet talking from Hannah could get her to open it.

Angelique sat at her dressing table, the tears flowing so uncontrollably, her body jerked in random spasms, inconsolable in her pain as she tried to make sense of all that had transpired that afternoon.

"I am a pauper, utterly penniless," she wailed. "How could you do this to me, Jean Paul?"

But no answer came. The dead don't speak.

Chapter Seven

The next day, the sun came up as it does every morning. It was the only bit of certainty Angelique had in her life. She woke, fully clothed, the stays of her corset painfully stabbing her flesh right below her heart. *It is appropriate*, she thought.

The grim reality of her financial state came crashing down around her. *What is to become of me?* She thought. She needed a plan, of course, but had no idea where to begin, particularly since she was, for all practical purposes, alone and fully in charge of her destiny. Her cousin Lily, who lived in Charleston would certainly take her in for a month or two, but she was a newlywed, and Angelique was hesitant to invade the couple's privacy. Perhaps family friends would allow her to stay with them for a while, but how could she even ask without appearing pitiful and desperate? Besides, those plans were short-term, and she would need a more permanent solution. She could possibly rent a room in a boarding house, finding a job in a store that catered to refined ladies, but she had never worked a day in her life. Yes, the decision-making was much too overwhelming that morning; it could wait. Tears formed in her eyes as she thought of her privileged life, one that she had regrettably taken for granted. She vowed never to do that again, ever.

Hannah knocked on the door, and Angelique refused to answer it. But the old woman wouldn't give up and continued to pound until she gave in and rose to let her in.

"Chile, what is wrong with you?" she asked, setting the breakfast tray on the foot of her bed.

"Nothing. Leave me alone. I am not hungry."

"Well, you went to bed with no supper, so I am guessing that you is mighty hungry in spite of what you might say, and I ain't a leaving until you eat a bite or two."

Angelique eyed Hannah with the same stubborn look she had often given her as a child. "You can give me that look all you want, but you is eatin'," she said. If there was to be a battle of wills, it would be no contest.

Hannah sighed. "I am here when you need me, baby girl, you gotta know that," she said, her voice soft and soothing.

"I do," Angelique said, taking a tiny bite of a warm biscuit, tears welling in her eyes once more. She struggled to swallow the food, which lodged uncomfortably in her throat.

"Want to tell Hannah what's troubling you?" she asked, handing Angelique a cup of steaming coffee.

"No," she replied, wiping her face with the back of her hand.

"Well, you know Jesus himself say that if you share a burden you cut it in half."

Angelique thought of that for a moment. It was true, of course. Sometimes in talking about a difficult situation, the answers come. Besides, Hannah was all the family she had left in this world, the only living person who truly loved her.

The tears began to flow once more and Angelique swallowed hard. "I have no money. Jean Paul gambled it all away."

"Baby, that can't be true. Mr. Jean Paul was a tough man to understand sometimes, but I is having a hard time seeing him doing something as jack-ass stupid as that, especially since he had to know that you would have to pay the price.

"But it is true," Angelique said, "Mr. Devereaux at the bank told me so."

"I'm afraid I don't understand. But honey, you still got dis fine house and the plantation that he grew up on. That's more than lots of people would wish and hope to have."

"No, I don't," Angelique wailed. "He borrowed against them. This house and the planation no longer belong to me."

Hannah stood quietly as though trying to comprehend the enormity of the situation. She shook her head in disbelief.

"Come here, Baby," Hannah said, wrapping her big arms around Angelique. "It gonna be alright."

"No, it's not," Angelique wept. "It is never going to be alright again."

"My poor girl. You has seen some terrible sadness in your short life. De Lawd is testing you because he got some big plans for you."

"I doubt that," Angelique said.

"Well, you shouldn't doubt de Lawd. He done put some powerful strength in you for a reason, girl."

"I don't feel strong. Not one bit," Angelique lamented.

"I know, Baby, but you will. I knows you will," Hannah said, offering up a spoon of grits.

"Hannah?" Angelique asked.

"Yeah, Sugar. What?"

"Do you think that Jean Paul killed himself with that gun? I mean because of the money problems?"

Hannah shook her head. "Who is to know that one? It is a mystery. But if'en he did, he sure was a coward man,"

Angelique thought of that for a minute. "You are right. My goodness, everything I thought I knew about him was a lie."

"Well," Hannah said, "the way I figure it, we don't really know anybody on this green earth. We all just get fooled into thinking that we do."

"That's true," Angelique said. "You are the smartest person I know, Hannah. And I am grateful for your wisdom."

Hannah laughed out loud and shook her head. "All I got is common sense. If you think that is true, then, you is needin' to meet you some new people."

Angelique reached onto the breakfast tray and pulled out the two envelopes. "What's this?"

"Came this morning, two separate deliveries." Hannah said as she removed the tray. "I'm gonna leave you to read dem all by youself."

Angelina wiped her tears and took a deep breath as she tore open the first one and read. It was a follow-up from Mr. Devereaux with a note attached from the bank's lawyer. The lien against both properties included the real estate holdings; they were in foreclosure, a process that had been set in motion months earlier. In addition, the slaves, equipment, and furnishings at Terrebonne were to be liquidated within the week to meet the additional debt obligation, including the accrued interest. However, the personal items, including, but not limited to, the furniture, household slaves, and other items at the New Orleans house were hers. He included the name and address of a local auctioneer who would help her to sell off what she could not keep. And she was given three weeks to vacate the premises.

"Hannah," she whispered, "at least you are safe,"

It made her sad to think of the lovely things that had graced the halls of Terrebonne being sold like common items at a bazaar. She wished she had brought her mother's porcelain china with her to the city house. That would be gone forever, along with so many sentimental treasures. But she was grateful for what remained and wondered how on earth she would part with them. Worse than that, she had no idea what to do next.

"I have twenty-one days to come up with a plan," she said out loud. "It will do me no good to feel sorry for myself, crying over what I cannot change. No, I have no time to mourn my fate. I have things to do, starting with figuring out where I will go from here."

Spying the other envelope, Angelique opened it and began to read the enclosed letter.

My Dear Angelique,

News travels faster to us here at the plantations than you might imagine, and we were heart sick to hear of the aftermath of Jean Paul's passing. Your father was my best friend in this world. We grew up together and our bond only grew stronger after living next to each other for so many years of our adult life. He loved you more than anything in this world, chèr and he would be angry to know that through no fault of your own, you find yourself in such a predicament. I wonder if he sensed that the old Frenchman you married would somehow cause you grief. On his deathbed, he asked me to look after you, and I promised him that I would, with pleasure. I extend to you my most willing helping hand, if you will allow me.

We have room here at Maison Blanche if you would like to come and live with us. You know what life is like here. It is a good one, and you will want for nothing as we will view you as our daughter. There is nothing that would please us more than to have your company.

But I also know you, Angelique, and your spirit will never be happy visiting with the ladies and riding horses through the fields. You have always wanted adventure, and New Orleans will offer you opportunities that you cannot have here in the country. My wife's distant cousin, George Wilson is the general manager of the St. Charles Hotel. Weeks ago, I took the liberty of penning him a letter, telling him of your plight, and he most graciously offered you a room there, without charge, for as long as you would like. Since you are already in the city, I think that might be a wonderful opportunity for you to meet some people and begin your life anew. If you would like to do that, go to the hotel and ask for him directly. He knows who you are and will be discreet.

You are young and beautiful, Angelique. Please don't resign yourself to a future of sadness. Life has been cruel to you, chèr, but the world is not a terrible place. Never forget

*that you have friends here and that our door is always open
to you. Find your happiness.*

With my best regards,
Alphonse Bourgeois

Angelique read the letter twice for good measure.
She was taken aback and mortified by the fact that her
father's friend had obviously known of Jean Paula's
devastating financial betrayal even before she did,
which she supposed was a result of the pending
auction at Terrebonne. It hurt her pride to think of her
sullied reputation, to be the subject of idle gossip. But
she was also grateful for his intervention on her behalf.
Without it, she would have had few choices. Was it
possible that she was to be given a place to live at the
St. Charles Hotel? Mentally calculating her financial
future, she figured she would have a little bit of money
from the auction and could probably find a job in one
of the fancy shops on Royal Street. She wasn't afraid to
work, even though she lacked experience. After the
utter despair of the previous day, she was surprised to
feel something akin to hope stirring deep within her
very soul. She clung to it.

Maybe Hannah was right, she thought. *The Lord does
work in mysterious ways.*

Chapter Eight

The auctioneer walked through Angelique's fine New Orleans home, tagging the various furnishings, occasionally clearing his throat and raising an eyebrow as he turned over the vases and figurines to check the trademarks. In such instances, a pedigree was important, but that was also true of the people considered to be the elite of New Orleans, as family lineage and social connections often opened doors that might have otherwise remained closed. Angelique was grateful to have long-established Louisiana roots and loyal friends who had come to her rescue. She shuttered to think of what her fate might have otherwise been.

And although she had worked through the details of what was to be sold, it was nevertheless unsettling for her when, two days later, she came down the stairs to find that a large group of people had gathered on her doorstep, waiting for the sale to begin. She tried to blend into the crowd as she mingled among them, but saw the pointed stares and heard several people speak in hushed tones as she walked by. As a Creole lady, she had been taught to hold her head up with pride, but those lessons were hard to remember in light of these humiliating circumstances.

To watch perfect strangers carefully examine her grandmother's cut crystal punch bowl, running their fingers around the edges, looking for flaws brought tears to her eyes, and she fought hard to contain her emotions. She felt much like those items that were soon to be placed on the auctioneer's block: she was being observed, scrutinized, and ultimately, judged. Angelique sensed that all-too-familiar anger rising in her very soul. It is one thing to have to pay the consequences for your own reckless behavior, but to suffer for the actions of another was cruel and unfair. The decisions that Jean Paul had made in the short five years of their marriage had wreaked havoc on her life, altering her path in ways she could not have imagined on the day she had agreed to be his wife. And sadder still was the fact that he was gone, unable to explain why and how he had chosen games of chance over loyalty to her, dashing their future together with the shuffle of a deck of cards. She wondered what other secrets she was yet to learn about her husband, a man she thought she knew so well, but realized was a stranger to her in so many ways.

The auctioneer ceremoniously pounded his gavel and cleared his throat as his lackey held up a small cane-backed rocker for the crowd to see. Angelique pinched her hand, which had become a painful habit, trying to concentrate the hurt on that very spot in an effort to keep from crying out.

"What will you give for this walnut rocker? Can I get an opening bid of twenty-five cents?"

"Twenty-five," came a voice from the back of the room.

"Do I hear thirty?"

"Thirty," said another.

The bidding continued as the people grew restless, anxious to see what the next item might be.

"Sold, for one dollar," he pronounced, pounding his gavel once more.

Angelique wanted to scream as the winner grinned at having scored his prize at a bargain price. And with that, the nursing rocker that three generations of mothers had used to nourish and soothe their fussy babies left her family forever. She whispered an apology to her great-grandmother, most certainly in heaven, for having to sacrifice the irreplaceable heirloom. The value of some things far exceed their material worth.

Unsure of how much of this she could stand to witness, Angelique made her way to the safety of the kitchen where Hannah was carefully wrapping the few items that she had managed to keep, determining that she simply could not part with them.. The silver flatware had been polished to a shine and placed in the velvet-lined mahogany box. The tiny tea set that she had played with as a child and delighted Josephina with one rainy summer morning, had also been packed away.

"How is you holding up, chile?" Hannah asked as she poured a cup of dark black coffee for Angelique and sweetened it with milk and sugar.

"It is just hard, so hard," Angelique replied taking a sip.

"I know, baby, but sometimes you got to get rid of the old to make you some room for the new."

"I hope that you are right," she said.

"I know I is," Hannah said, nodding her head.

Angelique finished her coffee and returned to the parlor where the auctioneer was holding up a small delft blue and white china clock. She gasped. It was one of the items she had intended to keep, not only because it was small enough to take with her to the hotel, but because it was among the things she cherished the most. She and Jean Paul had been strolling along Peachtree Street in Atlanta on their honeymoon when she had spied it in a shop window.

"Oh," she had exclaimed, "it is the most perfect little timepiece."

"Do we need another clock?" Jean Paul had teased.

"No, of course not," she had reluctantly agreed as they continued on their walk.

But later that evening at dinner, when he handed her a brightly wrapped package, she squealed with delight to see that he had gone back to the shop to get it for her as a surprise. It reminded her of happy times before her world had come crashing down around her.

"Sold," the auctioneer announced, pointing to a man in the crowd.

Angelique surveyed the room until she spotted the gentleman, who stood out among the Creoles. He was tall and fair, a blue-eyed blond, and incredibly handsome. She wondered if he was Scandinavian and that perhaps the clock's color and design had reminded him of his homeland.

She considered what she should do and gathered the courage to approach him

"Excuse me, Monsieur," she said.

He turned, his eyes fixed on her. They were the color of the sky, and she wondered if they matched her own. He smiled.

"Yes?" he asked.

She blushed. "I see that you have just purchased the little blue and white clock. I was wondering if you might consider selling it to me."

"Well, Ma'am, were you too afraid to bid on it yourself?" he asked.

Angelique searched for the right words, but let out a little embarrassed giggle instead. "I am afraid that I was in the kitchen and missed the whole thing. You see, this is my house. Well, it was mine. And these are my things. Regrettably, the clock was included in the sale, but it was not supposed to be. I had hoped to keep it."

"I see," he said. "And how much are you prepared to pay? I am afraid that I have my heart set on having it. It is so lovely."

He was toying with her. Could he not see that she was a widow in mourning and that such flirting was inappropriate? She lowered her eyes; she could not bear for him to witness her shame.

"I can give you what you have bid for it since you have not yet taken possession of it."

"I will need to think about that," he said, obviously enjoying watching her squirm.

"I hope that you will, sir. It would mean so very much to me."

He bowed low and turned away from her. She was left standing there, feeling only the flush of redness returning to her cheeks.

Thankfully, the rest of the day was uneventful and the auction ended by mid-afternoon. Items for pickup had been carefully marked and smaller pieces had been carted away by the victorious bidders, Angelique looked around at the remnants of her once gracious home. It was a tangled mess, much like her life.

The auctioneer approached her with his leger. "It was a successful day, Madame Latour," he said. He handed her a velvet pouch. She carefully opened it, looking at the various denominations of coins that would have to see her through the months ahead.

"Three hundred and forty five dollars," he said. "That is a tidy sum of money."

"Thank you, Monsieur," she said. "This is now the total of my fortune. I will have to use it well."

"Bon chance," he said, "I wish you luck."

"Merci, Monsieur. I am going to need it."

"Oh," the auctioneer said, "I almost forgot this." He reached into his satchel and pulled out the blue and white clock. "For you," he said. "The man who purchased this said he wanted you to have it."

Angelique clutched the object to her bosom, tears welling in her eyes once more. She had become a widow, dependent on the kindness of strangers, and this meant more to her than she could possibly explain.

Chapter Nine

Angelique sat at the kitchen table, dipping her pen into the ink well before her. She wrote slowly and deliberately, finally adding her signature and wax seal to each of the three legal documents. She handed them to Hannah and carefully counted out three ten dollar gold pieces.

"Hannah," she said, "you have been like a mother to me ever since I took my first breath. My gratitude for your faithful years of service to our family can never be repaid. Truly. But I can give you this. I want for you to live the remainder of your life as a free woman, owned by no one other than yourself. These letters will provide you with safe passage to the North, where I hope you are able to reunite with your sister."

Hannah wiped the tears from her eyes. "Goodness chile, I sure is going to miss you, but I never thought I would be as free as a bird up in the sky. Not in this lifetime. Lawd be praised. God bless you."

"I am going to miss you, too," Angelique said as she rose to hug the old woman one last time. "I can't imagine my life without you in it. But I pray that you will find happiness."

"I want that for you, too," Hannah whispered.

Angelique smiled. "I'd like to give you a goodbye gift, if you will accept it."

"No, chile. You have given me enough," Hannah said, reaching for Angelique's hand.

"This one is a sentimental indulgence on my part, Hannah," Angelique replied, as she held out a small brocade pouch.

Hannah looked at her with confusion. "I don't understand."

"Open it," Angelique said.

Hannah gasped as she removed the small gold locket emblazoned with a blue enamel star. "It's Miss Emma's. I remembered how much she loved it. Why, she wore it all the time."

"Open it," Angelique whispered.

Hannah smiled as she flipped the clasp to reveal a blurred photo of Angelique as a baby. "I am always gonna think of you as my little chile."

"Something to remember me by," Angelique said.

"I ain't never gonna forget you," Hannah promised.

"Nor I, you." Angelique responded. "Now you need to be on your way. You have a long journey ahead. Amos and Bertha are waiting outside. They have been given their freedom as well. Here are their papers for safekeeping. I have no need for household servants where I am going, and I will not sell the people who have shown me such loyalty and care. I know that you will see to it that they find their way to a new life."

"Sure enough," Hannah agreed. "And Miss Angelique?"

"Yes?"

"You don't forget what I done told you. The Lawd made you strong. You is gonna do something mighty powerful good in your life." She held up her freedom papers and kissed them, "You done gotta believe that you already has."

Angelique stood in the doorway as she watched the threesome make their way down the cobblestone street. With Hannah's departure, it was time to say goodbye to her old way of life and embrace the new. She had to laugh at her childhood dreams of adventure. It was true that a person needed to be mighty careful about what they wished for in their life.

She looked around at the empty house she had shared with Jean Paul, the place where Josephina had been born and died all too soon. The walls spoke to her as though bidding their goodbyes. She and her little family had packed a lot of memories into a few short years. And it was time, she supposed, for her to make new ones. She took a deep breath.

Closing the front door behind her, she made her way to the waiting carriage.

"Is everything loaded?" she asked as she looked at the carpetbags and trunks tied to the overhead rack.

"Yes, Madame," the driver said.

Extending her hand into his palm, she spoke quietly, "I want to thank you, Robert, for all of those early morning rides to the cemetery, for waiting for me as I shopped like a frivolous woman, for always making me feel protected and safe. I do so appreciate it. This carriage has sheltered me from the rain and sun."

"It was my pleasure, along with my duty, Madame," Robert said.

"And for your loyal service, I want you to have it. Begin your life anew, just as I will. These horses have served me well. And now, they belong to you. Treat them with care.

"Madame. That is not possible. I cannot accept such a generous gift, not under the circumstances," he protested.

"They are mine to give and yours to receive," Angelique said. "It is final."

The driver stood in utter amazement, a tear formed in his eye, and he quickly blinked it away.

"Thank you, thank you. I will never forget your kindness, Madame," he whispered.

"This will be our last ride together, Robert. Please take me to the St. Charles Hotel, if you will. And if you don't mind, take the long way there."

"Of course, Madame," he said. He tried to conceal the crack in his professional demeanor and as though she sensed his emotion, she hugged him on impulse. He kissed her gloved hand and then smiled as he helped her into the carriage one final time. Proudly climbing onto the high leather seat once more, he thought of the woman who had been his employer for the past five years. Unlike so many of the shallow women he had met in New Orleans, this little filly not only had plenty of horse sense, she had heart as well.

Chapter Ten

The lobby of the St. Charles was dazzling, a hub for the social life in New Orleans. The newly rebuilt hotel had risen out of the ashes of the fire that had consumed it and much of the surrounding area only five years earlier. Angelique liked that idea since she, too, felt much like a phoenix, being reborn on the heels of such personal tragedy. Standing among the sparkling chandeliers and polished marble floors, she made her way to the reception desk and quietly asked for Monsieur Wilson.

His greeting was warm and sincere, a quality she assumed he had reserved for paying guests.

"At your service," he said politely, "I wish for you to feel at home here. The premises are only enhanced by your gracious presence."

Angelique was grateful for his kindness, but was at a loss as to how to express it. "Monsieur," she said, "You have no idea what you have done for me. Your benevolence has saved my life. I hope to be able to repay you in due time."

"That is not necessary, Madame Latour. Someday, we will all be judged by how we have treated our fellow man. I hope that my God will smile favorably on me, His poor servant."

"I will pray for your good health and abundant happiness, Monsieur," she whispered.

Mr. Wilson snapped his fingers and a bellman appeared at once. "Please escort Madame Latour and her belongings to Room 410."

"Thank you," Angelique said as she followed him into the massive elevator.

Her room was small, but well-appointed, with a beautiful carved bed, a massive dresser, a marble topped washstand, and a velvet settee. Large windows overlooked busy St. Charles Street, flooding the chamber with bright sunlight. She opened the trunk, which had been carefully packed by Hannah, and methodically began placing her belongings in the armoire and drawers. The beautiful party dresses and feathered millinery would have to wait until her prescribed time of mourning was over. Her jewelry, which she had managed to save, went into the silk-lined tapestry roll. She stuffed it into the toe of a pair of boots for safekeeping. Someday, if she wasn't forced to sell them, she would once again don the fancy baubles that she treasured so dearly. But not now. To Angelique, it seemed rather foolish to continue to wear the black attire of sadness after Jean Paul's betrayal, but she had loved him once, she reminded herself, and she would respect his memory in spite of her feelings about what had transpired. Besides, it was expected of her. To appear in public dressed otherwise so soon after his death would be scandalous. She pinned the broach, a tin type of her husband's face to her bodice. In eight months, she would discard the black veil forever, the final step toward reclaiming her life.

Carefully placing the blue and white clock on the table near her bed, she smiled at the memory of the handsome stranger who had so gallantly saved it for her. *I wonder who he was*, she thought, and then told herself her curiosity was merely to pen him a note of thanks.

At half past six, Angelique realized that she had eaten nothing all day and feeling the hunger churning in the pit of her belly, she made her way to the table for ladies in the hotel restaurant. She thought it quite clever of the management to have made such an arrangement since widows like herself and unaccompanied single ladies found it quite awkward to dine alone. There were two other women there, already seated, and she introduced herself to them as she made polite talk about the weather and the varied items on the menu. They were visitors in the city, on their final evening there, and she invested little time in them beyond the required conversation, since she knew that they would be replaced by new dinner companions on subsequent nights.

Dinner was an elaborate affair, a fixed prix meal, with so many choices that Angelique's head was swimming at the possibilities. She settled on spicy cold shrimp, crabmeat mushroom salad, beef brisket with aromatic vegetables and horseradish sauce, and chocolate tart. It was served on the finest hand-painted bone china, with gold charger plates and matching flatware. The white-gloved service was impeccable. She was delighted. When the waiter presented her with the bill, however, she almost fainted. She had eaten a three dollar meal! Her room came to her without cost, but she soon realized that if she dined this way on a nightly basis, she would very quickly gobble up all that she had in the way of money. She determined that she would have to find suitable employment soon as well as a cheap eatery.

After dinner, she toured the hotel, making mental notes as to where she might sit to observe the comings and goings of the well-heeled, who frequented the hotel's bar and restaurant. Angelique had always been charming, a genteel Creole lady. If she was going to have to use her wits to survive, she needed to begin right away. She whispered a little prayer of thanksgiving to the nuns who saw to it that she was schooled in the social proprieties of the day and even though she had entered the convent school kicking and screaming as a child, those lessons would serve her well as a grown-up woman.

She returned to her room and slipped on her nightgown. Climbing into bed, she began to pray and for good measure threw in a petition to St. Jude, patron of lost and impossible causes. She would need all the help she could get.

Chapter Eleven

Angelique was up early and after tending to her toilette, walked through the lobby and out into the bright sunlight of St. Charles Avenue. She had decided to forgo breakfast after the large evening meal of the previous night and felt a bit of regret as she thought of the extravagance. But it would be an occasional splurge in the future, she assured herself; she had no intention of living the life of a pauper, even if, for all intents and purposes, she was one.

Six months earlier, she could have never pictured herself walking the streets of New Orleans alone, on her way to seek employment. She imagined the disappointment that her mother would have felt in seeing her daughter in such a dismal state. It was not exactly the kind of existence that a young cultured woman, to the plantation born, was destined to live. And she often longed for those days punctuated by fancy parties and mindless female pursuits. But feeling sorry for herself seemed like a futile gesture, although she certainly had her moments of indulging in self-pity. *Life is not without its twists and turns*, she thought, *and we are obliged to play the hand we are dealt because there isn't much of a choice.* Besides, she considered herself fortunate to have the social connections that enabled her to live at the hotel. She shuddered to think of what her fate might have been otherwise. Angelique was much too proud to have to resort to unsavory means of supporting herself, although she wasn't so naïve not to think that many a proper young woman had fallen into the abyss of morale decay just because she had to eat.

Spying a millinery shop nearby, she entered and asked to speak to the proprietor. She introduced herself, adding that she was looking for a job. The shopkeeper was quick to say that no, he was not hiring and, offering nothing more, returned to his task of decorating a hat for a customer. Angelique was struck by the irony that only a few months earlier, she might have been the lady for whom that lovely chapeau was being created, and she vowed never to take such luxuries for granted again if they ever came her way.

As she made her way down the busy street, she stopped by a dress shop where she was told that it would be improper for a lady in mourning to sell ball gowns and Sunday church attire.

"It would upset the customers, Madame. I am sure that you understand," the tailor said.

Angelique received equal rejections at the curiosity shop and antiques store, where she was told in no uncertain terms that such positions were reserved for men. Her final hope rested on the magasin that sold linens and lace. The merchant looked at her with such distain that she had to resist the urge to flee the premises immediately.

"A woman of your position, Madame? Working in a simple shop like mine? I cannot fathom it." And she was momentarily grateful that he had refused her since she could only imagine how difficult working for him might have been.

Feeling utterly dejected, Angelique stopped into a café for coffee au lait and a sweet bun. The sugar temporarily lifted her spirits, and she tried to think of what she would do next. Before returning to the hotel, she detoured on her route and entered the quiet sanctuary of St. Patrick's Church.

"Mon Dieu," she prayed, "please help me to find my place in this world." If Hannah was right about The Lord's big plans for her, she would have appreciated His letting her in on them as soon as possible. She went through the litany of prayers she had learned as a child, hoping that the spirits of her mother, father, and Josephina, most surely residing in heaven, would intercede for her and aid her in her plight. She left Jean Paul off of the list, convinced that he must be in purgatory because of his misdeeds while on this earth. It was a thought that brought her just a little satisfaction since she was in her current predicament because of him, and she could not bring herself to pray for his release. She rounded off her discussion with God by asking Him to bless Monsieur Wilson, whose kindness had given her a roof over her head. And for good measure, she spent a penny to light a candle, just in case Jesus needed a reminder of her pressing needs.

Safely back at the hotel, she took a position on one of the overstuffed chairs in the lobby and picked up a discarded *Picayune*. Flipping through the society pages and pressing news, she focused on the advertisement for jobs. Nothing for her. Whether or not she wanted to admit it, she had two strikes against her: she was a woman, and she had no marketable skills, in spite of her excellent education. She almost laughed at her optimism of the previous day when she felt with such surety that she would find employment immediately, enabling her to preserve her nest egg for a rainy day. Now, she began to calculate how long it would last her if she was able to get by with one paltry meal a day. She thought it quite ironic that as she sat among the magical splendor that was the St, Charles hotel, she might very well end up as a chambermaid.

Chapter Twelve

Andrew Slater entered the busy lobby of the St. Charles. He was early for his meeting, but that did little to alleviate his anxiety. He was looking for his third cousin, the impressive Captain Michael Schlatre, but since he had never met the man, he had no idea how to find him. Thinking that he might have left word at the reception desk, he walked over and made the inquiry. When the clerk pointed to a tall distinguished-looking gentleman sitting in an overstuffed chair, Andrew breathed a sigh of relief.

"Captain Schlatre?" Andrew asked, extending his hand. "So pleased to meet you, sir. I want to thank you for taking the time to meet with me on such short notice. I hope I haven't kept you waiting. I am really a long way from being acclimated here in New Orleans, even though I have been here for two weeks now."

The man, who was surprisingly younger than Andrew had imagined, smiled warmly in response, putting him at ease immediately. "Please don't call me 'sir.' There is not that much of an age difference between us," he said, "And I am happy to do so. Your father is my favorite second cousin, although please don't tell his sister that. When I received his letter that you would be residing here, I was glad to offer my services to help you get settled."

"And I appreciate it, most kindly," Andrew replied.

"So why don't you tell me a little about what you are doing here in our fair city."

"As you've read in my father's letter, I finished my schooling in New York last year, and through good fortune was able to secure employment with the new Smithsonian Institution in Washington City. I was fortunate to know the Secretary of the Institution, Professor Joseph Henry at the College of New Jersey, who recommended me. Of course, I am in his debt."

The Captain leaned back in his chair and puffed on a fat cigar. "Good for you. It's often who you know in this world that makes the difference. I have certainly learned that much. But as you have probably already discovered, education doesn't always carry you very far in this neck of the woods. In spite of what the gentry of this city, might otherwise profess, New Orleans is a working man's town. You'd be better off knowing something about navigation and steam ship boilers. You aren't afraid to get your hands dirty, are you?" He laughed.

Andrew smiled. "No, not at all," he replied. From what he had seen, he was inclined to agree. The city was unlike any place he had ever known, and he was working hard to get over his culture shock.

"So what does the Smithsonian Institution have to do with New Orleans and Louisiana, in general?" the Captain asked.

Andrew carefully thought of his answer. "Professor Henry has a great interest in all things scientific. His closest friend on the Board of Regents is a man named Alexander Bache, also an avid scientist, and involved in matters that might be of some interest to you, Captain. He's very involved with the study of weather in this country, and he has also been very influential with regard to the recently changed regulations regarding steam boiler safety and inspections."

Captain Schlatre turned to look at the younger man, who had piqued his interest. He paused to ponder the point and then offered, "Hmmm... I have an obvious concern for both of those areas. In fact, I am proud to say that I purchased my steamboat, *The Blue Hammock* just last year, and the inspections we had to endure were far beyond anything we had to do prior to 1852. But if they mean safer transport, then, I am all for it."

Andrew nodded his head in agreement.

"Tell me more about what they're thinking regarding weather," the Captain continued, "You know, we had quite a storm last year that did considerable damage. Luckily, it wasn't as bad as it could have been, but as we are situated below sea level, there is always a concern about water."

"It's a valid worry, Captain," Andrew replied, "And one that is shared with both of my mentors in Washington City. In fact, it is in the area of weather that I am currently employed. We are beginning to gather data daily here in New Orleans and several other cities in North America with regard to temperature, air pressure, cloud conditions and wind direction and speed. That information is being telegraphed to the institution where they are being plotted and incorporated onto a large map of the country. The plan is to grow this network until it covers the entire country so that weather assessments may be made and predicted."

"Sounds like interesting work," Schlatre said.

"It is," Andrew replied. "And as my father mentioned, I am on temporary duty, assigned to this area for the next six to twelve months to oversee those data collection efforts. But, there are other unofficial tasks my mentors are requesting, and they can make those daily now that the telegraph is in place and so convenient."

"Well," replied the Captain, "It must be exciting to be on the cusp of such great discoveries. A young man with your intelligence and ambition can go far. The motivation to excel must run in the family." He paused to laugh at his own joke. "Where are you staying while you're in town? Here at the St. Charles?"

"No, for now, I am at the St. Louis," Andrew replied, "until I can find a more permanent arrangement, of course."

"I can help you locate a suitable place, if need be," his cousin offered.

"I may call on you for that," Andrew said with a smile.

Although reluctant to draw their discussion to a close, Michael Schlatre had his own pressing schedule to keep. "Listen, Andrew, I would greatly enjoy hearing more of what you have to say, but I'm afraid I must take my leave. Perhaps we can get together later this week and resume our conversation?"

"I would like that very much," Andrew said.

And then, as though he had come up with an even better idea, he continued, "I know what; why don't you join me and the missus at Last Island next Friday? *The Blue Hammock* makes occasional runs, so I can give you a ride on my little vessel. We have a nice summer cottage there with ample room for guests. It would give you a chance to see the beautiful Gulf of Mexico and enjoy a little relaxation. Plus, you'll get to meet some of your Louisiana family."

"Why, yes, of course. I would be much obliged and grateful for the opportunity," Andrew said with a smile.

"Then it's done. Maybe if we are lucky, Mother Nature will put on a show for us, and you will get to do some weather studying while you are there," the Captain said as he rose from his chair. "I'll leave word for you at the St. Louis. My driver will be there to pick you up Friday morning at eight."

"Thank you, kindly," Andrew said, offering his hand.

"By the way," the Captain whispered conspiratorially, "have you had a chance to meet any of the Creole ladies here in New Orleans?"

Andrew blushed. It wasn't the time or place to tell the man, if ever, about his tattered love life. "No, I'm afraid not."

Michael Schlatre laughed in reply as he patted his cousin on the back. "You will, in due time. You most certainly will."

Chapter Thirteen

For the next three days, Angelique fell into her daily routine of visiting the shops and inquiring about employment. She was able to expand her search when she learned how to board the streetcar, which took her to the French Quarter with its vast array of glittering stores, selling wares of every possible description. But each day, she returned to the hotel feeling lost and dejected. She thought that she had heard every possible excuse for being refused. She was either too genteel or too female or too qualified or too late. Her state of mourning was off-putting to many. Either way, the answer was the same: nobody would hire her.

And every afternoon, she would settle into a chair in the hotel lobby to peruse the morning paper, hoping that through some miracle, she would find a clue as to how she should proceed with her life. On that third day, however, an article on the front page caught her eye and she read with interest about the proposed building of a grand hotel on Last Island by the owners of the St. Charles. It was to be called The Trade Winds and the description of its opulence would make it second to none as the vacation destination for the well-heeled of South Louisiana.

"Last Island," she thought. It was a lovely place, with its white sand beaches and gentle Gulf breeze. She had visited the popular resort with her mother and father, the summer before her thirteenth birthday. They had surprised her with the trip as a reward for doing so well in school. When the end-of-term letter from the nuns came, lauding her exemplary conduct and strong work ethic, her father laughed out loud, claiming that he must have received the report meant for some other child. And Angelique had protested loudly, claiming that she had indeed been on her very best behavior, although she didn't mention the incident when she had been caught giggling in church, and she was grateful that the good sisters seemed to have forgotten about it as well. She could tell that they were pleased, and so when planting was done and her father could leave the maintenance of the crop to the slaves and overseer, he proudly announced that they would be boarding the steamer *Vesta* for a week-long holiday.

Angelique had spent the warm summer mornings sea bathing as her father admonished her to be careful, lest she drown in the powerful surf. But she was a daredevil of a child, fearless, even though she couldn't swim, diving in and out of the waves as they came crashing to the shore, and when her mother came to check on her, she almost fainted at the sight of what she perceived to be daughter's near-death encounter with the Gulf. She had collected shells and cleaned each with care, placing them in the sun to bleach to a snowy white. When she let her father in on her secret intention of fixing them to a box as a surprise gift for her mother, he joined her in the hunt, pointing out the smoothest and best specimens to add to the cache.

They stayed in a tiny cottage as the resort was just growing as a summer destination for folks wanting to escape the heat of the city. But steamships arrived regularly with visitors on day trips and Angelique was never without a playmate or two to pass the time away. It was among the best times of her life, and she often returned to that memory when life became unpleasant, and she needed a diversion.

She wondered how the island had changed in the ten years that had subsequently passed, and she wondered if perhaps The Trade Winds Hotel might be the key to her future.

Approaching the reception desk, she asked the clerk if she could speak with Mr. Wilson, who promptly emerged from his office to greet her.

"My dear Madame Latour," he said, taking her hand, "I hope that you have found your accommodations satisfactory and that you are adjusting to life with us here at the St. Charles."

"I am, Monsieur," she said. "It is such a lovely place, and I am grateful every morning when the sun greets me to usher in a new day."

"I am so glad to hear that," he said.

"I have a question that I would like to pose, if you don't mind," Angelique said.

"Of course. What is it?"

"I was reading in *The Picayune* about the Trade Winds Hotel that is to be built on Last Island. It is my understanding that the owners of the St. Charles are behind that endeavor."

"Yes, indeed. And it will be quite a grand place, I have heard, although very difficult to build given the island's location. Why do you ask?"

"I hope that you won't think it too presumptuous of me, but I was hoping that perhaps I might be able to be a part of it. I could help design the ladies' spaces and even host some of the events."

Mr. Wilson chuckled and Angelique blushed a crimson red. "Well, that's a rather progressive idea, Madame, but I am afraid that it will be quite a while before they are to that point, perhaps a year or so."

"Of course. It is still in the planning stages. I am so sorry. It's just that…" she carefully considered how she could phrase this so that she wouldn't sound like the charity case that she already was. She did, after all, still have some pride.

"Yes?" Mr. Wilson asked.

"Monsieur, I need a job," she said, although she was sure that it came out much less refined than she had hoped. "I am well-versed in the needs of ladies of a certain status, although my own fortune is long gone. I thought perhaps that Isles Dernier, Last Island, might be a place for me to earn my keep, while using my talents as a hostess. It would be a lovely place to begin again."

The expression on Mr. Wilson's face softened. He felt sorry for her, and she hated it. "Well, Madame, while that is a wonderful idea, I am afraid you will have to wait a long time for The Trade Winds. However, Monsieur John Muggah, the owner of the Oceanview Muggah Hotel, which is already established and fully operational on the island, keeps a suite here at the St. Charles. And, in fact, he is staying with us this week, along with his brother, David, the owner of the *Star*, whom I do believe also operates the adjacent Billiard Hall. I have it on good authority that he takes tea in the lobby every afternoon at four, although I have also heard that he chases it with a swig or two from the whiskey bottle he keeps in his waistcoat pocket." He laughed at what he considered to be his own private joke. "Perhaps you might approach him with your novel idea and see what transpires."

Angelique smiled and extended her hand. "Thank you, Monsieur. You have been most kind to me in so many ways. And now, you have given me just a bit of hope."

"At your service. Always." The manager smiled and bowed, quickly turning on his heels to return to his office. Last Island may have been Angelique's last chance to find her way out of her current mess. And she intended to make the most of it.

Chapter Fourteen

Angelique looked at the blue and white clock on the side of her bed. "Three-thirty," she said out loud, as she studied her reflection in the mirror. She adjusted the black hat, drawing back the veil ever so slightly. It wouldn't do. And finally, in an act of defiance, she folded it above the brim of her bonnet, fully exposing her face. Her steel blue eyes were her best feature, and she needed every bit of charm at her disposal for her encounter with Monsieur Muggah. She pinched her cheeks until the color bloomed like a budding rose and as she bit her lips, they responded as well. She looked presentable, although she wished she could simply put on one of her low cut party dresses. She had never met a man who couldn't be persuaded by a properly presented bosom.

Making her way to the lobby at exactly four o'clock, she scanned the room for the place where Mr. Wilson had told her she might find the man who was her last hope. And indeed, just as he had predicted, the burly man sat, sipping from a tiny teacup. Mercifully, he was alone. She slowly crossed the room and headed in his direction. He looked up just in time to see her approach, nodding his head in deference to her widowhood.

"Captain Muggah?" she inquired, smiling ever-so-sweetly.

"Monsieur," he corrected her. "The Captain is my brother." She blushed. The first words out of her mouth were a faux pas.

"I am so sorry. Of course. Monsieur."

"Yes?"

"I was wondering if I might have a moment of your time."

He began to chuckle. "When a beautiful woman makes such a request, then the answer is most certainly yes."

Angelique blushed. She was woefully out of practice. Her coquettish days were long behind her, and she hoped that she could pull this off, especially dressed like a sixty year old hag.

The man pointed to an adjacent chair. "Please sit. Would you like some tea?"

"Oui, merci," she replied, "thank you."

He snapped his fingers and a waiter quickly appeared. He ordered another cup to be brought for her, along with some biscuits.

"And to what do I owe this honor?" he asked.

He was charming. She hadn't expected that and was pleasantly surprised.

"Monsieur, my name is Angelique Latour, and I have a most interesting business proposition for you," she said matter-of-factly.

He raised his eyebrow. She was glad that she had emphasized "business" before the word proposition. He was a man of the world and her choice of terminology hadn't gone unnoticed. She willed herself not to blush again in response.

The waiter appeared with a fresh pot of tea and the biscuits. She ceremoniously poured more into his half empty cup and then some for herself. In a graceful move, she dropped two sugar cubes into the steaming brew. He reached for a biscuit and then offered one to her. Her stomach was growling, but she resisted the urge to eat. She would have no chance with him if she had a mouth full of food.

"Go on," he said.

Angelique took a tiny sip of tea, fixing her gaze on the man who held her fate in his hands. Placing the cup on the table, she dabbed the corners of her mouth with her napkin and began.

"Monsieur, as you can see I am a widow. Through a serious of most unfortunate events, I find myself in a precarious financial position, which has caused me to rethink the course of my life."

"Hmmm… Sounds serious," he said. She wasn't sure if he was being empathetic or condescending. She didn't have the time to figure it out.

"I assure you that it has been most difficult for me. You see, I was brought up on one of the finest plantations in Louisiana, given the best possible education, and certainly taught the proprieties associated with being a Creole lady. It is not where I expected to find myself."

"I can see that, Madame, and while I am sorry for your regrettable circumstances, I am not sure what it has to do with me."

While it was humiliating for her to explain her plight in such blatant terms, Angelique knew she had to show him where her motivation came from, and so she continued. "Monsieur, you are the owner of the Oceanview Hotel at Last Island, are you not?"

"I am," he said.

"And if I may be so bold, may I inquire about the clientele at your establishment? I was under the impression that you attracted the finest and most well-established families in the area."

"That is true. We pride ourselves on catering to a wide variety of folks who visit the island."

She took another sip of tea and paused as her steel blue eyes locked onto his. "May I ask what kind of ladies' programs you have in place? Do you have a hostess prepared to receive your guests and plan your parties?"

Monsieur Muggah leaned back in his chair and looked straight at her. He began to laugh. "Is this what you are offering, Madame? Your professional services?"

Angelique's face reddened. It sounded tawdry when he put it in those terms. She ignored his question. "Sir, you do realize that cultured Southern ladies require more in the form of entertainment than sharing idle gossip, don't you? Afternoon card parties, sewing lessons, and rounds of croquet would keep them occupied while the men go about doing whatever it is they do. And everyone loves the idea of attending a grand party, but one that is held so near to the gentle Gulf breeze would be quite the draw. And what's more, you would sell lots of that expensive champagne that I am certain that you stock for your guests."

"Hmmm," he said. "I think you may have a point."

"I most certainly do," she replied. "I am well versed in the needs of pampered ladies, Monsieur, and you will not regret my assistance if you were to hire me in that capacity."

Monsieur Muggah sat in silence, as though processing all that she had presented.

"But a woman in mourning, planning parties seems a little out of place, don't you think?"

"On the contrary, Sir. You see, because I am in mourning, I present no threat to anyone at the hotel.

Forgive my suggestion, but the women need not worry about me flirting with their husbands."

He laughed out loud again as he quietly reached for the flask in his coat pocket and took a swig. She pretended not to notice. "I guess you have a point."

"My black mourning attire will lend a sense of seriousness to the job I will perform for you, I think."

He paused once more as though considering her words. After what seemed like an eternity to Angelique, he turned in his chair to look at her squarely. "Madame Latour, you are most persuasive. I will indeed offer you the position that you propose. You will, of course, receive free room and board at the Oceanview, as well as ten dollars a week in salary. Our agreement will extend through October first, at which time we will meet once more to determine if the arrangement has been mutually beneficial. The *Southern Star* shall leave with us onboard in three days. We shall set our course for Last Island at 8 a.m." He held out his hand to shake hers. She was both surprised and flattered to be treated as an equal in what she could only presume were negotiations.

"Merci, Monsieur," she said. "I promise you that you won't be sorry."

He laughed once more. "I certainly hope not."

He reached into his waistcoat pocket as he took a long swig from the flask and then, realizing that she was watching him, added as an afterthought, "I would offer you some," he said, "but I am reminded of your status as a lady."

Angelique had to stifle a laugh herself.

"Before you leave me, may I ask you a question?" he said.

"Of course," she responded.

"The widow's broach. Is that your husband?"

Her hand went to her throat, and she touched the tintype by instinct. "Yes Monsieur, it is. His name was Jean Paul."

"Oh," the gentleman said. "He looks much like a fellow I recently met. But they called him 'Bellafry or Ballfort,' something like that. Obviously, it was a different man, but the resemblance is uncanny. So sorry for your loss, Madame, and I hope my question did not cause you an undue stress."

Angelique's momentary joy was replaced by confusion. Surely, she had misunderstood Monsieur Muggah, whose memory was undoubtedly clouded by the effects of whiskey. Her husband, the cad, was gone. That was the only certainty she had in her disordered life.

Chapter Fifteen

Trying to shake off the strange conversation of the previous afternoon, Angelique turned her attention to the task at hand, packing for her journey to Last Island. She carefully folded her nightgowns and chemises, along with the whale bone corsets and an extra pair of high top boots. She sensibly wrapped the fragile blue and white clock to be sure that it made the trip intact. The additional black mourning attire had been pressed and went on top. She would forgo the bonnet and veil, except for traveling, a concession she would have to make, given the more informal atmosphere at the resort. Besides, she knew that wearing them made her seem staid and unapproachable, which could be an occupational hazard for somebody with the title of hostess. But she felt no regret in shedding that black albatross and looked forward to having a little more freedom at the resort than she had enjoyed in the city. She longingly fingered the smooth silk of her party dresses with the matching tapestry slippers and pondered whether she should take them along. In a moment of weakness, she decided to take two of her favorites, as well as four house dresses, her sea bathing clothes and her jewelry. It would be better to be prepared for any eventuality than to be caught without, especially given the island's isolated location.

She made her way down to the reception desk and inquired about Mr. Wilson's availability. He quickly appeared and greeted her in his usual affable manner. "Madame Latour," he said. "I take it that your meeting with Monsieur Muggah went well?"

"It did," Angelique replied, "thanks to your prompting. It seems that I am in your debt once more."

"Not at all," he replied. "So what are your plans?"

"I leave with both Monsieur Muggahs tomorrow. From what I have gathered, we take the Morgan Rail Road to Bayou Boeuf and then onto the *Star* for the final leg of our journey. I am most grateful to be in their capable hands as I am certain I would be completely lost on such a circuitous route."

He laughed. "All packed then?"

"Well, that is why I am here." Angelique said. "I do hate to impose upon you yet again, but I have two trunks with me, containing a few household items and clothing that I am unable to take along. Is there, by chance, a place here at the St. Charles where I might store them until my return?"

"Of course, Madame, and I will gladly accommodate you in that regard. I can assure you that your possessions will be safe here with us. And when shall you be coming back?

"Our agreement allows for a reevaluation on October first, at which time, either of us may continue or part ways, if mutually acceptable."

"My fervent wish is that you find happiness and healing in the gentle pleasures of the sun and sea. And please know that you indeed have a place with us here should you decide to return."

"Thank you, Monsieur Wilson. You are the kindest and gentlest among men."

And in his signature style, he bowed low as he departed for his office.

Angelique started to return to her room to complete her packing and then, on second thought, turned on her heels and entered the hotel dining room. She was escorted to the ladies' table, where she once again dined on the finest cuisine New Orleans had to offer. She gladly paid the three dollars for the meal and left a generous tip for the waiter. In light of the change of events in her life, this time, she had something to celebrate.

***

Early the next morning, she called for a bellman to retrieve her trunk. Donning her black bonnet and veil, she made her way to the lobby. The large clock chimed musically, and Angelique was pleased to discover the she was fifteen minutes early. It wouldn't do to have her employers worrying about her punctuality and when they appeared precisely on time, they seemed delighted that she was not one of those silly women who kept men waiting.

Monsieur Muggah cheerfully greeted her and introduced his brother, the Captain. She could see the resemblance between the two men immediately and was happy to discover that he also had a sense of humor as he laughed loudly, often at his own jokes.

"Pleased to make your acquaintance, Madame," Captain Muggah said, "My brother here tells me that you are to entertain the ladies on the island."

"Yes, Captain," Angelique replied. "I am looking forward to the opportunity to do so." He laughed. "Well, chèr, you may have your work cut out for you with some of those damsels, who complain about everything from the insects to the heat of the sun to the temperature of the food. There seems to be no pleasing some of those coddled socialites."

"I certainly will do my best to try," she replied.

And the Captain punched his brother on the shoulder. "Hear that, brother? Your guests are in capable hands."

Angelique tried to stifle a giggle. She expected that she would enjoy the company of these men on the journey and looked forward to getting to know them in the months to come.

They boarded the train at half past nine and enjoyed pleasant conversation throughout the journey. Angelique once thought she saw Monsieur Muggah examining her widow's broach, which bore Jean Paul's likeness, but she later contributed it to nerves and her overactive imagination. Coincidences are one of life's great mysteries, and she wouldn't spoil her happy mood by pondering this one.

They reached the busy steamboat port four hours later. Being with the owner of the vessel afforded them some privileges, as they were quickly whisked away to their sparse quarters while the porters loaded their luggage and trunks. Due to fluctuations in the tide, it was determined that the steamship would remain anchored for an hour longer and the passengers cheered with wild abandon once the longshoremen finally untied the massive ropes, which kept the ship moored to the dock. Within minutes, they were underway.

Angelique stood at the rail and watched as the shoreline grew smaller and smaller, fading in the distance. Her heart raced in anticipation. She had brazenly talked her way into a job, but she had never worked a day in her life and had no idea where she would begin in this new role. She hoped that the ladies of Last Island wouldn't see through her inexperience and that her own ingenuity would serve her well. For good measure, she whispered a prayer to St. Jude, and smiled as her words were lifted up to heaven by the Gulf breeze. She seemed to be talking to him on a regular basis and hoped that he was still listening.

Chapter Sixteen

Strolling around the ship gave Angelique a chance to get a preview of the group of merrymakers who would be disembarking at the hotel. They were in such good spirits, and she had to admit that their frivolity was a little contagious, even though her state of mourning required her to conceal any kind gaiety on her part. She walked along the deck, nodding politely to the ladies she encountered. It was far too early for her to introduce herself, but she figured that she would make the acquaintance of these and others within the coming days at the hotel. Angelique thought it quite ironic that Monsieur Muggah had called a place surrounded by the Gulf of Mexico The Oceanview, but now that she had met the man and understood his sense of humor, she didn't find it surprising at all.

A little under five hours after leaving port, as the steamship made its way through the calm sea, Last Island came into view. Angelique joined the other passengers at the rail to get her first glimpse of the place that was to become her home for the next five months, for sure, and perhaps indefinitely. At first glance, it appeared that the island had been plopped in the middle of the sea by the hand of God himself. The land mass rose from the like water a sentinel, when as far as the eye could see there was nothing but the vast stretch of the Gulf. But it was beautiful, awe-inspiring in its isolation and Angelique, struck by the fact that so many cultures had viewed a communion with nature as a rite-of-passage into adulthood, a transition from one stage of life to another, thought it was an ideal place for her own reinvention, and she hoped that she would find peace here. Yes, she was anxious for the adventure to begin.

The *Star* entered Caillou Bay and then slowly navigated Village Bayou until it reached the quiet harbor. The hotel, easily the largest structure on the island, stood directly before them, and the large adjacent dock was filled with slaves and other guests, who greeted the ship with loud cheers. The travelers waved back in response, anxious to disembark and begin their holiday. And soon, the vessel had been moored as one by one, people made their way down the gangway to shore.

There was a frenzy of activity as some passengers hurried to waiting carriages to be whisked off to private cottages, while others entered the hotel lobby for check in at the Oceanview. Angelique was unsure of where to go, so she was relieved when she spied Monsieur Muggah, who simply said, "Come with me."

She followed him into the lobby's reception area, which was sparse in comparison to the grandeur that was the St. Charles, but she was impressed by the simple beauty of the architecture and décor, the rustic cypress paneling contrasting with the delicate crystal chandelier that hung from the vaulted ceiling. The French doors that led out to the verandah were open, and a soft Gulf breeze cooled the room. Various groupings of plush furniture, covered in blue brocade, were arranged in such a fashion to create an atmosphere conducive to idle conversation among the guests. Angelique paused to take it all in, marveling at what a feat it must have been to coordinate the logistics of construction, given its secluded location.

Monsieur Muggah entered the small, but well-appointed office near the rear of the massive counter where the clerk stood, welcoming the newcomers, and she followed him obediently.

He pointed to a rattan chair, and Angelique sat to face him as he took his position behind the desk. He was serious and professional, which reminded her that she had been hired to do a job.

"Madame Latour," he said with a calm authority, "your quarters will be on this level down the hall to the left. I will escort you there in a moment. I have arranged to have your trunk delivered right away so that you can begin to settle in. There are no numbers on the staff rooms, so you will need to take care to locate yours, lest you enter one of your colleague's by accident." He chuckled and she made a mental note to keep hers locked, if that possibility existed. "You may eat in the small room next to the kitchen set aside for employees, but I suspect that you will also be mingling among the guests at meal time, so you may also eat in the main dining room. I expect you to be a visible presence among the visitors. I will want to meet with you every morning promptly at eight, where you are to give me an itinerary for the day's events, subject to my approval, of course. In addition, your presence will be required to greet the ladies as they disembark from the steamships, which occurs, at this point, on Monday, Thursday, and Saturdays. You will also attend any social functions currently in place, although I am sure that under your watchful eye, we will see quite an expansion of those. Do you have any questions?"

Angelique's head was spinning. The idea of being a proper hostess made such sense in her mind when she had proposed it, but now, she worried that she was woefully unprepared for the responsibility he placed on her. She had no intention, however, of letting him in on that.

"No, Monsieur, your instructions are straightforward, and I am anxious to begin."

"Good," he replied as he rose from his chair. "Let's tour the hotel, shall we?"

They walked into the lobby where he introduced her to the various members of the staff as he encountered them. She hoped that she would remember their names and tried to give herself some clue to help. And with that, she met Monsieur Cheinnoir, the front desk manager, who indeed reminded her of a black dog with his pointed nose and ears that were larger than his head. She noted that Sistine Leblanc, who directed the kitchen, and a large staff of slaves, had a white streak in her otherwise jet black hair. And Gertrude Thibodaux, head of housekeeping, who had a warm and inviting smile, would soon be her friend, of that she was certain. After a while, she gave up on any chance of keeping them all straight in her mind, and she figured that as she worked with them, the problem would fix itself.

Monsieur Muggah, strolled into the various reception rooms, including the ballroom, pointing to the most prominent features he wished for her to notice. They walked each of the two floors as he designated which rooms were the most sought after and, as such, commanded a fetching price. Finally, he escorted her out onto the wide verandahs, stopping to speak to guests who were enjoying the late afternoon breeze. And there, she got her first sight of the pristine beach, dotted with sea bathers and shell seekers. The cerulean blue of the water, which undulated in white tip waves as they crashed to the shore took her breath away. And she noted with interest how calm the bay side seemed in contrast, one side so calm, peaceful and the other most fully engaged in a war with Neptune himself.

As the tour came to a conclusion, Monsieur Muggah escorted her to her room, the third door on the left, she reminded herself, and he ceremoniously presented her with a key tied to a black velvet ribbon. "May this be the beginning of a mutually beneficial professional relationship," he said.

"Thank you, Monsieur. I will do my very best to make you and your guests happy."

"Then, I cannot ask for more," he said as he walked away.

Angelique entered her room and walked across it as though magnetically drawn to the view from the floor-to-ceiling windows. Such beauty Yes, she could be very content here. Last Island, she had determined, was indeed a lovely place for new beginnings,

Chapter Seventeen

Upon discovering that her trunk had been delivered to her room, Angelique made quick work of putting away the things that she had brought with her. She was hungry and tired, and would have easily chosen a meal, followed by a nap, but she knew that her first evening at the Oceanview needed to be spent in more industrious pursuits. She poured a bit of water into the bowl on the washstand and splashed her face; it momentarily refreshed her. Repining her hair, which had been smashed flat by the insufferable black bonnet, she sighed in relief that she was able to discard it for the time being. She took a deep breath for good measure and walked out into the hotel proper.

Angelique entered the lobby to find many of the guests, sitting in groups engaging in conversation. She put on her most cheerful face and made her way to three ladies, whose excited chatter grew louder as she approached.

"So what shall we do tomorrow?" one of them asked.

"Whatever we please!" the other exclaimed, as the three of them erupted into laughter.

"Pardon me," Angelique said tentatively, "I hope that you will forgive me for interrupting you, but I wanted to introduce myself. My name is Angelique Latour, and I am the ladies' hostess here at the Oceanview."

They stopped short and looked at her with confusion. She wondered if perhaps she had a bug on her face, or worse. But none of the women spoke to her.

"I had hoped that you might give me some ideas of what I might do to make your stay with us more pleasant." It was a question, even though she had not phrased it as such.

There came no answer.

"I had thought perhaps afternoon tea would be lovely, with some sandwiches and sweets. And I had planned a morning game of croquet on the beach."

Again, there was no response.

"I will post an itinerary for the day in the lobby each morning, and I hope that you will find something that piques your interest. I am always open to any suggestions you might have, of course. But please know that I am at your service."

As the ladies sat in continued silence, Angelique could feel the blood rushing to her face. She didn't know what to do, so she simply said "thank you," smiled, and walked away.

"She's in mourning," one of them whispered, loud enough for her to hear.

"It is scandalous," the other said.

"I cannot imagine what could have possessed the owner of this hotel to hire someone in grief to be a hostess. It goes against all manners of propriety," the third one agreed.

Angelique made her way to the upper verandah. She smiled as she introduced herself to each of the ladies she happened upon, but was largely received in the same cold manner. She hadn't counted on this and wracked her brain for some solution. Momentarily, she thought of changing into the house dress she had brought along, but then considered that it that would only raise all manner of questions, given that her conspicuous appearance had been already noted. She was at a loss as to what to do.

Quietly, she entered the staff dining room and ate her dinner in silence, while those around her chattered on about the new arrivals and their hopes for big tips from the richest among them. They tried to engage her in mindless talk, but she didn't feel the least bit sociable and hastily made a retreat to her room where she threw herself on the bed and cried until she was certain that she was unable to shed another tear. As the gulf breezes lulled her to sleep, Angelique wondered what she had gotten herself into and like a woman drowning in the mighty surf that pounded the shore outside her window, realized that she was in way over her head.

***

The next morning, she woke with the early light and sat at the desk to pen the day's schedule. She would propose her plans to Monsieur Muggah and, if he agreed with them, contact the appropriate staff to make arrangements for the set up. She hoped that news of her status as a pariah among the ladies had not yet reached him, but she steeled herself to be put back on the earliest returning steamboat if it had.

At exactly eight o'clock, she knocked tentatively on his office door. "Come in," he said.

"Bonjour, monsieur," Angelique said, trying to sound cheerful.

"Ah, Madame Latour, you are punctual. I like that. I trust that you slept well."

"I did, monsieur," she lied. "I do have the plans for our ladies. If this meets with your approval, I will post it in the lobby and begin to get everything ready."

He took the list from her and went over each item, smiling when he noticed that she had arranged for tea at four. "It is such a civilized custom," he said, "and I am pleased to see that you remembered."

"Of course, monsieur," Angelique said.

"This looks very promising," he said, "I look forward to hearing how it all goes."

Angelique resisted the urge to further comment. She had no idea what to expect. "Then, I will get started," she said as she got up to leave.

"Good luck," he called.

I am certainly going to need it, she thought.

The itinerary listed croquet at ten, followed by a game of hunt the ring on the lower verandah. After lunch, there would be bead work or sampler sewing in the ladies' lounge. At two, the first chapter of Harriet Beecher Stowe's *Dred: a Tale of the Great Dismal Swamp* would be read aloud, with subsequent readings each day at the same time. Finally, tea time would begin in the main lobby at four.

At ten, Angelique had the croquet course set up and the mallets at the ready, but no ladies showed and when she approached those who passed her by, they gave the excuse of having other plans. She sat alone at the appointed hour for the ring game and had no one attend the sewing classes. By two in the afternoon, she was utterly dismayed as she opened the book she had so cleverly purchased the day before she left New Orleans, convinced that no one would attend that event either. So when she heard the footsteps of someone approaching, she sat upright in anticipation.

An elderly woman, who hobbled along with a golden-tipped cane, appeared in the doorway. "Is this the book reading?' she asked.

"Yes, Madame," Angelique said, rushing over to greet her. "Welcome. Please come in and make yourself comfortable. I am Angelique Latour, the ladies' hostess. I am so pleased that you could attend."

"I know who you are," the old woman replied, "I am Countess Maria de la Martinique," extending her hand.

"Countess," Angelique replied with a slight curtsey as she gently embraced her wrinkled hand. "I am honored by your presence."

"No need for such formalities here, child. But I have to admit to throwing my title around a bit to get my way." She laughed.

Angelique smiled in response. She liked this woman immediately. "Shall we begin with our reading?"

"In a minute," the Countess replied. "I see that the ladies of the hotel have been quite cold to you. I observed the way you were received yesterday and heard the idle chatter at dinner last night."

"It is true. I am afraid that my status as a widow is most disconcerting to them."

"Foolish hens," the old women replied matter-of-factly. "I think it simply reminds them of their own tenuous positions as wives."

"Sadly, my future rests in their hands. If Monsieur Muggah learns of this, I will be sent back to New Orleans, tout suite. And my fate will be uncertain, to say the least."

The Countess smiled. "Tell me your story, which I am sure is much more interesting than anything contained within the pages of that book you hold."

Angelique hesitated, unsure of how much of her shattered life she should share with this genteel woman. But when Countess Maria leaned forward and nodded, the kindness in her eyes was reassuring, and Angelique began to reveal her tumultuous past.

My husband was to preserve my holdings for me, but I later learned that he borrowed from it until nothing remained. He died in a hunting accident, and while I believed that I was to receive his river plantation and home in New Orleans as his widow, I soon discovered that those had been liquidated as well. For all practical purposes, I am penniless." She omitted the details of sweet Josephina's short life, convinced that revealing that chapter of her story would indeed portray her as a tragic, pitiable figure. Besides, she found it difficult to talk about losing her baby, a memory she kept locked deep inside her heart.

"My goodness, child, how on earth did that happen?" she asked.

Angelique's face turned a crimson red. It was humiliating to admit, but she had already revealed so much to the woman, a stranger and prominent guest of the hotel. "He was a gambler, Madame. Of course, I had no idea of it. And he lost every penny we had in games of chance."

The Countess shook her head. "How heartbreaking. To suffer for the actions of another, especially one you have deeply loved, is unfair. Life has a way of bringing such cruel turmoil our way sometimes."

"Yes, it does," Angelique replied. "But I have been fortunate to meet great kindness in this world. People like yourself assure me that not all are bad. I am most grateful for that."

"You flatter me, child, but I do think that the only difference between you and me is that my husband died a rich man with a title. I had the good fortune to inherit both from him. But in different circumstances, I might very well have been right where you are."

Angelique pondered that thought for a moment. "I doubt that your husband was also a cad. But yes, I am glad that my fate escaped you, Countess. I would wish this on no one."

The old woman smiled as she looked at the clock on the wall and extended her hand once more. "Help me up, child. I do believe that tea begins in fifteen minutes."

When they walked into the lobby, the Countess holding firmly onto Angelique's arm, all eyes focused on them. They made their way over to the settee where the tea had been set out on the large coffee table by the servants. A two tiered platter held tiny sandwiches and sweet biscuits. They sat and Angelique poured a cup for the dowager, who looked around at the women sitting in various spots. "One would think," she said loud enough for them to hear, "that ladies of good breeding would relish the opportunity to have afternoon tea, especially if it meant they could keep company with a Countess. But I suppose, it is more gratifying to be judgmental and narrow- minded instead, a position I find rather detestable."

There was a silence in the massive room, and Angelique held her breath. Out of the corner of her eye, she saw first one woman and then another get up and move over to where they sat, smiling and introducing themselves to the ladies' hostess, the newest addition to the staff at the Oceanview Hotel. And behind the reception desk stood Monsieur Muggah, who looked over at Angelique and grinned.

Chapter Eighteen

The next day and those that followed, the women at the Oceanview Hotel eagerly participated in the activities that the ladies' hostess had created for their enjoyment. They giggled their way through Blind Man's Bluff and I Spy. Casting off their high top boots, they strolled along the beach, participating in shell-seeking contests. They shot archery, and when one of them announced that she imagined the bull's eye of the target to be her husband's face, she quickly apologized profusely to Angelique, who took it as a sign that they no longer viewed her as the poor widow and instead, to them, she was just another woman.

"Please, Madame, do not concern yourself. If you only knew the story of my husband's failings while he was on this earth, you might understand that I could say the very same thing."

And while the group gasped at the scandalous statement, they laughed even more in response and hugged her tightly.

Every afternoon at two, they met in the ladies' lounge to hear Angelique softly read from the Harriet Beecher Stowe book as some of them slowly drifted off to sleep. And promptly at four, they rendezvoused in the big lobby to take tea with the Countess, who was always the first one in attendance.

As some of the ladies bid their tearful goodbyes, they were replaced with new visitors who quickly learned, in quiet whispers, of the remarkable Angelique, the ladies' hostess, a widow, who was kind and fair and fun. And as each new group embraced her, she became more confident in her ability to do the job she had been hired to do. In fact, Monsieur Muggah was so pleased with the enthusiastic reports he had received from his female guests, that he no longer required the morning meetings, instead giving her carte blanche to create a schedule of events.

The summer of 1856 was a lovely time to be on Last Island. There was a variety of hotel guests and cottage owners, who spent time in leisurely pursuits at the playground of the well-heeled. Sober old men strolled the beach in the early morning, later retreating to the wide verandahs to talk politics until they were called to lunch. Young children built sand castles and frolicked in the waves as their nannies admonished them not to get burned by the sun. And romance blossomed among many a young couple, put together by fate and circumstance.

Boats of every size imaginable transported men out into the deeper water beyond the shoreline for fishing. And stories of the amazing specimens that got away were told with great animation around the dinner table at night.

The sea air and salt water was considered by many to be a cure-all for many ailments and the island became known as a place of healing. But all agreed that the gentle ocean breeze and bright blue skies, the roll of the waves as they rushed to the shore, provided a respite not just for the tired and weary, the high strung and nervous, but for everyone who came under the spell of this place.

Angelique took to visiting the equestrian area in quiet moments when she had no pressing duties. She loved watching a young girl of fourteen jump over logs and barrels with grace and speed and often thought of her with longing of her precious Josephina, wondering what she would have been like at that age. And when she had the time, she took long rides on horseback as she fondly recalled her carefree days on the plantation.

She tried not to think back on that time in her life, which seemed so long ago. Even though he had only been gone for six months, Jean Paul seemed like a distant memory. So much had happened to her in a short expanse of time, and she knew that such experiences changes a person forever. And yet, in some ways, she liked this new version of herself and was ever so hopeful that the peace and tranquility that Last Island offered its guests would work its magic on her as well.

Chapter Nineteen

The vast array of hotels and cottages were situated on the western end of the island, providing spectacular sunset views. And the vacationers used that location to their advantage, participating in the evening ritual of strolling along with beach as they exchanged pleasantries and made small talk. Once darkness enveloped the beach, they retreated indoors for other pursuits.

There were several eateries, and the abundance of fresh bounty from the sea meant that guests were treated to a vast array of sumptuous dishes, often at the Last Island Dining Club, where Captain Muggah, who considered himself to be quite the gourmand, attended to the catering when he was in residence.

Angelique dined on most nights with the Countess, where the finest table in the hotel had been reserved for her. She enjoyed the old woman's company and listened with rapt attention as she told romantic tales of adventure with the Count. She pictured the places they had visited, exotic locales that only existed in the pages of a book for Angelique.

"I have lived quite the life, child," she had told Angelique. "I have been one of the fortunate ones."

And indeed, the idea of living in a European castle, furnished with rich tapestries and ancestral portraits, seemed like a beautiful fantasy, something that only existed in fairy tales, and she found herself imagining what it might be like. The more time they spent together, the more Angelique came to like the Countess, who became her favorite guest and her trusted confident.

Serious about her job as the consummate hostess, Angelique took to heart the comment from one of her ladies about the lack of opportunity to wear her party dresses, since there existed only bi-monthly dances, with a sole fiddle player providing the music. In addition, she overheard mumbling about the fact that the hotel management charged the men fifty cents to take a lady to the dance floor, a practice that Angelique thought both strange and inappropriate.

She made an appointment to meet with Monsieur Muggah right away and pled her case on behalf of the female guests. By the next week, the bounty had been eliminated and the dance floor was occupied on Saturday nights with happy couples, who twirled to the music of a full band that he hired from New Orleans and had dispatched to the island immediately. Angelique's gentle touch as hostess was felt all over the hotel.

On evenings, when the men disappeared to the Billiard House or bar with club rooms for playing cards, Angelique had additional activities in place for the ladies and on more than one occasion, she received a whispered word of thanks from a grateful husband who was happy to be able to escape the nightly duties of keeping his wife entertained while he engaged in more manly pursuits.

Angelique continued to wear the customary mourning attire and, as she had suspected, it provided her with an air of respectability. But her approachability came through to all who met her, and her warmth enhanced the free and easy life the guests enjoyed at the seashore.

On one particular evening, as she was dining with the Countess, Angelique noticed a fashionably dressed man who continued to look her way. At first, she thought it was her imagination; his curiosity obviously piqued by her position at the hotel. It was not usual for new arrivals to wonder about her presence, given the gloomy black apparel, which seemed out of place in such a lively environment. He appeared to be alone, and she found that his stares made her uncomfortable, as she avoided his stolen glances.

"That man is looking at me," she whispered to the Countess.

"Of course he is, Angelique. You are a most beautiful woman."

"No, Madame. It isn't that kind of gaze. It is as though he knows me and is trying to figure out how."

"Then, go over and ask him," the Countess said with a laugh.

"I could not. It would be improper."

"Then live with your curiosity," she replied. Angelique loved the way the Countess was able to size up a situation so swiftly and express the truth, however bluntly it came out.

As was her custom, upon completing her meal, Angelique made the rounds of the restaurant inquiring among the ladies about their evening plans, offering her services and bidding them a good night. She approached the table of the strange gentleman and resisted the urge to ask him if perhaps she had grown a third eye in the middle of her forehead that caused him to look at her so intently. Instead, he spoke to her as she passed.

"Pardon, Madame," he said, "I hope that you won't think it rude of me to have stared at you for much of the evening."

"Well, as a matter of fact, I do," Angelique replied. "I find it most confusing."

"I don't mean to trouble you, of course, it is just that I found this on the floor as I entered the dining room, and I thought it might belong to you as you appear to be in mourning."

"Excuse me, Monsieur?"

He held the widow's broach in his hand which he extended to her. "You do wear the image of your late husband, do you not?"

Angelique's cheeks flushed, and she nodded her head. "Thank, you Monsieur. I didn't realize that I had dropped it."

"Not at all," he replied, "and let me express my sincere condolences."

"You are most kind, Monsieur."

"I am sorry. This is remarkably awkward. It is just that I had no idea that he had left this earth, especially since I was in his company just a month ago."

Angelique was dumbfounded, unsure that she had heard him correctly.

"Pardon?" she said, expecting the man to clarify.

"I did not know that your husband had passed, Madame, having met him so recently."

Her mind began to race; she was bewildered. "That is not possible, Monsieur. My husband, Jean Paul, passed six months ago. I am certain that you are mistaken."

The man's face turned a crimson red. "Please forgive me, Madame. I am incorrect, of course. It is just that the scar on your husband's face is much like that of the man I knew. But he went by Balafré and I think his given name was John, not Jean Paul. It is an honest mistake, no doubt. I humbly beg your pardon."

Angelique felt as though her feet were nailed to the floor as she stood in stunned silence. Had she misinterpreted? The man rose and bowed slightly. "If you will excuse me, I am late for a card game. I do hope that if we meet again while I am here, you will not hold this regrettable indiscretion on my part against me. I am mortified at my boldness and I pray that I have not caused you any distress."

But Angelique was unable to speak as she struggled to catch her breath. She searched for some logical explanation for what she had just heard, but none came. She grabbed a nearby chair to keep from fainting and found herself falling, falling, falling into an abyss, deeper than any she could have possibly imagined.

Chapter Twenty

The color drained from Angelique's face and she rushed over to where the Countess was seated.

"I am sorry, Madame, I must take my leave from you."

"What's wrong, child?" The Countess asked, concern rising in her voice. "You look troubled."

"I most certainly am," she replied. "I am afraid my explanations will have to wait until a later time. I presently have a mystery to solve." And with that Angelique walked out of the dining room and into the lobby. She was in search of someone who might help her unlock the puzzle.

"Monsieur Muggah," she said, moments later when she located him outside the ballroom. "May I have a word with you?"

"Of course, Madame. Do you have some new idea for our ladies that needs my immediate attention?" he asked.

"No, I am afraid it is something a bit more serious."

"Then please, come into my office where we will be afforded some privacy."

She followed him, taking her customary seat in the rattan chair as he sat behind the desk.

"Pardon my candor, but you look as though you have seen a ghost, Madame?"

Angelique thought for a moment at the irony of that observation. "I think perhaps I have."

He leaned back and looked at her intently. "I am afraid that I don't understand. Go on."

"If you recall the day we had tea at the St. Charles, you asked me about the picture of my husband on the widow's broach I wear."

"Yes, I remember."

"You said that not so long ago you had met a man who looked much like him, a man you called Balfort."

"Yes. And at the time, we confirmed that I was mistaken, a mere coincidence."

She hesitated. Taking a deep breath, Angelique asked the pivotal question, knowing that the answer could alter the course of her life forever. "Could you have possible meant Balafré?"

He paused before replying. To Angelique, it felt like an eternity. "Why yes. Yes, I do think that's the name," he said.

"Can you tell me the circumstances under which you made his acquaintance?" She asked.

Monsieur Muggah thought for a moment as though trying to retrieve a memory. "I believe it was in Memphis. I was there on business and found myself in a particularly spirited card game, with rather high stakes, I might add. The man, whom they called Balafré, was there. But I think he went by another name, a common one, like James or John. I assumed that he was a regular. I would not have remembered him except that I thought it odd that his name means scarface in French and indeed, he bore a semi-circle mark on his face."

Angelique could feel her heart racing in response. She tried to maintain her composure, nodding her head to indicate she understood. "Go on," she prompted.

"That is all, really. He referred to himself as a professional gambler, and I told him of our small games of chance here on the island. I indicated that while we simply had a few nightly hands to be played, the men who did so had deep pockets. I told him that if he found himself so disposed, he should pay us a visit."

Feeling as though the room was spinning, Angelique held tightly to the arms of the chair, pinching her hand to divert the emotional pain.

"Are you okay, Madame?" Monsieur Muggah asked, suddenly aware that there were implications to what he had revealed, although not aware of just how enormous they were.

"I don't know," she replied. It was an honest assessment as she tried to process all that had transpired that evening. She took a deep breath. "Monsieur," she continued, "I do believe that you have met my husband."

The hotel proprietor sat looking at her in disbelief. "Your husband? How could that be? Pardon me if I sound too straightforward, but isn't he deceased?"

"Yes, at least I thought he was. But there is no other logical explanation, I'm afraid," she said. "Yours was not the first encounter with the man we presumed to be dead since now I have learned of another. His use of the name John is bewildering, of course, but it could be an alias. No, it is all too coincidental. I suppose that he never thought that such a twist of fate would reveal his existence. It is, after all a big country and should be easy to lose oneself."

"You have had a bit of a shock, Madame," he said. "Please, let me get you a glass of brandy."

"No, I need a clear head in order to think. I do thank you for your help. And now, if you will excuse me, I have a lot to process."

"Of course, Madame," Monsieur Muggah said as he rose from his chair.

And with that, Angelique, feeling emotionally numb and overwhelmingly confused slowly made her way to her room, where she sat in the darkness for

much of the night with only the sound of the surf to
comfort her.

Chapter Twenty-one

Angelique woke with a start. She had dozed for a bit in the overstuffed chair, and as she lit the lamp near her bed, she glanced at the blue and white clock. It was after midnight. The events of that evening assaulted her brain, forcing her to catch her breath. Her heart clinched in painful response, and she wiped away a tear. There was little breeze entering the room, which suddenly felt airless and oppressive.

Walking to the window, she scanned the beach. It was deserted. The light of the waxing gibbous moon reflected on the water, and she left her room, tiptoeing through the quiet lobby and out into the sand. She glanced at the hotel. It was dark, the guests having turned in for the night. After removing her high topped boots, she waded into the water, which was still warm as though the kiss of the sun still lingered. The black taffeta of her dress felt like lead as it became soaked and with some difficulty, she continued her trek to the deeper parts of the Gulf. It seemed so easy to simply drift away with the tide, allowing the briny water to perform a soothing cleansing, washing away her pain until she felt nothing at all. She hoped that death would come quickly as she whispered a prayer, begging God to forgive her. Resigned to her fate, Angelique wondered if sweet Josephina and her mother would be waiting for her at heaven's gate.

"Da Lawd done made you strong, chile," she heard the voice say, as clear as if the speaker lurked nearby. "You is going to do something big," whispered the wind. She paused to listen.

Suddenly, her despair turned into anger. How dare Jean Paul do this to her? He had robbed her of everything, her money, her home, her dignity. Would she give him her life as well? Wasn't it hers to fashion as she pleased?

"No," she whispered. "You bastard. I will not die because of your transgressions. They are your sins, not mine."

In a fit of rage, she removed the wedding ring she had once so proudly worn and threw it into the churning current. She unpinned the broach, bearing her husband's face and hurled it into the darkness. Finally, she shed the black gown of mourning that she had worn out of duty. If she was no longer a widow, she was under no obligation to continue to don it. And she watched with satisfaction as the waves bore the oppressive garment far out to sea.

Slowly, she made her way out of the water and stood for a moment on the shore, looking out at the vast expanse of the briny deep. She smiled. This had been her baptism, she reckoned, and with a certainty in her soul that could only come from God Himself, she knew that she would begin her life anew. Clothed only in the pure white of her undergarments, she made her way back to the safety of her room. She could manage a few hours of sleep before the sun would come up, ushering in a new day.

***

Andrew Slater could not sleep so he decided to move from his bed to the coolness of the verandah of his cousin's cottage. He had experienced many a sleepless night since Anita had broken off their engagement only eight months earlier. He considered himself a man of science, a pragmatist, and yet, he had no way to biologically explain the pain in his heart, the intense longing he felt for the love he had lost. He had accepted the position in New Orleans to escape the places that reminded him of their days together. Far away from the North and challenged by the possibilities of a professional adventure, he had focused on erasing the memories of their courtship. For the most part, it had worked. But in the quiet moments of the night, the aching resurfaced, stabbing him like a sharp saber. Time, he knew, was a great healer, and he hoped that his time at Last Island would go far in helping him restore his sense of wellbeing. A change of scenery would do him good. As his cousin so aptly put it, it certainly couldn't hurt.

Looking out onto the wide breadth of sea, Andrew marveled at the splendor of the moon reflecting off of the water. The sky was clear and the stars twinkled in their glittery splendor. He looked up to see the summer triangle high up in the sky and wondered how many seamen had used those familiar constellations to navigate their boats through the dead of night. He thought of Odysseus, who had followed the handle of the Big Dipper in the long desperate voyage to his homeland. He hoped it would point the way for him as well.

He speculated about the time and remembered that his pocket watch was on the dresser in his room. If he didn't get some sleep, he wouldn't be very good company the next day. Stifling a yawn, he rose to return to his bed. Looking out at the sea once more, Andrew became momentarily distracted by movement in the water. It must have been a giant fish, he reasoned, but when he saw an undeniable figure moving slowly into the surf. It aroused his curiosity. Was it some late night swimmer, he questioned, and then thought it a dangerous bit of folly to go out into the unpredictable tide in the middle of the night. As he stood there in rapt curiosity, he was shocked to see that it was a woman, a most beautiful one from what he could see in the darkness. She hurled something into the water, then, undressed until she was only in her unmentionables. And he stared in amazement as he watched her make her way to the water's edge and then to the steps of the hotel where she disappeared from sight.

Chapter Twenty-two

Angelique appeared at the office door at eight the next morning.

"A meeting, Monsieur?" she asked.

He looked up from his desk and then did a double take. He hardly recognized her in the pale blue dress, which accentuated her tiny waist. The dangling sapphire baubles hanging from her dainty ears moved when she turned her head. She was stunning.

"Madame Latour," he said, rising to greet her, "I... I," he didn't know what to say.

Angelique laughed. "I look a little different, don't I, Monsieur?"

"Yes, and quite lovely, I might add." He blushed. She was, after all, his employee and he wondered if his comment had crossed the line of propriety. "Please, come in," he said.

"I did not want to appear to the guests of the hotel dressed in this manner until I had discussed it with you, but in light of the events of last night, I will not put my widow's dress back on, Monsieur. And if you insist, I will tender my resignation at this very moment and leave for New Orleans on the first available steamer."

"Oh, no, Madame, no. That is not necessary. Of course not. But are you sure that your husband is alive?"

"No, Monsieur, one can never be completely sure of situations that are surrounded by such mysterious circumstances. And his death certainly left me with many unanswered questions. However, for two people to have met a man who looks so much like my husband, a man who was called by the name given to him by his friends, and who bears the identifying scar on his face. Well, I think you must agree that it is more than a mere coincidence."

"It is true."

"But worse than that is the fact that if he lives, he did this to me by his own choice. He deceived me, letting me fall into the depths of sadness and poverty, utterly alone. No, Monsieur, that is inexcusable. It is cruel beyond all imagination. And even if he lives, he is dead to me, just as surely as if his body lies in the tomb. My days of grief and sorrow are over."

"I understand your plight, Madame. And your story is safe with me," he reassured her.

"I appreciate your discretion, Monsieur. I will simply say that my time of mourning has come to an end. It is a plausible excuse for those who are here on extended stay; the new arrivals won't know any different."

"Very well, Madame."

"So if we are in agreement, I will be off to set up the activities of the day for the ladies."

"Yes, yes," he said, "carry on."

Angelique exited the lobby and immediately went in search of the Countess. She thankfully found her sipping coffee in the dining room having just finished her breakfast.

"My dear Countess," Angelique said as she slipped into the chair opposite her. "I hope that you weren't worried about me, but I had a very eventful night."

"I can see that by the way you are dressed, my dear. May I presume that you are no longer in mourning?"

"I guess you could say that," Angelique replied.

The Countess leaned in and whispered conspiratorially. "Tell me everything and spare no details. I can only assume it had something to do with the man you met last night."

"Yes, but you must promise to keep the secret."

"Of course. Do you think I would share such private things with the silly hens here?"

Angelique laughed. "No, of course not. Let me begin by saying that the man you saw in this same room last night had found my mourning broach. I hadn't realized that it had fallen from my dress. When he returned it to me, he said he knew my husband, having seen him just a few weeks ago."

"What?" the Countess asked, "is he not dead?"

"I have my doubts, especially since Monsieur Muggah also seems to have met him months ago at a card game in Memphis."

"Are they sure it was your husband and not some case of mistaken identity?"

"Well, they called him by his childhood name, Balafré, given to him because of the scar on his face. It is hard to call that a mere coincidence."

"I am afraid I am woefully confused," the Countess said, "Start at the beginning, child." And Angelique related the story of Jean Paul's hunting accident and her inability to identify his bloodied body She told of how unsettling it had been at the time, how difficult it was to not have that moment of closure to say goodbye.

"Now, I can only pray that I never, ever see him again except perhaps in a court of law where I will plead for a divorce."

"My poor child. I can see why you might feel that way, but that is against our Catholic faith as you well know."

"Well so is faking your death!" Angelique, said, trying to keep her emotions under control, "I need time to make sense of it. But now, I wonder if I will ever learn the truth."

"Yes, of course, so many unanswered questions. Let's hope that the truth will become clear. For now, we will tell anyone who asks that your time is over. They will be none the wiser."

"Thank you Countess. You are my closest friend."

"The pleasure is mine, child."

And Angelique bid her goodbyes, the blue dress fluttering in her wake.

Chapter Twenty-three

Jean Paul Latour removed the gold pocket watch that had belonged to his father from his breast pocket. With one swift move, he popped open the cover, glanced at the time, and returned it to its safe place. He had an hour to kill before the high stakes card game was to begin, and he was filled with nervous anticipation. Carefully removing the leather pouch from the secret compartment in the bottom of his satchel, he counted out five hundred dollars. He had done well in Chicago, but as he was painfully aware, Lady Luck was an unpredictable mistress and didn't often stay in one place very long. He was always smart enough to hold back enough of his winnings to buy a train ticket on a moment's notice, a lesson he learned when he had to jump a box car like a common vagrant.

Fleeing a town in a hurry had become a way of life for him, and he had become quite adept at avoiding angry men, who often didn't take too kindly to his way of gaming. Besides, he reasoned, he was very much out of his cultural element in the North and eagerly anticipated his return to the South and a more cultivated way of life. Regardless of what the night's cards might hold for him, he would be headed that way tomorrow.

Upon returning the pouch to its hiding place, he found a slip of paper that had previously eluded him. He opened it to reveal the information that had been passed along to him. He read out loud, "Monsieur Dave Muggah, Oceanview Hotel, Last Island, Louisiana." *Hmmm*, he wondered, trying to remember where he had met the gentleman. So many of these encounters ran together, an occupational hazard for a professional gambler, and then he suddenly recalled the night in Memphis when he had lost hand after hand, along with a tidy sum of money. Monsieur Muggah offered to buy him a whiskey as a consolation prize, and they had talked at the bar for a few moments. He told Jean Paul about his hotel at Isle Dernier and the gentlemen's rooms he and his brother maintained for card games, whispering that the rich men who frequented the games had deep pockets and often, poor skills. They laughed at the folly of such fools and Jean Paul had invited him to call him Balafré, a name he went by only among those he considered friends and fellow gamblers. He carefully placed the piece of paper in the pouch. *I might need this someday*, he thought.

Jean Paul looked around the small room he had occupied for the past two weeks. It was beginning to feel confining and sterile. He certainly wouldn't miss it when he moved on to what he hoped would be greener pastures. A stroll around the city streets would clear his mind and calm his frazzled nerves, he reasoned. It always did. Grabbing his hat, he walked out the door, through the lobby and out into the cool of the summer evening. He took a few steps, getting his rhythm, and then turned the corner which led directly to a small city park.

It had become his nightly custom to take such walks though the green oasis, which reminded him of the verdant fields of Terrebonne, with its fragrant flowers and lush foliage. It seemed like a lifetime ago when he had spent the idyllic days of his youth there, riding horses and fishing in the ponds, immune to the responsibilities of adulthood. He tried to will himself not to think of the other memories that the plantation held for him, particularly those of his life there with Angelique. It was in these quiet moments that his thoughts turned to her, the vision of her beautiful face, so etched in his mind that he could see her as plainly as if she strolled along beside him.

The loneliness was intense. How he longed for her. Just to spend a moment in her presence would be a gift, one he knew he didn't deserve. He would never see her again, a sad reality that he had learned to live with and begrudgingly, accept. But he had done what he was compelled to do seven months earlier. His mounting gambling debts had, unfortunately, put their property in jeopardy, but worse than that, it had threatened their very lives. Jean Paul was loathe to admit that he had sunk to some underhanded dealings in the process, but he was confronted with the reality of his desperate choices every day of his life. He had once promised Monsieur Chauvin that he would protect Angelique with his last breath, if need be, and in the end, that is what he had done. She would never understand that, of course, how could she, given all that had transpired? But then, she would never know.

He wondered what kind of life she had created since he had faked his death, and prayed that she had escaped harm as she dealt with the aftermath. He guessed that she would find happiness eventually, even though it would be without him. After all he had put her through, she certainly deserved it, although the thought of her in the arms of another pierced his heart like a knife.

Pausing to light a cigar, he puffed on it as the smoke billowed around him. He rarely allowed himself to indulge in such moments of nostalgia, and he knew it would not do much for his concentration. Fearful of throwing off his game, he was determined not to think about it and instead pondered the night ahead as his heart began to race in anticipation of the possibility of a big win. He would always be chasing after the next victory, the pot of gold that could be his with one well-dealt hand. It was who he was, and who he would always be.

Chapter Twenty-four

Andrew Slater sat alone at a table in the dining room of the hotel. He was pleased when he was escorted to a window seat where he could look out at the water and the people on the beach. He wondered if perhaps he might get a glimpse of the sea nymph he had witnessed taking a midnight swim. And then he realized that he probably wouldn't recognize her if he did. She remained a beautiful phantom of the night to him, one who had had been on his mind all morning.

He looked around the room. The other gentlemen had wisely removed their jackets, a concession made to the oppressive July heat, and he followed suit. He took out his handkerchief to wipe his brow. It would take a while for the fella from Baltimore to get used to the Louisiana humidity, he reasoned. And even though Washington City was technically below the

Mason Dixon line, the dog days of summer were more like Great Danes here in the Deep South. But he was grateful: his work on the island had provided him with an escape from New Orleans, where it was at least ten degrees warmer.

In quite a twist of fate, the weekend trip with his cousin to the resort had turned into an eight week professional project. On a whim, he had collected some random data during that first visit and telegraphed it back to Washington when he returned to his pied a terre in the city. His information was met with great interest, and when he wrote his supervisors with a description of the location of the landmass, along with stories of how the area had changed with annual storm activity, he was given the assignment to remain there for a month, collect the various statistical information and write it into a report at the conclusion of his stay. It seemed like an exciting project to Andrew, one which could possibly help budding meteorologists gain some new insight into climate changes, so he packed his bags immediately and headed back on the first available steamer. When the Captain and his family were in residence, he stayed with them, but once they left, not wanting to impose on their hospitality, he moved into the hotel, as he had that morning. It provided him with a more convenient base of operations for his experiments.

Andrew observed the sea bathers splashing around in the surf. They seemed so carefree and he envied them for that. He remembered that feeling of overwhelming joy of life, a phrase he had learned from the French of New Orleans as joie de vivre. He hadn't felt anything akin to that since his relationship with Anita ended. They had been engaged for eighteen months after a whirlwind courtship, but he knew that she was the one he wanted to marry within weeks of meeting her and all he wanted was for them to begin their life together. She had delayed setting a date, even when he pushed for one, which she contributed to the myriad of details that planning a wedding involved. But as the months passed, he began to feel uneasy about her commitment to him. When she broke off their engagement, he was heartbroken, but not completely surprised. He was stunned, however, when three months later, she announced that she would be marrying, John Ashington, the son of a prominent banker. Andrew surmised that his position as a budding scientist with relatively empty pockets, made him a less suitable catch, especially in her family's mind. They were always looking for ways to increase their social position and would use their attractive daughter for that purpose as need be. But in the end, he knew that it was ultimately Anita's decision, and if she willingly went along with them, the culpability rested with her as well. Acceptance, he was learning, is a hard won lesson.

Pulling out the pad of paper, he began reviewing the data he had collected the previous day. Last Island, it seemed, was a perfect place for such a study. The weather could turn in an instant and popup squalls were commonplace. He made a note to check the rain gauge he had installed behind his cousin's cottage so that he could compare it to previous amounts. He looked through the chart he had constructed where he carefully recorded his daily observations of temperature, barometric pressure, humidity, wind and cloud conditions. On another sheet, he wrote down the data he had collected that morning and placed it in an envelope, which he sealed and addressed to the telegraph station in New Orleans. He would meet the incoming steamer bearing tourists within the hour and hand it to the purser, who would give it to a waiting courier at the dock. This relay system worked well in conveying the information to his employer at the Smithsonian, and he received word at the end of his first week there that they were pleased with his efforts.

Andrew paused to wipe his sweaty brow once more when she caught his eye. The tiny brunette entered the restaurant, her blue dress rustling with each movement. She stopped to speak to a group of ladies whose animated chatter filled the room, and they giggled in response. She weaved her way through the tables until she found an empty one in the corner and sat. Using the menu to fan herself, she brushed a wisp of hair from her brow. She was enchanting, and he tried not to stare.

Returning to his paperwork, he occasionally looked up to catch a glimpse of her. She tilted her head slightly as she studied the bill of fare. She smiled at the waiter who took her order, called him by name, and then rose from her chair as she crossed the room to the nearby window. Closing her eyes, she let the gentle breeze wash over her as she sighed in relief. When she spied the server, who set the dish of cold shrimp at her place setting, she returned to her table. Andrew watched her with keen interest. There was something oddly familiar about her, and he searched his mind for where he might place her. He prided himself on having a sharp memory, especially when it came to people, and he was certain that he would have remembered an encounter with one so lovely. Nevertheless, he was determined to meet her.

Chapter Twenty-five

After a frenzy of morning activity, Angelique was tired. She had gotten little sleep the night before and the fatigue overcame her much like the waves rolling just outside of the hotel. The incessant questions about her discarding her mourning attire were beginning to get on her already frazzled nerves. The Countess was right: these women were much like a brood of hens, and she had been thoroughly pecked.

At half past twelve, she made her way to the dining room in search of something to satisfy her urgent sense of hunger. She had hoped that trading in the oppressive black taffeta for the blue cotton day dress would provide some relief from the oppressive heat, but she discovered that it was inescapable. Angelique longed to shed her corset and pantaloons for a sea bathing costume and a dip in the water. Maybe, she thought, she could come up with a diversion for the ladies that would enable her to do that, although she couldn't imagine what form it might take and still fall within the clearly delineated rules of propriety. She was, after all, an employee, not a guest.

As she waited for her food to be prepared, she walked to the window in the hopes of catching a bit of the breeze. The room felt unusually stuffy, but perhaps it was because of the heat from the nearby kitchen, she reasoned. And then, she considered herself fortunate that her position at the hotel kept her far away from the confines of places that were like an inferno on such scorching July days. She felt sorry for her colleagues who weren't so lucky.

Looking out at the sea of visitors to the resort, she scanned the beach. Angelique tried not to giggle as she imagined her black gown bobbing around in the waters of the Gulf. Her venture out into the surf the previous night had been an impetuous decision, but in light of the events which seemed to indicate, with reasonable certainty, that Jean Paul was still alive and walking this earth, it had been the only thing she could think to do. And it had been empowering, a ceremonial step toward reclaiming a life that had been hers all along, but she had most certainly lost in her despair. Now, she wondered if that same act of emancipation would come back to haunt her and in the process, raise some unanswered questions. She looked as far as she see could along the shoreline. No sign of the dress. Breathing a sigh of relief, she whispered a little prayer to St. Anthony, patron of lost things. This was one item she hoped would never be found.

Chapter Twenty-six

The mid-afternoon sun was brutal and many of the sea bathers sought the shade of the verandah or opted for a nap. Andrew Slater placed a straw hat on his blonde head, adjusted the long sleeves of his shirt, and walked out to the beach. Even with that protection, he figured he was good for a half hour or so before the scorching rays would turn his fair skin a bright red, a hazard he attributed to his Scandinavian heritage. But he had data to collect, and he knew that this was peak time for gathering information on wind velocity.

He headed west and stopped to plant the anemometer in the sand. Having worked with this particular piece of equipment for years, he knew that based on the size of the cups, he need only adjust the dial to count the number of turns of the shaft over a set period of time and multiply that by two. It would run the experiment twice for good measure. He pulled out his watch and began the count. He was a minute into his experiment, when he spotted something tumble to shore with a wave. Watching the surge pull it back out to sea, he waited for the next roll of surf to see if it would reappear, and when it did, he was standing there, ready to retrieve it. He grabbed at the object and carefully washed the sand away. It was a broach, bearing the face of a dark haired man with a bushy moustache. *Somebody is missing this, a sentimental treasure, no doubt* he thought, and upon examining it further, he recognized it as some sort of mourning jewelry. He thought of the mysterious woman of the night before and remembered seeing her fling something into the briny deep before she removed her dark clothing. As a man of science, Andrew was familiar with the concept of solving puzzles, and he wondered if perhaps the two incidents were related. He stuffed it into his pocket and made a mental note to turn it in at the hotel.

Returning to the task at hand, he once again began to count the rotations as he watched the second hand on his timepiece. He turned his back to the wind and made two marks in ink on a small pad of paper. Wind out of the south, at ten miles per hour, he wrote.

Andrew walked back toward the hotel, his mind preoccupied with the day's events. He entered the lobby and immediately saw her standing near the reception desk, her blue dress matching the color of the sky beyond. She was even lovelier than he remembered her to be only a few hours earlier. Placing his hand in his pocket, he withdrew the broach. In a bit of serendipity, he saw this as an opportunity to speak with her.

"Excuse me," he said, removing his hat.

She turned to face him, "Yes, Monsieur?"

He studied her face. That all-too-familiar feeling of having met her before briefly distracted him. "You do work here, do you not?"

"I do, Monsieur. I am Angelique Latour, the ladies' hostess. Can I be of assistance?"

She was even more beautiful at such close proximity. Andrew felt his face flush, and he stammered in response. "Uh, uh, I am Andrew Slater. I am staying here at the hotel."

"Wonderful, Monsieur. And I trust that you are enjoying your visit."

He chuckled, afraid that he was coming across as woefully awkward. "I am actually here on a professional assignment, gathering weather data for the Smithsonian in Washington City." He hoped that she might be impressed.

"Oh, my," she said, "that sounds incredibly interesting. I have often wanted to visit our nation's capital," her voice trailing off. Her wanderlust never seemed to wane.

"It is a very interesting city and much different from New Orleans."

"I can imagine, Monsieur. Now, did you say that you needed my help?"

He had momentarily been sidetracked, but had to admit that he was enjoying her company. She was as charming as she was attractive. "Oh, yes. I was on the beach this afternoon and found this. I thought that perhaps one of the hotel guests might have lost it." He held out the broach for her examination.

She paused before taking it from him, her face growing pale. "It is mine, Monsieur. Thank you," she whispered.

He looked at her, a confused expression on his face. "Oh, I am so sorry, Mrs. Latour. I didn't realize that you were a widow," he said, eyeing her blue gown.

Angelique blushed. Her situation was far too complicated to explain to this handsome stranger. "I am. My days of mourning have come to an end." She paused, tilting her head slightly as she examined his face, "Have we met before, Monsieur?"

And suddenly, in one brief instant, all of the mysteries of the day had been solved. It came to him with a reasonable certainty: this vision of loveliness was indeed the Venus he had seen being born from the foam of the sea on the previous night. But even more interesting to him was the fact that he suddenly recognized where he had met her before fate put them together again on Last Island. He smiled at the memory.

"Mrs. Latour," he said, "may I be so bold as to inquire if you have a small blue and white china clock?"

Angelique turned to him and gasped. "My goodness! It is you," she said, extending her hand, "how lovely to see you again."

He bowed low and took her hand. "It is wonderful indeed."

Chapter Twenty-seven

The lightening illuminated the night sky and the clap of thunder which followed it woke Andrew with a start. He rose and made his way to the window to take in the show. Mother Nature's ever-changing moods had always fascinated him, even as a child. The idea of being a part of the trailblazing research on weather patterns was exciting, and Last Island provided him with an exceptional opportunity for study. But meeting Angelique again was an additional bonus, a delightful surprise, and he marveled at the universe's timing. His pragmatic mind told him it was merely coincidental, but his romantic heart said otherwise. Looking out over the water, he thought of how he had watched her a couple of nights before. What a vision she was! And she had no doubt had secrets to tell that he hoped she would readily share with him in the days to come.

Andrew contemplated going back to bed, but when he looked out into the distance, he saw that the skies had cleared and daybreak was imminent. He quickly dressed as he decided on a walk along the beach before the scorching rays of the sun would threaten to burn his fair skin. It was one of the advantages of his job that he often enjoyed. He had done some of his best thinking on those outings, the calm of the sea clearing the cobwebs from his mind, provided him with great clarity.

Grabbing his straw hat, he walked out of the hotel and onto the sandy shore. The air was clean and renewed after the rain and he breathed deeply, filling his lungs with its freshness. The sun began to peek above the horizon, putting on its brilliant display of color and light. He stopped to contemplate the beauty of such simple moments, the promise of a new day, which came with the dawn. His professional responsibilities had brought him to the island, but like so many, he had found healing there, and he could feel himself open up to the possibilities of his future. Time, along with the climate, had done wonders for his broken heart. With gratitude, he sensed that had begun the process of reclaiming his life.

He looked down the beach where he saw the lone figure of someone, who obviously had the same idea of an early morning stroll. It was a woman, he determined, and she was alone. He contemplated turning and walking in the opposite direction. He certainly didn't want to frighten her, and it would be improper to speak to an unaccompanied lady under such circumstances. But as he stood for a while watching her gaze out at the sea, he recognized her form: it was Angelique. He studied her silhouette. She was captivating and as the morning light began to illuminate the scene, she took on the ethereal form of an angel. He found himself riveted as he saw her reach into the rolling surf to retrieve something, which looked like a tattered piece of cloth.

She turned and made her way back to the hotel and as she grew closer, she waved in recognition.

"Well, Monsieur Slater. We meet again," she said as she reached the place where he stood.

"We do, Madame, and the pleasure is all mine."

She blushed in response. "Are you studying weather this early in the morning?" she asked.

"No, no," he said, "just couldn't resist the sunrise."

"Me, too," she said with a laugh. "It is the best part of the day. Besides, it is the few moments that are mine before I begin my responsibilities here at the hotel."

Andrew smiled. "Then please, don't let me interrupt you." He was trying to be chivalrous, but he wanted nothing more than to spend the time with her. She had been so gracious the night before, which was her manner with everyone. She was not just lovely; he found her to be quite intriguing as well.

"No interruption. And this gives me the opportunity to properly thank you."

"Thank me?" Andrew asked.

"For the clock," she said. "It was so kind of you to see to it that I was able to keep it, especially since you had won it quite fairly in the bidding."

"Well, if anything, my late father always told me that I should never pass up a chance to impact another soul through a good deed."

"Your father was a wise man," she said.

"Yes, he was. Besides, I could tell that it was of great sentimental value to you."

Angelique's face grew solemn. "Well, I thought it was. Now, I'm afraid that I am not so sure."

"Really?" Andrew said. "I must admit that you have piqued my interest now."

"And it is quite the story, Monsieur, although I don't think that we know each other well enough for me to share."

Andrew pointed to the piece of wet black taffeta that she held in her hand.

"Does it have anything to do with that bit of material you have retrieved from the water?" he asked.

She nodded her head, obviously embarrassed, and unsure as to how to continue with the conversation.

Andrew wondered if it was wise to reveal what he already knew of it. He cleared his throat. "If I may be so bold, I probably should mention that I saw you shedding your dress in the sea two nights ago. May I assume that this is the remnants of that garment? I hope that this knowledge won't cause you any distress as I can assure you that it was quite by accident."

Angelique blushed again. She searched for an appropriate response. "My goodness, Monsieur, you have seen me in my underwear, then?"

Andrew tried not to laugh, which he knew would only contribute to her anxiety. Instead, he tried to assuage her concerns. "It was very dark, Madame. I can assure you that your virtue was not besmirched. But I must admit that it did around my curiosity as to what might have prompted your actions."

She held up the tattered piece of black material for his inspection. "Well, yes, the morning brought me out looking for this. It would not be in my best interest for it to come tumbling to shore while the hotel guests are out and about. How could I possibly explain? And I hope that it is all that remains of my mourning attire."

"And if I might ask without seeming too forward, why did you feel compelled to throw it into the sea in such a clandestine way?"

Angelique sighed and carefully considered whether she should share the events of the previous days. It was humiliating, of course, but it seemed that fate had already brought them together, and she figured she had little dignity left to lose with this man who had already witnessed her surreptitious act of desperation.

"It seems that my husband may not be dead after all," Angelique said, more bluntly than she had intended, "a fact that brings me great pain rather than joy."

"I am afraid that I don't understand," Andrew said.

"Can you keep a secret?" she asked, as she gazed intensely into his eyes.

"I believe that I already have," he said with a chuckle.

Angelique considered the validity to that as she began to divulge the story of Jean Paul's bizarre accident and the financial consequences of his gambling. She told the details of her chance encounter in the dining room with the stranger, who recognized his face on the mourning broach, and relayed how it coincided with the same kind of recognition from Monsieur Muggah at their first meeting at the St. Charles.

"Unless it is some inexplicable coincidence, everything points to the probability that my husband is indeed alive."

Andrew was unable to respond. His mind was reeling at the story he had just been told. He felt compassion for her. What a complicated situation, a real dilemma! And he tried to disguise his disappointment because it meant that Angelique was not a free woman.

"I am so sorry, Madame," he said, wanting for his words to sound sincere, He was struck by the irony of expressing his condolences at her revelation. Under different circumstances, there would be rejoicing at the news. "How awful for you and what a curious twist of fate."

"Indeed," she said, "And now, I am at a loss, hopelessly confused as to how to proceed with my life. There are many questions for which I must find answers."

"I can only imagine. If you won't think it too presumptuous of me, I'd like to offer my services in any way I can. I may be able to use my connections at the Smithsonian to help you uncover the truth. I do have the ability to send and receive telegraph messages. And at the very least, I can be a sympathetic ear and a supportive friend." He meant it. She was a damsel in distress if he had ever met one, and he hoped that he could be of some help to her.

"I do thank you, Monsieur. It is most kind of you. And I must implore to you to keep my story from the other guests of the hotel. It would be scandalous if the truth were known." Her eyes met his, and he could feel his heart respond. It wasn't an altogether unpleasant feeling, but he reminded himself that she was a married woman and unavailable to him.

"Of course, Madame," he said. "Rest assured, my lips are sealed."

"Thank you Monsieur. Your discretion is most appreciated."

On an impulse, he added, "Would it be improper for me to invite you to dine with me tonight so that we can discuss how to proceed in our quest for the truth?"

"Our quest?" Angelique asked, confused.

"Well, I did offer to help.

Angelique paused for a moment as though carefully weighing the consequences of her answer. "Well, as far as anyone knows, I am a widow who is out of mourning, and you are a single gentleman, a guest of the hotel. It may raise a few eyebrows, but yes, Monsieur Slater, I will have dinner with you tonight."

"In that case, you must call me Andrew."

"Very well, Andrew. And you may call me Angelique. But now, if you will excuse me, I have ladies to entertain."

"And I have data to collect."

"Au revoir," she said as she made her way back to the hotel.

Andrew watched as she disappeared from sight. What a mystery this woman was, what a delightful mystery.

Chapter Twenty-eight

There was a gentle breeze wafting through the lobby and the laughter of the ladies filled the room as they gathered for tea. As the days passed, Angelique had fallen into the rhythm of her daily routine at the hotel, planning activities and parties. She was the consummate hostess, and it was difficult not to join in on the gaiety of the guests. The diversion was good for her because it kept her from thinking about Jean Paul and his wicked deception. She was anxious to learn the truth, which she deemed necessary in order to pick up the pieces of her shattered life. Goodness know that she was grateful to the Muggah brothers for the opportunity to live and work on the island, but she couldn't imagine that she would remain there indefinitely. And regardless of whether she did or not, her marital status was a key piece of information about her life that she certainly couldn't ignore. She simply had to know the truth, although she had no idea where to begin.

When tea time was over and the ladies moved to their rooms to nap before dinner, Angelique began to clear the dainty cups and saucers. The Countess, who remained in position on the settee, reached out for her young friend's hand. "Shall we have one more cup, chèr?" she asked.

"If you wish, Countess. I do believe that there is enough remaining for the two of us to share."

"This one will be special," she whispered.

Angelique looked at her quizzically. "In what way?" she asked.

"I have an extraordinary gift, my dear, one that I rarely reveal, but am aware of every moment of my life."

"You have many gifts, Countess," Angelique said with a smile.

"This one is rather specific. And if you will pour our tea, I will tell you all about it."

As they sipped, the Countess began to weave a tale of growing up on Dauphine Street in the Faubourg Marigny section of New Orleans. She had a variety of colorful friends as a young woman, including one with an elderly grandmother, who was both fascinating and frightening. Once, before she was a Countess and only known as Maria, she had gone to visit and happened to be left alone in the parlor with the old woman as she waited for her friend to appear.

"You don't know, do you, child?" the woman had inquired with her shaky voice.

"Know what?" Maria had asked.

"Those special powers that the Lord above has bestowed upon you."

"Excuse me? Powers? What powers?"

The old lady had cackled in response. "You'll see soon enough. When the voices begin to speak to you, know that they tell the truth. Use the magic for good, and it will be returned to you tenfold. Stay strong in your faith to God; He will guide you."

Maria had been relieved when her friend appeared, but she thought of the unsettling encounter for days afterward. And on an unseasonably warm November morning, when she had tripped as she emerged from mass at St, Louis Cathedral, falling into the arms of The Count, she heard the words loud and clear. "He is to be your husband." She had mumbled her apologies, but it scared her so greatly, that she quickly fled his presence, returning to church for another hour to light a candle and pray for protection against the forces of evil.

Three months later, when she had been invited to attend a lavish Mardi Gras Ball, Maria was left breathless when he approached her, bowing low and offering to catch her should she fall during the evening. She had blushed in response, but was flattered that he had remembered such a brief encounter between them. When he informed her that he had filled her dance card for the remainder of the night, she had been both flustered and pleased. By the end of the party, she hadn't been the least bit surprised when the voice told her that she would be married within the year. And in a beautiful fall ceremony, filled with pomp and circumstance, she had become The Countess Maria de la Martinque.

As she grew older, the voice had grown stronger. It had once saved her youngest son from drowning when she found him in the pond, his head slowly disappearing under the water. She pulled him out just in time, and she shuddered to think what might have happened if she had ignored the words, "find Edward," which went off in her head with alarming certainty.

When the Count went off to war, she didn't worry about his safety as long as she heard "he's protected," each night as she drifted off to sleep. And through the years, she had come to depend on the Divine Intuition, which told her what was to happen, especially to those whom she loved.

Angelique took the final sip of tea, placing the porcelain cup on its matching saucer. The Countess patted the spot next to her, and Angelique moved beside her obediently. "Give me the cup," the Countess whispered. Taking it in her gnarled hands, she began to study the leaves left at the bottom, the random patterns spelling out some bizarre secret code that made no sense to Angelique, who leaned forward to hear the story, the mysteries, that it revealed.

"Ah," the Countess said, "I see the snake."

"You do?" Angelique asked in wide-eyed wonder.

The Countess pointed to a thin line of tea. "This indicates a falsehood that has come into your life."

"Like a husband suddenly brought back from the dead?" she asked. "That's no surprise."

"Hush, child," the Countess admonished. "I also see the mountain, which means that you will have many obstacles to overcome in your journey for the truth."

Angelique stifled a giggle. She didn't need any supernatural powers to predict either of these, but out of respect, she continued to listen intently.

Suddenly, the Countess began to laugh. "Ah yes, she said. There it is."

"What?" Angelique asked.

"The heart," she said with great satisfaction. "My dear girl, you are about to fall in love."

Chapter Twenty-nine

Panic rose in Angelique's heart. Love could make a person blind and stupid; it was a sure-fire way of destroying yourself. She certainly was proof of that. And the thought of giving herself so completely to another again terrified her.

My dear Countess," Angelique said, "I have no intention of falling in love again. Ever."

"But you will," came the reply, "of that I am certain."

Angelique took the old woman's hand in hers, "I know that you are a hopeless romantic, who steadfastly holds onto the idea that love conquers all, but life has taught me to be a little more realistic. I was almost crushed beneath the weight of my grief. I have cried enough tears to fill an ocean and prayed enough prayers that I am certain that The Almighty Himself has grown tired of the sound of my voice."

The Countess shook her head sympathetically. "My dear Angelique," she said, "when we are at our lowest point, we must acknowledge what we know for certain, that life must change. And it is in that change that we find hope."

"I have had to adapt to far too many changes in the past few months. I am afraid that I have lost my ability to adapt."

"Nonsense. You are a strong young woman. Goodness knows you have handled these overwhelming challenges quite well."

"I don't know about that. But it isn't like I really had a choice, did I?" Angelique offered.

"No, of course you didn't. But sometimes, we must simply allow the universe the guide us as it unfolds its magnificent plan."

"I am a social director for spoiled ladies at a hotel in the middle of the Gulf of Mexico. I have a lying, cheating husband, who may or may not be dead and barely a penny to my name. Some magnificent plan, if you ask me."

The Countess patted Angelique's hand. "Be patient. It will come. Great things are awaiting you, my dear."

Suddenly, Angelique could clearly hear Hannah's voice, admonishing her to stay strong in order to fulfill her destiny. She shuddered as she heard the words.

"Well, regardless," Angelique said, "I can't even think about falling in love when I am far too busy falling to pieces. Besides, even if I was so inclined, I am not free to love anyone, not until this business with Jean Paul is laid to rest."

"Well, now, that's an interesting play on words," the Countess laughed.

"You know what I mean. I just want to be happy, although I think I have forgotten what that feels like. Honestly, sometimes, I think that happiness is just the absence of drama and chaos and pain."

"And I understand why you feel that way, chèr. But I want you to promise me that you won't let the past destroy your future. All of us have been through something that has changed who we are. You have to let go of what should have been and look at what is while you hope for what will be. Go bravely into the storm, safe in the knowledge that you won't drown. That's how the healing begins. And then, you will rebuild your life one moment at a time. And don't you worry about that husband of yours. The universe will find a way to bring him to his knees. He will pay for what he has done to you."

"Do you really think so, Countess?" Angelique asked.

"With every breath I take," she replied.

"Well, I hope I get to witness it. Is it wrong to feel so filled with anger? I can't help it!"

"Of course not. You are only human," the Countess said, "but remember, vengeance belongs to God alone."

"I know that you are right. And I must remember that even though Jean Paul took so much from me, I cannot allow him to destroy what I have left or my very soul will be gobbled up by his deceit."

"That's my girl," the Countess said, clapping her hands. "Keep your heart open. There is a great power at work here, which we are not meant to understand. Just trust that good will come. Give yourself an opportunity to recognize your own glory."

"I'll try. I promise to try." Angelique said. She paused. "How did you get so wise?" she added.

"I have lived, my dear. Goodness knows, I have lived."

And with that, the Countess rose and gestured toward the reception desk, where Andrew Slater stood, waiting.

Chapter Thirty

Andrew smiled as Angelique approached. She held out her hand, and he took it in his, holding on for a moment longer than perhaps he should have. Her touch was electrifying, and he struggled to subdue the emotions that bubbled to the surface of his conscious thought. "Good to see you again, Madame," he said, "Looks like you were having quite the intense conversation."

"The Countess is a remarkable woman. I am so fortunate to have her advice and counsel."

"Loyal friends are rare and more precious than gold, Angelique," Andrew said.

"That is most certainly true, especially during difficult times."

Andrew took a step closer. "I hope that you will someday count me among those who are here to support you."

Angelique was struck by the sincerity in his voice, but unsure how to reply, she simply nodded her head. "Did you want to see me about something?" she asked.

He cleared his throat and pulled a carefully folded piece of paper from the pocket of his waistcoat. "I have an idea that I hope will be met with your approval. I have taken the liberty of penning a message to a friend of mine, who works for the North-Western Police Agency in Chicago."

"Police? I don't understand."

"Actually, the name is a bit of confusing. They are not into enforcing the law, but are rather trailblazers in a new field called private investigating."

"What's that?" Angelique asked.

"As the name implies, they do research on people who may be into some unsavory dealings, background checks and such. But they also locate missing persons."

"I see. Go on."

"With your permission, of course, I'd like to send Benjamin this telegram, requesting his aid in determining the whereabouts of Jean Paul."

Angelique took a step back and looked Andrew squarely in the eye. Her blues locked onto his. For a moment, he was afraid that he had overstepped his bounds. After all, he had only known her for a short time, and he worried that she might have thought his actions presumptuous.

She softened, reassuring him with her smile. "I am overwhelmed by your kindness, Andrew. Do you think it might be possible that this friend of yours could find Jean Paul?"

"If anyone can, he can."

Angelique looked up at the ceiling as though trying to process the possibilities. She furrowed her brow. "I am not sure that this is wise. I can't imagine what I would say to him if indeed he was located. In fact, I would have an overwhelming urge to shoot him myself."

Andrew stifled a laugh as he thought of Angelique wielding a pistol at her wayward husband. "If I may be so bold as to suggest that finding him is the only way you will discover the answers you seek."

"Of course," Angelique replied. "He is most certainly unfinished business in my life. And at the very least, it will settle the mystery as to whether he lives or is simply an inconvenient ghost."

"Precisely," Andrew said.

"But, Andrew," Angelique began. She paused, then blushed, her face turning a crimson red. "I am afraid that I barely have the funds to pay your friend Benjamin. Frankly, I would rather not know the truth. No, I would prefer to live my life in this terrible limbo than ask anyone for money."

He had embarrassed her, and it pained him to see the agony on her face. "Let's begin with this telegram as a form of inquiry and see where it leads. My friend is a kind sort, a most agreeable man, who would never miss an opportunity to help a damsel in distress, especially an incredibly beautiful one."

Angelique felt her cheeks burn once more. This man had seemed to arouse so many of her emotions in the course of a brief conversation. "You flatter me so," she said with a smile. "Truly, you are becoming a dear friend."

Andrew returned her smile. "And that is my greatest wish," he said. "So I have your permission to send this?" he asked, holding the paper tightly in his hands.

"Yes," she replied in a barely audible voice. "And we shall let fate decide what we uncover in the process."

"And may it conspire to bring you the peace you seek."

Andrew bowed low and turned to walk away. Her eyes followed him until he was well out of sight.

What a curious twist of events has brought this man into my life, she thought. Angelique sighed as she felt something stir deep within her heart.

Chapter Thirty-one

Jean Paul removed the handkerchief from his pocket and wiped away the beads of sweat forming on his brow. He hated that his own body had betrayed him by producing such tangible evidence of his frayed nerves. They were only into their fifth hand, and he had already lost most of his money. He had bet recklessly, against his better judgment, on hands that had been less than stellar. But the winning cards had been elusive and with each round, he was easily beaten. It was an ominous beginning to a night that had been so full of promise.

As the dealer shuffled the cards with great fanfare, Jean Paul, who had always been a bit superstitious, felt for the St. Christopher medal he kept in the left pocket of his waistcoat. The amulet, which he considered his good luck charm, had been given to him by his great uncle, who had taught him how to play this very game when he was nine. Oh, how he loved those lazy afternoons when they sat in the parlor at the square table, the old man pointing out the best strategies for a win. When he was twelve, he was introduced to the idea of gambling, anting up his stash of sweets against his uncle's silver coins. And when he won, he squealed with delight, quickly becoming seduced by the euphoria that accompanied a victory. By the time he was sixteen, he was an accomplished card player and had taken the weekly allowance of many a boyhood friend. The medal had seen him through every game he had ever played. He stuck his fingers deep into the pocket and tried to conceal his alarm when he couldn't find it. And then, he began a search in earnest. First, he examined his right jacket pocket, then, that of his trousers. He felt the carefully starched linen of his shirt, but it was nowhere to be found. Panic rose in his heart and he wiped his sweaty brow once more.

"Lose something, old man?" one of the players teased as he puffed on his fat cigar.

"Uh, uh, no," he stammered, trying to conceal his ever-growing anxiety.

The men around the table laughed. "Don't be nervous. The night is young, and you will have plenty of time to win back what we have taken from you," one of them said.

Jean Paul took a deep breath and reached for the five cards that he had been dealt. Slowly, he moved them to reveal three jacks and two tens. He smiled. Full House. He would hold this hand rather than risk getting something less desirable by discarding.

The wagers moved from man to man. Two of the players folded, leaving the three remaining to battle it out. Jean Paul watched as the pot grew larger with each raise, figuring there was close to eight hundred dollars in the middle of the table. He licked his lips; he could almost taste triumph. When the bet was at a hundred, he did the mental math. He had just enough to raise one last time and remain in the game. Silently, he prayed that one of the players would call, and he could claim his winnings. If he walked away with a three hundred dollar profit for the night, he would be well satisfied.

"Call," the cigar smoker said as he chewed on the end of the stogy.

The dealer pointed to the man at his left. "Two pair."

Jean Paul was next. "Full House," he called as he laid his cards on the table.

He was poised to scoop up the pot when the cigar smoker began to laugh out loud. "Looks like this is my lucky night," he said, "I have a Straight Flush, jack high here." And he placed the five ordered cards on the table with one hand as he began to grab at his winnings with the other.

The men grumbled and one of them suggested a whiskey break. "You are buying," he said to the winner, who rose from his chair.

Jean Paul sat in disbelief. What were the chances that his opponent would draw the one remaining jack? Rotten luck. Clearly, he was out of the game, but he was also out of money. With the exception of his emergency fund, he was broke. He was glad that he had been smart enough to have a contingency for just such moments. He nodded his head in deference to the winner.

"If you guys don't mind, I am going to call it a night," he said, trying to be cheerful.

"What's the matter, Balafré, have you lost your nerve, along with your money?"

Jean Paul managed a weak chuckle and patted his belly. "Naw, I could beat you fellas on any given night if I sat here long enough. Unfortunately, the pork roast I had for supper seems not to be agreeing with me, and I have one hell of a case of indigestion."

"Sure, you do," one of the men teased. "I would hate to think that you are losing your guts, or worse than that, a poor sport."

"Tomorrow night, I will return for my revenge," Jean Paul said dramatically. "Be ready and bring your money."

"We will, sir. We will," another called.

Once outside, Jean Paul had little time to relive the events of the night. He had to formulate a plan. Sadly, he didn't have enough money to pay both the hotel bill and buy a train ticket out of town. Life was about choices, quick decisions made out of necessity. It had become his way of life. He entered the hotel, grateful that the lobby was deserted. Making his way to his room, he quietly opened the door and slipped inside. He removed the satchel and felt for the secret compartment. He retrieved the four twenty dollar gold pieces, along with a five, and stuffed them into his pocket. Hastily, he packed his clothes, pausing to feel for the St. Christopher medal with each garment. *Where on earth could it be?* He wondered. When he gave up all hope of finding the precious charm, he closed the valise and tiptoed out into the hall. He was relieved to see that the night clerk was still absent, asleep on the job, no doubt, and that the lobby was unoccupied.

Jean Paul knew that it would be impossible to find a driver at such a late hour and justified walking the six blocks to the train station by thinking of the money he would save. By the time he reached his destination, the large clock showed that it was close to 2 a.m. He approached the ticket window and asked when the next train going south would be leaving.

The clerk looked at him incredulously. "Your destination, sir?" he asked coldly.

He thought of the piece of paper in his pocket. Last Island. All he needed was a couple of lucky streaks at the tables, and he would be back in business. And hadn't the gentlemen who owned the resort mentioned the deep pockets of the unskilled players? It would be a risky trip, since he was required to return to the place where he might indeed be recognized, but he figured that he had been dead long enough to have been forgotten. Besides, he considered himself much too clever to be exposed. Yes, he had a plan.

"New Orleans," he said.

"Day after tomorrow," the clerk said as he yawned.

"No," Jean Paul said. "No, that won't do. You see, I have a bit of an emergency that necessitates my arrival in New Orleans as soon as possible."

"Sorry, sir, but I can't help you," the clerk replied nonchalantly.

Jean Paul reached into the pocket of his trousers and pulled out the five dollar gold piece. "Would this help?" he asked, placing it on the counter.

In one swift move, the clerk retrieved the coin and looked at Jean Paul. "I have no control over the railroad timetables, sir. But I can put you on a freight train arriving within the hour. There is a small passenger car behind the engine, usually reserved for crew. I can give you a ticket at a reduced price, if you don't mind a rough ride and no conveniences."

At that point, Jean Paul would have hitched a ride with the devil himself just to get out of town. He readily agreed. The clerk handed him the leger, asking for a signature and with a flourish, he signed his name.

"Good evening, Mr. Smith. I am glad that we were able to accommodate you."

Jean Paul took the ticket and moved to sit on a nearby bench. He could feel the rapid beating of his own racing heart, and breathed a sigh of relief when he finally heard the distant whistle of the train as it rounded the bend. His chariot to freedom had arrived, and he wondered what fortunes he was to make at the resort. Luck might had eluded him on this night, but he fully intended to take her along on his next adventure.

***

The following morning the chambermaid entered the deserted hotel room. Assuming that the guest had checked out early, she quickly attended to the task at hand, readying the room for the next occupant. She was almost done when a shiny object caught her eye. As she bent down to retrieve the medallion, she carefully examined it. "Why, it looks like a St. Christopher," she said, "It must be my lucky day." And she slipped the medal into the pocket of her apron.

Chapter Thirty-two

After a restless night, Angelique gave up on trying to sleep and rose before dawn. Exhausted from replaying the events of the previous days in her mind, she quickly dressed and set out in search of coffee. As she popped into the kitchen, she was happy to see the cook standing over the large drip pot and closed her eyes as the comforting smell of the brew awakened her senses.

"You're up mighty early," Sistene Leblanc observed, handing Angelique a dainty cup of dark coffee.

"Couldn't sleep," Angelique replied, trying to muster a weak smile.

"Happens to the best of us," the kitchen manager said. "Our problems seem to be magnified in the stillness of the night."

"C'est vraiment; true words," she confirmed, pouring cream into the steaming cup.

Sistene turned to look at her colleague. "I don't know your whole story, but this is a small hotel and people talk. I have heard bits and pieces. Seems to me that you have more than your share of heartache."

Angelique blinked away the tears she could feel forming in her eyes. "Yes, I suppose I have," she whispered.

"Honey, you just keep the faith. Bad times don't last. Besides, you strike me as a strong woman. Why, look at all you have done here in such a short time. Don't forget, there is always a tomorrow. That's what gives us hope." She offered a smile. "Now, you take your coffee out on the verandah and enjoy the sunrise." And with that, Mrs. Leblanc turned to attend to the pot of grits bubbling on the massive stove.

"Thanks, I will," she called as she made her way to the quiet of the porch.

Settling into a rocker, Angelique thought about the fact that everybody seemed so hell-bent on calling her strong, when she didn't feel that she was in the least bit. Sure, she had survived difficult circumstances and incredible loss, but she was all out of resilience, having emptied that well months earlier. She thought of the battle that lay before her if Jean Paul was indeed alive.

Did she have the wherewithal to fight him, especially given his history of control and manipulation? She tried to examine her emotions where her husband was concerned. The anger and pain of his betrayal was palpable. But she knew with reasonable certainty that the only way she would ever find peace was to know the truth, whatever that might be. She would adjust her sails and head into the wind because it was the only way to reach a safe harbor. She prayed that she could muster up the courage she would need in the weeks ahead. And then, she laughed to herself. What choice did she have? She would have to fight or die a slow death herself. Yes, she would choose to fight.

Lost in her reverie, Angelique was suddenly aware that she was not alone. Andrew stood a few feet away from where she sat. "Good morning," she said quietly.

"Good morning to you," he replied, "looks like you were quite engrossed in some deep thought."

"Yes," she whispered. "Sometimes, it is hard not think too much."

"Understandable," he said, trying to sound supportive.

"And then, I keep trying to formulate a plan of action in the process," she added.

"So have you?" he asked.

"Not yet. I guess a lot depends on what your friend from Chicago has to say."

"Yes, of course. I am so pleased that he has agreed to do some simple investigating. Who knows? It may turn up nothing, but if anybody can solve the mystery regarding Jean Paul, Benjamin can."

"And I suppose I need to know what to do when that information comes to me. If he is indeed dead, then, I am afraid that I will feel relief, rather than sadness."

"Well, after all that you have learned about him and his actions, your response is a reasonable one."

"But if he is alive, then, I must find him, confront him, and divorce him."

Andrew heard Angelique sigh. The early light of the breaking dawn illuminated her beautiful face, and he felt his heart soften.

"I know that will be hard, but peace of mind is often hard won. And you certainly deserve a harmonious life after all of the strife you have endured."

"Thank you, Andrew," she said as she turned to face him. "You have been such a supportive friend."

I would like to be much more than that, he thought, but he kept that to himself. "I am so glad to be of service to you, Angelique."

Emptying the contents of her cup, she rose. "Guess it is time to get ready for the day," she said.

"Me, too," he agreed. "I have data to collect." And then, as though struck by a great idea, he added, "I will be done by 10. How about you? Can you take a mid-morning break and join me at the shooting range?"

Angelique thought for a moment. Why not? She was woefully out of practice, but maybe sharpening her marksmanship would be a good idea. "Yes," she said. "That might be fun."

And as they parted company, each thought of the possibilities the day might bring.

Chapter Thirty-three

Angelique grabbed her straw hat from the hook on the hall tree and slipped quietly out the back door of the hotel. The sun, although still low in the sky, was already shining brightly, and she squinted as her eyes adjusted to the glare. The heat and humidity were oppressive. *It is going to be another hot day*, she thought, glancing at the sea bathers who splashed merrily in the cool surf.

Surveying the paths surrounding the inn, Angelique set out for the firing range. Andrew was waiting for her and when he saw her, his face broke into a wide grin. "So glad that you could get away," he said, offering his hand.

"Thanks for thinking of it, Andrew," she replied, removing her hat and shielding her eyes from the sun as she looked up at him. "It has been a while since I have done any shooting, but who knows, it might come in handy someday..." She stopped short, figuring there was no need to elaborate. While she spoke in jest, Angelique wondered if there was a bit of truth in her words. Some days, she felt capable of cold blooded murder where Jean Paul was concerned.

Andrew led Angelique to the table where two shiny Allen and Thurber single-shot pistols were being carefully loaded by the hotel shooting instructor, Ralph Dubois. He tipped his cap to acknowledge the pair, and then proceeded to go through the safety regulations he had implemented for anyone who entered his realm. "Wouldn't want anybody to get hurt by accident," he said soberly. When he was satisfied that they were dully prepared, he pointed to the bench. "Ya sit here, and use the table to help steady your hand. Aim first at the nearest target, then you will work your way to the one farthest away."

Angelique held the strange-looking gun in her small hands. It felt heavy as she awkwardly tried to balance it. Andrew tried not to chuckle. She looked fierce, yet adorable, wielding the pistol. He admired the fact that although she was soft and feminine, she was fearless. Her boldness mesmerized him.

"Ladies first," he said.

She smiled and pointed the gun at the first target. Closing one eye, she furrowed her brow in intense concentration. Gently, she squeezed the trigger. The lead ball left the barrel with a resounding boom and Angelique's body jerked in response. "Did I hit it?" she asked.

"Looks like you just grazed it," the instructor replied.

Angelique frowned. "Your turn, Andrew," she said.

Assuming the same position, he fired the pistol, hitting left of the center.

The pistols were reloaded. "Try concentrating on the target. Line up the center of the firearm with the exact spot you want to hit."

Angelique nodded. She picked up the pistol once more. Andrew watched intently as she took a deep breath and held it. In one swift move, she pulled the trigger.

"Little lady, I think you have a bull's eye there," Ralph said with a grin.

Andrew clapped enthusiastically. "Well done!" he cheered.

Within the hour, they had shot six rounds and Angelique had won five of them handily.

"Remind me not to make you angry," Andrew teased. "You are quite adept with a pistol."

"Just luck," she said with a grin, "although I suspect you let me win."

"Not a chance," he replied. "Men are notorious for having an ego where marksmanship is concerned. I would have gladly taken victory over you. You won fair and square."

"Then, good for me," Angelique laughed. "Of course, I used to shoot all the time on the plantation. But those days seem like a lifetime ago."

"Well, clearly, you haven't forgotten. How about a glass of lemonade before lunch?"

"To celebrate my triumph?" she asked.

"Well, yes, and to cool off after being out in this heat."

Angelique smiled as she placed the hat back on her head and took Andrew's arm. He blushed, completely enchanted.

The dining room was a pleasant oasis from the oppressive temperature of the sunny outdoors. The lunch crowd hadn't fully arrived yet, and Andrew was grateful to have a few moments of quiet conversation with Angelique.

"So tell me some more about your work," she began, "it seems so interesting."

"It is. You have seen me collect data on everything from wind speed to barometric pressure and rainfall amounts. There are others doing the same all over the country. The idea is to plot these numbers on a huge chart to determine certain patterns. It is the first step toward predicting the weather, which will have greater implications."

"True. People will have a better idea when to plan their picnics," she said with a laugh.

"Well, we hope to save lives as well. If we can warn people about excessive rains that could mean potential flooding or storms with destructive winds, we can do something good for the nation."

"That's true." Angelique said. "It is noble work, Andrew, and you should be proud."

"I will be when I can see this come to fruition. I hope to be part of the team that works on analyzing the results when I return to Washington City. That's when things will really get exciting."

The expression on Angelique's face changed. Andrew secretly hoped it was because he had mentioned leaving Louisiana, and her, behind. But he quickly changed the subject. "No science needed to predict this weather. It looks like today is going to be clear and unreasonably hot."

Angelique gazed out the window at the vast expanse of sand and sea. Billowing clouds drifted in the blue sky above. "When I was a child I used to lay in the grass and stare up into heavens, watching the puffy cotton-like clouds take shape. I imagined them to be animals or monsters or pretty maidens dressed in their finery. I could spend hours, there, lost in the stories I made up in my mind."

Andrew laughed. She was charming. "I used to do that, too. Simple entertainment, I guess."

Angelique leveled her gaze at Andrew, her blue eyes twinkled, which never failed to disarm him. "But you know what?" she asked.

He got the idea that the question was rhetorical, so he simply locked eyes with her and shook his head.

"In all of those days, I never looked for rainclouds."

He looked at her quizzically as she continued.

"You know, Andrew, I think that life is a lot like the weather that you study. Sometimes, a storm comes out of nowhere and catches us unprepared. And we have to run like the dickens for cover. Do we have control over it? No, of course not. So it does little to worry if tomorrow will bring sunny skies or rain showers; all we can do is embrace whatever comes along. And even though it is hard to see past the clouds, we have no choice but to adapt."

"Yes, I do believe that to be true, Angelique."

"But then," she continued, "there are moments that take our breath away like a rainbow that suddenly appears, bringing with it the certainty that God is still in charge."

Andrew reached across the table and took her hand in his. "Angelique, you are the most fascinating woman I have ever met."

She blushed. "Forgive my ramblings. I was just hoping that this bit of quiet isn't the calm before the storm."

"Were you referring to a tempest named Jean Paul?" he asked.

"I suppose I was," she responded.

He squeezed her hand. "Just remember that even after the most violent hurricane, quiet and order returns."

Angelique smiled. Andrew always knew just what to say.

As they parted company, Angelique thought of the serendipity that had brought Andrew into her life. She remembered his kindness at their first chance meeting at the auction in her New Orleans home. It had seemed like a lifetime ago. He had gallantly returned the blue and white clock just because he understood that it was important to her. And without the intervention of the universe, she would have never been able to properly thank him. But the fact that he had so inexplicably appeared at Last Island gave her pause. As her grandmother liked to say, "You often meet your destiny on the most unlikely roads." And Angelique could not help but wonder if the dashing Northerner, who studied the weather, might perhaps be a part of hers.

Chapter Thirty-four

The sunlight was blinding and Andrew adjusted the brim of his hat in order to read the thermometer more clearly. He carefully entered the numbers onto the chart he had painstakingly constructed and did a quick comparison. "Ninety two degrees," he said to himself, "been in that same range all week. It is a blazing inferno out here." He wiped his sweaty brow with a handkerchief. Although he had been documenting weather patterns on Last Island for close to three weeks, he wondered if he would ever become accustomed to the unrelenting heat and humidity. But the unexpected assignment that had kept him at the island after visiting his cousin had been therapeutic; his broken engagement seemed like a lifetime ago. Of course, meeting Angelique had done wonders to heal his wounded heart. He glanced at the rain gauge, but knew that with no noticeable precipitation, there was nothing to record. His thoughts returned to her. She was beautiful, no doubt, but it was her spirit that had ultimately attracted him. Every moment he was able to spend with her was delightful, and he found himself looking for excuses to wander around the hotel, hoping their paths would cross during the course of the day.

He set the weather vane in the sand and watched as it blew in the wind. He had loved the way she had compared life to the weather. What a clever woman she was, how insightful. He recorded the wind direction. Her strength and determination in spite of the overwhelming circumstances of her life inspired him. But there was something else, something much more powerful at work, and he knew it. He was falling for her. His logical mind told him to run as far as he could from the charming Mrs. Latour, with her complicated history. His instincts warned him that her questionable marital status could potentially bring him heartbreak if he allowed himself to feel affection for her. But in the war against rational and emotional thought, the heart often wins. Andrew smiled at the possibilities. Although he may have been a man of science, he was a hopeless romantic. And Angelique was undeniably the object of his affection.

Looking over the data sheet, Andrew double checked the numbers, then, carefully copied them onto another form. He folded the page and placed it into an envelope marked for the telegraph office where the information would be relayed to Washington City. As he dusted the sand from his trousers, he headed to the dock to meet the steamer.

The purser disembarked after all of the passengers. He waved in recognition when he saw Andrew. The two shook hands in greeting; they were accustomed to these bi-weekly rendezvous, which were strictly business.

"Hello, Sir," Andrew said. "I take it the trip over was pleasant?"

"Smooth seas," the man replied, "which is always good."

Andrew nodded. "I have the most current information to be telegraphed," he said, handing him the envelope. "I do appreciate your help with this."

"Certainly," the purser said. "Glad that I can contribute to the process. Perhaps someday, the weather will no longer be a mystery."

"Well, we are doing our part, but yes, that is what we hope to accomplish."

"I almost forgot," the man added as he handed an envelope to Andrew. "This came for you as well."

"Thanks," Andrew said. And then, he stopped short when he looked at the return address. Benjamin Browning. Chicago, Illinois.

Chapter Thirty-five

Jean Paul stretched and yawned as the train slowly pulled into the station. The trip from Chicago to New Orleans had been a long, grueling one. He probably should have listened when the ticket clerk had warned of no comfort features on this particular train, one which had been designed to transport cargo rather than people, but his need to leave town was urgent. The saying that beggars can't be choosers came to mind and although Jean Paul hated to be in a vulnerable position, his weakness exposed, he had become accustomed to bending to the hand of fate. And ultimately, didn't luck always change in his favor? He smiled. Undistracted, the trip had offered him plenty of time to formulate a plan. Returning to his native land was risky, at best, since being recognized could threaten his very life. But what choice did he have? He would regroup and move out of the city as quickly as he could. And if Fortune had come along on this trip, as he hoped she had, he would replenish his coffers with the necessary funds to achieve his ultimate goal. He took a deep breath as he descended the steps, clutching his satchel. The familiar sounds and smells of New Orleans were comforting, yet terrifying all at once. For better or worse, Jean Paul was home and his first order of business was to find a barber.

The bell jingled softly as he entered the shop only two blocks from the station,

"Good morning, Sir," the barber greeted him, "How may I help you?"

"I need a shave," Jean Paul replied

The barber nodded, pointing toward the empty chair. "Have a seat. You're next," he said, returning to his customer.

Jean Paul picked up *The Picayune* and scanned the pages. He didn't know what he was looking for, but sighed in relief that there was nothing that pointed to him. After eight months, he was still safely dead and buried. He hoped that he had been forgotten as well.

As the barber shook the cape with great fanfare, Jean Paul slipped into the chair. "Sir?" he asked, which came as both an acknowledgment and a question.

"A complete shave," Jean Paul replied.

"All of it? Are you sure?" the barber asked, carefully examining the thick black beard and moustache. Jean Paul was relieved that the man had not questioned why he would shun conventional fashion of the day by requesting such a drastic thing.

"Yes," he said.

Jean Paul took a deep breath. He had worn the facial hair all of his adult life, and he thought that it made him look distinguished, more masculine. But this was not the time for vanity to rule and removing it would keep him from being recognized, he hoped.

"Have to charge you extra for that," the barber said, whipping the lather in the large mug.

"No problem," Jean Paul said as he did the mental math. His limited funds required frugality, a concept he detested, and he looked forward to his recouping his losses.

The barber deftly spread the foam, using a fluffy short-handled brush. Jean Paul closed his eyes. "You live here or just visitin'?" the barber asked in an effort to make polite conversation.

"Visiting," he said.

"I see," the barber continued. "Where are you from?"

Jean Paul cleared his throat. The time he had spent in the Midwest had trained his ear somewhat, and although he had practiced faking the accent of a man from Chicago, this was his first opportunity to actually use it. It would be hard to discard the distinguished cadence and pronunciation of his South Louisiana drawl, with its French influence. He had a lifetime of habits ingrained in him, his speech being only one of them. "Chicago," he replied, careful to emphasize the short "A."

"Long way from home," the barber commented as he continued with the lather.

"Yup," Jean Paul replied.

"Here on business, then?" the barber asked.

"Ah, huh," Jean Paul confirmed. He breathed a sigh of relief as the barber held his neck back and wielded the straight razor.

"No talking now," he said with a chuckle, "wouldn't want an accident."

With long strokes, the barber made quick work of the thick beard and ten minutes later, he placed warm towels on Jean Paul's clean-shaven face.

"Done," he pronounced, as he held up a mirror for closer inspection.

Jean Paul stared blankly at his own reflection. He hardly recognized himself, which is exactly what he had hoped for, but he felt naked and exposed. It was unsettling. The only remnant of his previous life was the distinguishing scar on his upper right cheek. He touched it by instinct. Anyone who had known him would recognize it immediately, but he had little recourse there.

"That will be fifty cents, Mr…" the barber's voice trailed off.

"Smith," Jean Paul replied, "John Smith."

The barber chuckled as he took the money. "Common name in Chicago, I am sure. Fortunately, for you, it is rare here in New Orleans."

Jean Paul nodded his understanding. He quickly donned his hat and grabbed his satchel as he made his way to the door before the barber could ask any more questions. He stepped out into the busy street and kept his eyes to the ground as he made his way to his next destination.

He had walked several blocks before he located the apothecary.

"May I help you?" the clerk inquired.

Jean Paul cleared his throat and concentrated on the accent. "I have a most unusual request," he said. "Do you have powdered henna?"

The clerk raised his eyebrows. "Don't get much call for that, but let me check." He moved to the rows of long glass cabinets behind the counter. After a few minutes of searching, he reached into one and pulled out a small packet. "It appears that we have it, sir," he said, placing the item on the counter. "That will be twenty-five cents."

Nodding his head, Jean Paul paid for the package and dropped it into his satchel.

"Anything else I can do for you?" the clerk asked.

"Yes," he said. "Can you give me a recommendation for a reasonably priced hotel nearby?"

"Certainly, sir," the clerk said, "I can tell by your accent that you aren't from around here."

Jean Paul smiled in response and nodded in affirmation.

"I would suggest The Cornstalk, which is four blocks north of here. It is nothing fancy, but clean and quiet," he said. And as an afterthought, added with a grin, "The cook there is famous for her biscuits."

The four blocks to the hotel seemed like a mile to Jean Paul, who was weary from the long train ride. Other than a short cat nap, he hadn't slept in two days. He breathed a sigh of relief when he saw the distinguishing sign, a brightly painted ear of corn on a slender green stalk.

As he approached the reception desk, he was mindful of his speech. "Hello," he said, "I'd like a room, please."

"Of course, Sir," the clerk said, "and may I ask how long you will be staying with us?"

Jean Paul thought for a moment. It was a good question, dependent entirely on how long his limited funds would keep him afloat. He was careful how much he revealed. "I am not certain," he replied. "My business in this area may only take a day or two, but it could be longer."

The clerk held the room key in his hand and tried not to show his exasperation. "Well, we ask for payment in advance, Sir, which is why I asked."

There would be no running out of this hotel, leaving the management to explain the unpaid bill. Jean Paul wondered how long he could afford to stay and still have enough money to stake a card game. "Let's make it two nights," he replied.

Turning the guest register for Jean Paul to sign, the clerk handed him the key. "That will be eight dollars, Sir."

After he paid, Jean Paul wearily climbed the stairs to his sparse room. He dropped his satchel and fell onto the bed. Within minutes, he was snoring loudly, oblivious to the sounds of the city below.

Chapter Thirty-six

Andrew stuffed the letter into the inside pocket of his jacket and made his way back to the hotel. The lobby was quiet as many of the guests had retired to their rooms for an afternoon nap. Angelique sat with a small group of ladies, who seemed to be doing some kind of stitchery. He nodded and waved in recognition, which she returned with a smile. Anxious to hear what Benjamin had to report, he didn't stop to exchange pleasantries with them. In fact, it took every bit of restraint he could muster not to run to his room and the privacy it afforded him. But once he had cleared the watchful eyes of the group, he quickened his pace until he reached his destination. Turning the key in the door, he quickly entered his room and making his way to the desk, he pulled out the envelope, studying it carefully. He took a deep breath. Only then, did he realize that his hands were shaking. His future with Angelique rested in the contents of Benjamin's letter, that much was certain. And the fact that it he was so concerned about the outcome of the investigation solidified his feelings for her. Yes, he cared more than he wanted to admit, even to himself. He opened it and began to read.

Dear Andrew,

I hope this letter finds you well and that you are continuing to enjoy your adventure in Louisiana. You lucky bastard! Spending the entire summer at the seashore under the pretext of working is my idea of heaven Yes, you are gathering random data on weather in order to earn your keep, but I know that you are in your element doing so. You have certainly fallen into a good situation as well as an excellent professional opportunity. As I run around the city, chasing after bad guys, I think of you with overwhelming envy.

From your telegraph, I sensed some urgency where your friend's husband is concerned, and fortunately, I have been between cases, which has afforded me the time to do a bit of investigating on her behalf. Under normal circumstances, such a hunt might take me all over the country as I followed up on possible leads and subsequently, it is a slow, and often expensive process. But on a whim, I began my search right here in Chicago; I figured, why not? The key to being a top-notch sleuth is to put yourself in the mindset of the person whom you are pursuing. You said that he was a gambler, first and foremost. As you may (or may not) know, there is a rather large community of card players in the city, many with deep pockets. You also said that he is presumed dead. I figured if I was a gambling man who wanted to cover my tracks, I would get as far away from my homeland as possible and then find a place with ongoing action and high stakes. Chicago certainly met that criteria.

I reached a few dead ends, at first, but that never stops me. The main clue that guided me was his French Creole accent, which I thought would certainly arouse curiosity and attention here. I figured that all on my own, old man, which is why I am such a good detective. The addition of the distinguishing scar on his face was a helpful bit of information that you passed along as well as the possibility of his using John or James as an alias. I am sure that I woefully mispronounced his nickname, Balafré and frankly, I was not sure that he would have even used it outside of his circle of friends in Louisiana, but armed with a description of the man, I had enough to begin the search.

An associate of mine happens to belong to a group who plays cards with some regularity, although I often tease him about the prudence of gambling on our paltry salaries. But he proved to be an invaluable resource and opened the doors to some of these card parlors, which might have otherwise remained closed to me. On the third evening of my search, through sheer luck, I happened upon a small assembly of men who had indeed met your infamous Jean Paul. And to further substantiate that I had found our man, they too, referred to him as Balafré. He has assumed the name of John

Smith, which made me chuckle a bit. No one knew him as using his real last name, Latour. And given his accent, he had admitted to his fellow gamblers that his name was indeed Jean Paul, but thought that the Anglicized John was more appropriate, considering their Midwest location. They laughed as they recounted the story of watching him sweat as he lost hand after hand, one fateful night, feigning illness so that he could be excused from the table. They hadn't seen him since, but it was my observation that he didn't seem to garner much respect among them.

Upon further investigation, I was able to identify the hotel where he had been staying. And I wasn't totally surprised to hear that he had sneaked out of the establishment, in the middle of the night, I might add. He left a sizeable bill in his wake and the manager seemed anxious to help me locate him in the hopes of recouping the money. I checked the stables as well as the coach and train stations, figuring he had left town. I was right. I was finally able to locate the rail clerk who remembered his identifying scar, prominent accent, and nervous demeanor. With a little coaxing, he was able to check the ticket leger and said that a Mr. John Smith had indeed bought a ticket on a southbound freight train to New Orleans. He didn't travel in style, that's for sure.

Depending upon how long it takes for this letter you reach you, I think it is safe to say that the phantom husband of your friend is alive and well and walking the streets of New Orleans. Or perhaps he is in seclusion nearby. I have learned that devious men often return to the scene of the crime, even if it is a risky move. And while I can't imagine that he would remain in a place where he could be so easily recognized, given his faked demise, investigative work has taught me never to try to understand the intentions of the disturbed and the desperate.

The fella sounds like a cad, and I hope that if you do find him, you give him a good thrashing, for the good of mankind. But somehow, I think you will do what is necessary to defend the honor of this lady, whom you obviously care for as well. Chivalry has always been your strong suit. And if it provides her with any reassurance at all, the fact that she holds a valid death certificate for him, should protect her in a court of law.

I am delighted that this was such a simple case. So much of what I do is lengthy and complicated. And I hope that you find this information helpful. You now owe me a favor and you know how much I enjoy having you completely indebted to me. Perhaps we will meet soon in Washington City, where I will expect for you to repay me with a fine meal and a bottle of the best whiskey money can buy.

Good luck and do be careful. I would advise caution where this man in concerned. I got the idea that he is motivated by his own agenda. Keep me posted. You know how much I love a good mystery, especially when a woman, who I can only assume is beautiful, is involved.

Your friend,
Benjamin

Andrew read the letter twice, trying to digest the details. While there had been several clues, sound indications that Angelique's husband was indeed alive, he had hoped those were merely coincidences. Of course, Benjamin's letter had indicated otherwise. And this new evidence raised even more unanswered questions. He knew that it was important that he share this information with Angelique as soon as possible, but he needed to think about how to proceed. The last thing he wanted was to cause her any undue worry, although he couldn't imagine how she would not be filled with dread and concern once she learned the truth.

Taking another deep breath, he folded the letter and returned it to the safety of his jacket pocket. As he entered the hotel lobby, he smiled. Sitting alone in an overstuffed chair was the Countess.

"My dear Countess," he said, as he approached her.

She looked up and him and greeted him with a huge grin, the wrinkles around her eyes becoming more prominent. Even though she was, by all practical standards, an old lady, she still possessed a youthful zest, which made her beautiful. "Well, if it isn't the dashing weather man," she said, extending her hand. She was charming.

Andrew bowed low, taking her hand in his.

"Would you care to sit with me for a while? Maybe we can stir up some gossip," she said with a wink.

"I would love nothing more," Andrew replied. "But, I had hoped for someplace more private."

The Countess laughed, "My dear man, are you propositioning me?"

Andrew blushed. "N-n-n-o, ma'am," he stammered. "I just need your advice."

"Then, take my arm and lead me to the library. The silly hens here don't read, so we will be undisturbed," she said, and then added, "Perhaps you can order us a bit of sherry?"

Andrew offered his arm, which she firmly grasped. The Countess stumbled a bit, but rose to her full height. "What secrets do you have to share, young man?" she asked.

"You have no idea, my dear Countess," he replied, "You have no idea."

Chapter Thirty-seven

Angelique was surprised to see the Countess and Andrew emerge from the library arm in arm.

"Are you two on a date? Unchaperoned?" She teased.

"I will never tell, chèr," the Countess replied with a wink. "But I am willingly going to turn him over to you, now. If you will excuse me, I am late for dinner." And she slowly made her way to the dining room, leaving Andrew and Angelique standing in the shadows.

"So it seems that you have had an eventful day," Angelique said.

"I have," Andrew said soberly.

"Is that what you were discussing with the Countess?" she asked.

"No. I solicited her advice on another matter," he answered.

"Hmmm... You are being awfully mysterious," Angelique said. "Would you like to share?"

Andrew blushed and pointed to the library. "I think we will be afforded some privacy in here," he said.

Angelique looked at him quizzically, but proceeded into the walnut- paneled room. It was by far, the most serious spot in the inn, a tastefully-decorated place of restful quiet with volumes of books lining the massive bookcases. But it was rarely used by those seeking lively entertainment, rather than intellectual pursuits, during their time at the hotel. She took a position on the large velvet sofa and waited for Andrew to join her.

Reaching into the pocket of his waistcoat, Andrew removed the letter and held it out to Angelique. "I have heard from Benjamin," he said, taking a deep breath.

"And?" she asked. The question hung in the air like molasses poured from a bottle on a cold day.

"I think you should read it for yourself," Andrew said.

They sat in silence as Angelique read. When she was finished, she folded it carefully and returned it to the envelope. Andrew wondered how many minutes had passed between them before she spoke; it felt like an eternity.

"I don't know what to say," Angelique said, tears forming in her crystal blue eyes.

"I know that it is shocking, something that you could not prepare for, even with the possibilities laid before you by others."

Angelique nodded her head in agreement.

"How can I help?" Andrew asked.

"I don't know that you can," she answered. "My husband, it seems, is alive, which I can't ignore. But with no way to locate him, my life is on hold."

"Do you really think so?" Andrew asked.

"Well, most certainly," she replied. "How could it not be? I am in limbo, a widow who is not a widow. I am as imprisoned as a caged canary, without the freedom to choose the course of my own life."

"But you have a valid death certificate, Angelique. For all practical purposes, and certainly in the eyes of the law, Jean Paul is dead and buried," Andrew said.

"It is simply a piece of paper, Andrew. And it does, in no way, overshadow what I know now to be the truth. I don't want to live my life in fear that someday, he will turn up like a reoccurring nightmare. No, until I am able to settle matters with him. I am not free."

Andrew reached for her hand. It pained him to see her so distraught, and he wondered if he had made a horrible mistake by launching the investigation. "This is my doing," he said quietly, "I should have left Jean Paul in the grave where he belonged."

"No," Angelique whispered, "you were only trying to help, to be my champion. I am grateful for your loyalty and friendship."

Andrew smiled weakly. It was so like her to spare his feelings when her own heart was in turmoil. "I'm sorry."

Angelique turned to look at him squarely in the eye as she often did when she was about to make a serious point. "Does the Countess know? Is that what you were discussing earlier?"

"No," Andrew said, "It would be unchivalrous of me to breech your confidence in that way. No one will hear of this unless it comes from your lips. And I will hold your secret until I go to my own grave, if that is what you want."

Squeezing his hand, she said softly, "thank you for that."

"It is the least I can do for you," he said.

She held tightly to his gaze. "Then may I ask what you and the Countess did discuss?"

Andrew's face turned crimson as he searched for the words. The silence between them was deafening.

"Andrew?" Angelique asked, shattering the stillness that enveloped the room.

He cleared his throat. "Would you believe me if I told you that we were discussing the weather?"

"No," Angelique replied.

Andrew chucked. "The Countess is a wise one, as you well know. I needed her counsel about a personal matter. "

"That is rather vague," Angelique replied. "Care to elaborate?"

"I am not so sure that is appropriate, given the current circumstances."

"I see," Angelique said, pressing her lips together. He had offended her. She had shared her confidences with him and yet, he remained closed to her. Understandably, she thought it was unfair.

He cleared his throat. "I told her that my affection for you grows stronger with each passing day, and that those feelings are confusing to me."

"Is that your truth?" she asked in such a simple way that it took his breath away.

"Yes," he said.

"And what did she say?" Angelique asked.

"She told me not to let anyone, living or dead, keep me from exploring what might bring me great joy. The heart, she says, is resilient. And just because it has been broken, doesn't mean it can't love again. She said that when the right person comes along and the feelings are undeniable, it is an opportunity to embrace the possibilities, rather than run from them. She suggested that there is great power in true affection and that in the end, no obstacle is too great for love conquers all."

"Do you believe that?" she asked.

"I do, Angelique, I must if I am to survive in this world."

"The Countess is judicious indeed, especially when it comes to matters of the heart," she said.

She turned away from him, and he could tell that she was crying. "Please don't cry," he whispered. "I can't bear to see you in pain."

"These are not tears of sorrow, Andrew," she said, facing him once more. "They are tears of joy because, you see, I have growing feelings for you, too."

Andrew smiled and gathered her in his arms. "Then, that's all I need to know," he said. "Somehow, we will find a way; we will not run away from what might happen between us. It is my promise to you."

Angelique had no words. She simply lifted her chin so that he could kiss her, and he happily obliged.

Chapter Thirty-eight

Jean Paul woke with a start. It took a few moments for his brain to identify the unfamiliar surroundings in the twilight, but he breathed a sigh of relief when he realized that, for the time being, he was safe. As he lit the lamp, a dim light illuminated the room. Pouring water from the pitcher into the washbowl, he splashed it onto his face, its smooth feel startling him. He removed his clothes and laid them on the bed. Then, reaching into his satchel, he pulled out the packet of henna. He laughed at the absurdity of what he was doing, and then shrugged as he wet his jet black hair and systemically shook the powder onto his head. It was a messy undertaking, and he soon realized that would have been a better idea to complete the task in the bathroom at the end of the hall, but fear of discovery kept him safely within the confines of his rented room.

An hour later, he studied his reflection in the faded mirror. He didn't recognize himself. The henna had turned his hair a deep auburn color and that, coupled with his lack of facial hair, had transformed him into a completely different man. It was exactly what he had hoped to accomplish. For added measure, he donned a pair of horned rimmed spectacles of plain glass he had sometime used when he needed a more subtle disguise. The affect was quite dramatic. He whistled a little tune to celebrate his victory as he redressed.

As he made a mental inventory of what his next order of business would be, his stomach growled in response. Food, no doubt, was first on the list. And then, he would find a card game. It was time to recover his losses. He licked his lips in anticipation of both.

With only fifty dollars left in his pocket, he ordered the cheapest item on the menu of the neighborhood tavern. He chose a table closest to the action, where he could eavesdrop on the conversations of the other patrons, hoping that someone would mention a game nearby where he could unobtrusively invite himself. And soon enough, a small couple of men gathered at the bar, ordering rounds of whiskey, which they quickly downed. When one of them announced that he had heard that there was a particularly interesting house for games of chance right next door, the others wholeheartedly agreed that they should pay a visit.

With one swift, move, Jean Paul headed in their direction and introduced himself.

"Good evening," he said in his practiced Chicago accent. "I hope you will forgive the intrusion, but I couldn't help overhearing your conversation about the card game. Let me introduce myself. My name is John Smith. I am here on business and looking for a bit of diversion. I don't know anything about gambling, but have always wanted to play. Would you be willing to take a novice along with you?"

The men looked at him incredulously. His appearance made him look comical, like a newspaper cartoon character come to life. "John Smith, eh? So you have never played poker?" one of them asked.

"No," Jean Paul lied. "I have thirty eight dollars in my pocket. Would that be enough to get me a seat at the table?"

The men laughed in unison. "Are you prepared to lose that money?" one asked.

"Maybe I will have beginner's luck," Jean Paul said in reply.

The oldest of the group looked at his companions and whispered. "It will be like taking candy from a baby," he said. And then, putting his arm around Jean Paul's shoulder added, "Come with us."

There was no sign over the door of the building next door, indicating what might be housed inside. One of the men knocked boldly and said something that Jean Paul didn't understand to the man who answered. Within minutes, they were escorted to a side room and a table with six empty chairs. A deck of cards rested in the middle, and one of the men picked it up and idly began to shuffle.

"Shall we go over the basic standard of play?" he asked.

Jean Paul anxiously nodded his head in agreement.

"This will be a training hand, so as to go over the rules with you," the man said as he carefully dealt each player five cards. "OK, John. Look at your hand." It was lousy and Jean Paul was thrilled. The dealer described the procedure for betting and Jean Paul placed a dollar in the practice pot. After the other players followed suit, they taught him the language of poker, and he eagerly asked the difference between raising and calling. When they questioned if he understood the ranking of hands to declare the winner, he grinned and said that he did. In unison, the men laid down their cards.

"I think I won!" Jean Paul exclaimed. "I have a king and a queen!"

The men at the table rolled their eyes. "Not this time, Monsieur," one of them said. "My pair would have beat you and my friend's full house would have beat us both."

"Oh," Jean Paul said, trying to look disappointed, smug in his acting ability. They played another round for good measure and then, the dealer announced that the next hand would count.

Jean Paul hastily bet on a bad hand and lost three dollars. When the waiter appeared, the winner ordered a bottle of whiskey for the table and handily poured two fingers for each man as the next hand was being dealt.

For the next three rounds, Jean Paul lost badly, but he remained sober, as the men downed glass after glass of whiskey.

Satisfied that he had won their confidence, and that no one had noticed his sleight of hand, he smiled. "How about we make this more interesting?" he asked, placing a ten dollar bill in the pot.

"It is really a shame to take your money so easily, Monsieur," one of the players said, his slurred speech indicating that the alcohol was taking effect.

"Maybe my luck will change soon," Jean Paul said.

The man laughed as one by one they looked at their cards. Soon, the betting began in earnest and Jean Paul was pleased to realize at one point that the pot had risen to one hundred dollars. He studied his hand, revealing the three queens. That possibly would have good enough to win, but for good measure, he slipped the forth queen from the waistband of his trousers into his hand, discarding the useless eight of diamonds in the process.

When Jean Paul laid his four of a kind on the table, the men gasped in amazement. "Well, Mr. Smith, it appears that you are a quick study."

Jean Paul grinned as he scooped up the money from the table. "It sure is better to win than to lose."

"True," they all agreed, the level of their intoxication becoming more pronounced.

By the end of the night, Jean Paul had exhausted the supply of prime cards from his jacket and trousers. More importantly, he was three hundred dollars richer. He gallantly shook the hand of each man at the table, and then bid them goodbye, as he slowly made his way back to the hotel. And, it seems, his ultimate lover, Lady Luck accompanied him. Of course, on that night, she had a little help.

Chapter Thirty-nine

Madame Bienvenue folded her arms and pouted. "I am bored to tears out here on this dreary island," she whined. "I was told that there would be fancy parties and chances to wear my ball gowns. So far, the nicest thing I have had on is my bathing costume."

Angelique's face flushed. She was afraid that she had been distracted from her responsibilities as hostess for the ladies. On most days, she simply went through the motions of entertaining the guests and was embarrassed to admit that she really hadn't planned a new diversion in weeks. She had hoped that no one had noticed, but the comment was a stark dose of reality. To be honest, she was preoccupied. Between the scheduled activities, she spent as much time with

Andrew as possible, taking romantic horseback rides and evening strolls along the beach. They dined together with such regularity, that even the Countess complained that she was being neglected.

"I am so sorry, Madame. Of course a woman as beautiful as you are would want to dress in her finery and dance the night away. I am afraid that our little parties are rather dull, given the relaxed atmosphere of the island, but if the other guests share your opinion, then, we should, most certainly, plan a gala summer ball.

The woman clapped her hands with glee. "Yes, yes," she said. "I know that your idea will be met with the utmost enthusiasm. So when will it happen?"

"Let me discuss it with Monsieur Muggah," Angelique replied. "We will have to secure a proper orchestra. And there are other details to work out, of course, if we are to have an elegant soirée. But it will be fun. I am so glad that you suggested it."

"May I add something?" Madame Bienvenue questioned.

"Your suggestions are always welcomed, Madame," Angelique said.

"What if we made it a bal masque, a masquerade ball?" she asked.

Angelique thought on that for a moment. "I am not so sure how we would accomplish such a feat. Where would we get the masks?"

"Why, we will make them!" the woman replied. "Surely, we can gather enough supplies between us to be creative. They don't have to rival those worn at the Mardi Gras, just something simple."

"And mysterious," another added with a giggle.

"Well, that's an interesting idea," Angelique said, She turned to the others in the group. "What do you ladies think?"

They nodded their heads enthusiastically.

"Well, I suppose that we have a consensus, then. I will see Monsieur Muggah right away and present the suggestion to him," Angelique said. "If he approves, then we will have lots to keep us busy in the days ahead."

The room was suddenly filled with excited chatter. Angelique rose and excused herself as she set out to find her boss. Perhaps a night of frivolity might do them all a bit of good.

Chapter Forty

Angelique had easily won Monsieur Muggah over to the idea of a grand masquerade ball, especially when she pointed out that it would attract guests from the smaller inns and privately- owned cottages. "We can sell tickets to those not staying at the hotel, Monsieur. It will be the social event of the summer and everyone will want to attend," she had told him, enthusiastically, "And a large crowd will no doubt mean additional revenue for the hotel since I am certain we will be totally booked. If we offer a lavish meal and sell champagne by the glass that will bring in even more money."

As he had leaned back in his chair and smiled, Angelique could see his mind at work, counting the potential profit. "Well then, I will procure the music," he had said, "but the rest of the details I leave to you, Madame Latour."

She had assured him that all would be well in her capable hands, but once she had left his office, her excitement waned. It was one thing to plan simple activities for bored rich ladies and a weekly dance, but she had no experience in organizing a party on such a grand scale. Besides, the event would take up most of her spare moments, meaning less time with Andrew. But Angelique reminded herself that she was most certainly indebted to the Muggah brothers and considered what her fate might have been had they not taken a chance on her with her nonexistent experience. She owed it to them and their guests to create an extraordinary event.

As she entered the lobby, Angelique was relieved to see the Countess sitting alone.

"My dear Countess," she said, "May I join you?"

"Well, well, well," the Countess said with a smile, "If it isn't my young friend. To what do I owe the honor of your company?"

Angelique blushed. "I deserve that. Please forgive me for neglecting you. It's just that…"

"You are having a grand time with your new suitor," the Countess said, completing her sentence. "Silly girl. I would never begrudge you the time you are able to steal away with Andrew. You are falling in love with him, no? Although I might add that the whole idea of falling means that it has already happened. And if I may say so, I had predicted as much several weeks ago."

Angelique thought on that for a moment. "Yes, you did," she said, "although at the time, I would have never believed it possible."

"My dear, this world is filled with infinite possibilities," the Countess replied.

"Well, it is still complicated, as you well know, but I am hopeful."

"Angelique," the old lady said, "life often seems riddled with complications. But it is really quite simple. Find who and what makes you happy, then, hold onto the dream as if your very life depended on it because, in reality, it does."

Angelique sighed. "I suppose you are right."

"I know I am, child. You must let go of the weight that holds you down. Jean Paul is an anchor that threatens to drown your happiness. He is dead, remember, and you have the paper to prove it."

"Well, we both know that isn't true. You have read the letter that came from Andrew's friend, Benjamin. He is alive and far too close for my comfort."

"Do you honestly think he would risk showing his face where he might be recognized? He is most certainly in a heap of trouble or he wouldn't have gone to such extreme measures to wipe away any trace of his existence. I do believe that he will be far away very soon."

"I hope that you are right," Angelique said.

"Must I remind you that I am gifted in such matters?" the Countess replied with her signature laugh.

"No. I have seen your powers at work, my dear Countess, and I would never doubt your wisdom."

"Good," the Countess said.

"Which brings me to the reason for seeking you out," Angelique said, changing the subject. "I need your advice on something that is much less serious."

"And what might that be?"

"I am to plan a ball, a huge soirée, and I have no idea where to begin."

The Countess giggled. "A ball? How wonderful! When the Count was alive, we had such lovely dances. Fortunately for you, my dear, I am also gifted at planning parties. Take out your pen and paper so that we can make a list."

Angelique breathed a sigh of relief. She scribbled wildly as the Countess dictated page after page of ideas. By the end of the hour, the menu, decorations, and refreshments had all been decided upon, and Angelique was filled with nervous anticipation.

Chapter Forty-one

Beads of sweat formed on Jean Paul's brow. His shoulders ached and his stomach growled in protest from lack of food. But he was not about to give into the protestations of his body, not on this night, when it seemed that he couldn't lose. He looked at the growing stack of gold coins that lay in front of him. In a matter of hours, he had managed to win a tidy sum of money, and he resisted the temptation to assess his prize as he concentrated on the cards in his hand. He pasted a scowl on his face, but inside he was laughing uncontrollably.

"I see your ten and raise you another twenty," he said.

"Fold," the player to his right said.

"Too rich for my blood," another said.

One by one, the players laid down their cards. Jean Paul smiled. "Then, gentlemen, I believe this is mine," he said as he raked in the sizeable pot.

"Show us your cards," one of the men insisted.

"No, Sir," Jean Paul replied in his practiced Chicago accent. "You must pay for that privilege."

"He was bluffing," the player, who sat across from him said, louder than was necessary.

Jean Paul sensed the tension building, which didn't surprise him given the outcome of the evening. His gut instincts had been developed on many such an occasion and he knew that flight would be better than fight. He systematically began to place his winnings in the leather pouch he pulled from his waistcoat.

"One more hand," another called, "give us a chance to get even."

"On any other evening, I would gladly oblige," Jean Paul said as he rose from the table, "but I have an appointment."

"At this hour?" one asked incredulously. "Sounds like a lame excuse to me."

Jean Paul could sense the man's agitation. It was time for him to leave as quickly as possible.

"No excuse, sir, just fact. I am leaving town tomorrow since my business here has ended. I have a professional obligation that I must attend to before I do so."

The men grumbled as he walked toward the door. "Good riddance, Mr. Smith," one of them called behind him. "Go back to where you came."

Once safely outside, Jean Paul exhaled. "Sorry losers," he said to himself. But he could hardly blame them. He had often felt the anger and frustration of being on the losing end, trailing behind in a race that couldn't be won; it was humiliating. But not on this night. Patting the heavy pouch, he smiled. No, on this night, he was very much a winner.

Whistling, Jean Paul walked the five blocks to the bar. He paused in the doorway to survey the scene. The piano player was pounding out a lively tune, which matched his happy mood. There were still a few patrons in the establishment, most of them intoxicated after hours of drinking. At a small table in the back on the room, a man sat alone. Jean Paul made his way over to him. The man looked up and nodded as though he was greeting a stranger.

"Ca va? How are you?" Jean Paul asked.

The man looked puzzled and then, trying to focus his eyes, did a double take. "It is impossible," he said. "My eyes deceive me."

Jean Paul began to laugh. "You look at though you have seen a ghost through those eyes, my friend."

"I do believe I have. Balafré? Is that really you?"

"It is indeed," Jean Paul replied, as he reached over to shake the man's hand. "How are you, Francois?"

Jean Paul signaled for the bartender to bring them whiskey.

"I have to admit to you that I almost didn't come," Francois said taking a drink. The message you sent was a strange riddle, and I thought perhaps it was some kind of prank. But in the end, my curiosity won out."

"And I am most grateful that it did. It is so good to see you. Having been on my own for so long, I yearned to see a friendly face. Of course, you understand that I am counting on your discretion. My existence must remain between us."

"Of course, of course," Francois said, shaking his head. "I am not sure that anyone would believe me if I did tell them about this night, my old friend, but yes, you can count on me to keep your secret. But in exchange, you must tell me how you managed to get to this place. What happened to you?"

For the next two hours, the two men downed most of a bottle of whiskey as Jean Paul related the events that caused him to fake his death. He told of his travels from one seedy hotel and card game to the next, relating tales of narrow escapes and near brawls, along with big pots and high stakes.

"And so, if I may be so morbid as to ask, are you legally dead?"

"I am," he said.

"And going by the name of John Smith?"

"Yes."

"Sorry, but that isn't very original." He laughed at the absurdity of his friend's name of choice.

"I realize that," Jean Paul said, "but it makes it very easy to blend in since it is the most common name in America."

"That's true. Crafty on your part, I guess."

Jean Paul nodded his head in affirmation.

"And Angelique?" Francois asked. "Does she not know that you live?"

The mention of her name stopped Jean Paul in his tracks. He had worked so hard to forget her, to pretend that he had never known her, never loved her. He was unable to speak.

"So sorry to have asked. By your hesitance, it is obvious that she does not."

He swallowed hard. "Is she well?" Jean Paul asked, afraid of the answer.

"I do not know," Francois said quietly. "I heard that she lost the house here in the city, but I am unaware of her whereabouts. I am afraid that your friends have been dismal failures when it comes to helping your wife. For that, I am sorry."

Jean Paul hung his head. "I had hoped that she would find some aid along the way. Indeed, I am ashamed to admit that I left her in a most dismal state. I wish that I could have chosen otherwise."

Francois nodded his head in acknowledgment. "Of course. Sadly, we never know what terrible things we are capable of until we are forced with difficult choices."

"It is the truth," Jean Paul said, "I had no idea that this is the path my life would take. I have created my own tragedy and must live with the consequences."

"So what are your plans?" Francois asked. "I will tell you that except for your scar and voice, I would have never recognized you, but I can't imagine that you will remain here in the city for too long."

"No, I won't. I can't. I have been rather lucky over the past week here, but I have exhausted the possibilities at the local halls. It is too dangerous. So I leave tomorrow on a steamer for Last Island. I made the acquaintance of a man who owns a resort and from what I am told, the money flows freely at the tables there. You know that I like nothing more than taking money from rich men with no talent for the game."

"You never change, do you? Forever a gambling man," Francois said.

"And it has cost me dearly," Jean Paul said. "It is my hope to make enough in a week or two there to fund my escape to France. Maybe then, I can begin a new life, one where I am not constantly looking over my shoulder."

Francois lifted his glass. "May you find peace, my friend."

"Ah yes," Jean Paul replied. "Peace. And maybe a little luck as well."

Chapter Forty-two

After finalizing the menu for the pre-ball feast, Angelique congratulated herself for having a successful meeting with Sistene Leblanc, who had only raised minor objections over the complicated bill of fare. It would mean a great deal of extra work for the kitchen manager and her staff, so Angelique was grateful that she was able to convince her that her efforts would be appreciated. She had hinted that there would be a little something extra in the way of financial compensation for her, and hoped that the grateful party-goers would tip appropriately in gratitude. She made a mental note to mention that to the Countess, in the most tactful way, of course, who would no doubt plant that idea among the other guests and make them think that they had thought of it all on their own.

She stopped at the ballroom and, with ink and tablet in hand, drew plans for seating. There would be tables and chairs around the perimeter of the room with centerpieces to add to the festive atmosphere. Crimson velvet curtains, trimmed in gold fringe had been brought out of storage and hung with care, gracefully framing the French doors and windows. Closing her eyes, she imagined the orchestra positioned at the far end as couples spun around the dance floor in time with the music. It was going to be enchanting! She had requested a long table for champagne flutes and glass buckets to keep the bubbly properly iced. Through sheer luck, she had managed to uncover two lovely cut crystal punch bowls with matching cups as she rummaged through the kitchen pantry as well as a beautiful lace tablecloth, used in the past for some bridal celebration, no doubt. She could picture the room set for the event in her mind's eye and was well pleased.

Angelique rushed through the lobby on her way to meet Monsieur Muggah. Andrew was waiting for her at the reception desk.

"There's my hard working little party planner," he said with a grin. "You will be my date to this grand affair, won't you?"

"Andrew! Yes, of course, I will," she said, winking at him, "But my goodness, I have so many details to attend to if I am to make it happen!"

"Well, being busy agrees with you. You are positively radiant."

Angelique blushed. "You flatter me, kind sir. But in truth, I am happier than I have been in a long time. Truly, I have found contentment."

"And I hope I have, in small part, contributed to that," he said.

"You are a big part of my happiness," she said, her blue eyes twinkling.

"That's music to my ears. Then I won't keep you from your work," he said, "I am off to collect the afternoon numbers."

"See you at dinner, Andrew. We are dining with the Countess tonight."

"I look forward to having the company of two beautiful ladies," he said with a bow.

At that moment, Monsieur Muggah appeared with a large crate that he placed on the counter.

"My goodness, Monsieur, what do you have there?" Angelique asked.

"It's a surprise for you and your ladies. Came in on the morning steamer. It's for your party, Angelique," he proudly announced..

She was thrilled to note that he, too, had been caught up in the excitement. Angelique clapped her hands with glee. "Really?" she asked, "what can it be?"

"Open it and see," he said with a wide grin.

She slowly removed the top to reveal brightly colored feathers and ribbons. There were iridescent stones made of paste and packets of glitter from finely ground glass. And there were mask forms, paint pots, and fine brushes. Flowers made of paper maché, which rivaled the beauty of real foliage, lay on top. Angelique gasped. "How on earth did you accomplish this, Monsieur?"

"You forget that I am well-connected, Madame. I have my ways." He was obviously pleased to see her excitement.

"Will you have someone bring this to the ballroom?"

"Of course," Monsieur Muggah said, and he dispatched the bellman to follow Angelique with the treasure trove.

Within the hour, Angelique had assembled her ladies, who squealed with delight as they carefully unpacked each item. "Tomorrow, we will make the masks," she instructed.

"It is going to be like a real ball," one of the ladies said. "We can all be princesses for the evening."

Angelique smiled to herself. Ah yes, and she most certainly had a date with a prince.

Chapter Forty-three

The steamboat slowly rounded the bend that led into the Last Island harbor. Within minutes, the dock was bustling with activity as the workers prepared to tie the massive vessel and roll out the gangway. Inhabitants of the island stood by, anxiously waiting for a glimpse of their guests and loved ones. A group of ladies huddled under parasols, giggling nervously as they craned their necks to get a peek at the renowned orchestra that was expected to arrive in preparation for the much-anticipated masquerade ball. There was an atmosphere of excitement as the passengers disembarked and made their way to waiting carriages. Luggage and cargo were quickly unloaded.

Jean Paul Latour adjusted the brim on his straw hat. It was an incredibly hot August day and he wiped his brow, hoping that the recently applied henna had stayed in place on his auburn hair. He grabbed his satchel and asked for directions to Mrs. Pecot's Boarding House. He was glad that he had inquired about accommodations on the trip over and readily determined that the smaller, low key guesthouse would serve him well as a base of operations. Although he figured that the remote location of the island might provide him with a certain amount of anonymity, the eight months following his death had taught him that being overly cautious was in his own best interest. Besides, he needed to get a lay of the land, so to speak, and thought perhaps a few friendly games at the smaller inn would give him an idea of what to expect at the tables of Moniseur Muggah's more respected establishment. He had time to make his move into the gaming club, where he had learned one must follow the protocol in order to find acceptance. The key to winning was always in the strategy.

Mrs. Pecot, a robust woman, with a warm smile, greeted Jean Paul at the door.

"Come on in, Moniseur," she said, ushering him into a sparsely furnished living room. "Can I help you?"

He removed his hat and placed his satchel by the door. "I was hoping that you might have a room available."

"Well, you are in luck," she said, wiping her hands on her apron. "I have one left."

"Then, good for me," he said, careful to remember his Chicago accent.

"You sound like you aren't from around here, for sure," Mrs. Pecot said with a laugh.

"No, I am from Chicago."

"Hmmm…. Long way from home. Kind of surprised you found our little bit of paradise. So, you here for the big ball at the hotel or on a holiday?" she asked.

"Big ball?" he asked, confused. "Uh, no, just here for some rest and relaxation."

"Yes, big dance Saturday night up at the Oceanview Hotel. Got the whole island abuzz with excitement and keeping me busy as a bee with a houseful of guests. Let me show you to your room."

"Thank you," Jean Paul replied. And he made a mental note to inquire about this ball. It sounded like a perfect opportunity to meet some of the well-heeled gentlemen whose pockets he hoped to pick.

"How long you planning to stay?" she asked, making her way to the stairs as he followed.

"A week. Maybe longer. Would you like for me to pay you now?"

She laughed. "No need. You can do that in the morning. It isn't like you can make a quick escape, now, can you?"

Jean Paul didn't respond. This poor woman had no idea what he was capable of doing in a moment of desperation.

The room was small, but adequate, with a big window facing the Gulf. Mrs. Pecot pushed back the curtains and opened the window. "It's plenty hot here until the sun goes down," she said. "You have time for a dip in the water before supper, if you want. We eat promptly at eight."

Jean Paul nodded his understanding.

"You have towels here and I'll bring up a fresh pitcher of water for washing up. Bathroom is at the end of the hall, but you may have to wait your turn. I am afraid I only have the one for all eight rooms."

"I'll adjust accordingly," Jean Paul said.

"Well, I'll leave you then."

After unpacking his satchel, Jean Paul donned his hat and set out for a walk on the beach. The soft breeze was a welcome relief from the heat. And although his travels had taken him to many a picturesque place, there was no denying the beauty of the island. If his luck held out, he might well spend a few pleasurable weeks here in this bit of paradise.

He walked for an hour or so, pausing to watch the sunset. Such moments seemed to amplify his loneliness. While he rarely gave into the waves of self-pity that threatened his resolve, sometimes, those feelings were unavoidable. And he fought the urge to think of his life before his death and the love he once had and lost. Jean Paul thought of his future. It was hard to acknowledge that it was his own foolish decisions and rocky past that had gotten him to this place of uncertainty. He was a lost man. Perhaps he would find himself here on Last Island. At the very least, he hoped this place would fund his new life, one filled with second chances.

Chapter Forty-four

Angelique took a deep breath and tried to calm her frazzled nerves. She had spent most of the afternoon dashing around the ballroom, putting the final touches on the lavish table décor and making sure that all was scheduled to go as planned. The masks that hadn't already been claimed by the ladies, were laid on the reception table, along with the plain black ones, which were to be given to the gentlemen in attendance. When the clock struck six, she reluctantly left for her room to dress.

It was with great anticipation that Angelique donned the royal blue taffeta and silk gown she had packed for her trip to the island as an afterthought. She was grateful that she had followed her instincts and included it, laughing as she imagined herself relegated to the somber mourning attire she had worn at her arrival two months earlier. The chambermaid had helped her with the stays of her corset, whittling her waist to tiny proportions. Although she had not brought along the customary hoop to wear with her dress, Angelique was nevertheless pleased with her reflection in the mirror. She fastened the sapphire and diamond necklace around her neck. It accentuated her bosom. The matching earrings brought a sparkle to her steel blue eyes. She was ready. Pausing to pinch her cheeks for a bit of color, she headed for the lobby to meet Andrew and the Countess.

Crowds of partygoers had already gathered, to share a drink and socialize. She scanned the scene, looking for her beau, and spotted him far across the room. And almost as though he could sense her presence, Andrew turned, waving in recognition. He smiled broadly as she approached.

"Angelique," he said, taking her hand in his. "I am left speechless by your beauty."

"Thank you, kind sir," she replied with a smile. "You look mighty handsome yourself."

Andrew shifted his weight from one foot to another and adjusted his ascot. The fancy suit was a borrowed one, generously loaned to him by Monsieur Muggah, and possibly left behind by a previous guest. It was a far-from-perfect fit, which made him concerned that he might look ridiculously out of place, but in her sweet and genuine way, Angelique had reassured him.

"I am a nervous Nellie, I am afraid," Angelique whispered. "I hope it all goes well."

"It will be wonderful," Andrew said, offering his arm to the Countess, who embraced Angelique before taking hold of him.

"Going to be a magical evening," the Countess said. "All these silly hens want is a chance to dress up, show off, and prance around like peacocks."

Angelique laughed out loud at the observation. "My dear Countess," she said, "you do have a way with words."

Couples strolled into the dining room to taste the lavish array of dishes that Mrs. Leblanc and her staff had carefully prepared and set out in a buffet that was a treat for the eyes as well as the palate. The sound of laughter filled the room as the champagne was poured and people toasted to a good time and good health. Once Angelique was convinced that all was in order, she turned to Andrew and the Countess. "Let's go in and enjoy," she said, adjusting her mask.

The ballroom had been transformed to into an enchanted wonderland, its opulence surprising, given the remote island location. Candlelight cast a soft glow across the room and the arrangements that Angelique had crafted with care glistened and sparkled. A faint scent of lavender, mixed with the sweet fragrance of perfume, permeated the air. The orchestra, which had taken its place at the far corner, began to play a waltz. As the masked revelers twirled around the polished wooden dance floor, the spectacle was a kaleidoscope of color. Angelique paused to take it all in.

"It's all so lovely! Why, I haven't been to a soirée this fancy since the Count was alive," the Countess said. "You did a wonderful job, my dear."

"And I agree," Andrew said. "You did the impossible! I am mighty proud of you."

"Thanks," Angelique whispered.

Andrew looked at the doorway and smiled. "And now, I get a chance to show you off. Come and meet my relative."

She turned to the Countess, "will you excuse us?"

"Please, please. By all means. And you two dance the night away. I certainly would if I could," she replied.

"Well, I expect at least one dance on your card, Countess," Andrew said.

She didn't reply as she waved him off, but Angelique knew that the old woman was secretly pleased.

Michael Schlatre and his wife Lodowiska entered the ballroom, their masks in hand. Andrew rushed over to greet them.

"Captain Schlatre," he said, extending his hand. "I am so happy to see you here."

"You didn't think we would miss the social event of the summer, did you?" the Captain replied.

"Well, I was hopeful that you would be in attendance. I know that you have been away for a while."

"New business venture, Andrew. Keeps me busy, although I would love nothing more than to idle away my time, enjoying the Gulf breeze. I should be here for the next week, however, a little respite from work. We hope that you will join us for dinner one night."

"I would like nothing more," Andrew said.

"I take it that you are being productive here?" Michael commented.

"Ah, yes. My supervisor is pleased with what I am doing. The island provides an interesting place to study the various weather changes. It is an exceptional opportunity."

The Captain turned to Angelique. "And I take it that you have provided my cousin with some diversion as well."

Andrew blushed. "May I present Madame Angelique Latour?"

"Madame?" Michael questioned.

"I am a widow, Monsieur," Angelique replied matter-of-factly. "It is lovely to meet you. Andrew has told me so much about you and your beautiful family. And I understand that it is through your efforts that he found his way here, so I am certainly grateful for that."

"It was just a lucky coincidence, but I am glad that it has worked out so well," he said. He turned to his wife, "Andrew, you know Lodowiska, of course. My dear, this is Angelique."

"My goodness," she said, "I have heard a great deal about you and your success with the ladies here at the hotel. I understand that you are responsible for this gala. How enterprising of you! It is nice to finally be introduced. And please, you must come to dinner with Andrew next week so that we may become better acquainted."

Angelique smiled. "Thank you for your kindness. I shall. I hope you have a good time tonight."

"I intend to enjoy every moment of it. Why I haven't danced in ages. I am afraid that I spend most of my days tending to the needs of small children, which is far from glamorous. This is indeed a treat for me," Mrs. Schaltre said.

Andrew took his partner's hand. "And speaking of dancing, I do believe that it is our turn. Angelique, if you will give me the honor, I would be most grateful."

Angelique donned her mask and smiled. "Certainly, sir."

The couple made their way to the ballroom floor. Andrew took Angelique in his arms and they slowly began to move in rhythm to the music. It was the first time they had ever danced together, but they moved as one. Their synchronicity didn't surprise either of them. They had, in fact, seemed to be in tune with each other since their first meeting. And although the room was crowded, to the two lovers, the orchestra played only for them as they gazed lovingly into each other's eyes. By the third dance, Angelique suggested that they rest for a bit, and Andrew led her out to the verandah.

The French doors leading to the porch had been opened wide. Candles, shielded by fat glass chimneys, graced the outdoor tables, enhancing the romantic atmosphere. And in the distance, the sound of waves crashing to the shore accompanied the music from the nearby ballroom.

"Goodness, it is warm," Angelique commented as she removed her mask. She closed her eyes to feel the Gulf breeze on her face.

"You are a wonderful dancer," Andrew said.

"Years of practice at all of those cotillions in my plantation days," she said, "but I could say the same about you. Who would have thought that a Yankee scientist could be so graceful?"

"I guess my mother would be pleased to hear that. She sent me to dance lessons as a boy. I hated every minute of it."

Angelique laughed. "I can't imagine you in knee pants, counting out the rhythm to a waltz with some blushing young girl."

"Well, that's a pretty accurate description of it. Of course, you failed to mention my sweaty palms and two left feet."

"Then, you must thank your mother for having such foresight."

"To hold you in my arms tonight has made my entire life worth it."

"Andrew," she whispered.

He took her hand in his and kissed it lightly. "Angelique, you must know how much I love you. I didn't think it was possible to feel this way, but I most certainly do. I want nothing more than to spend the rest of my life with you, to take care of you, to safeguard you."

Angelique looked deeply into his eyes. "Oh, Andrew, I love you, too. Truly, I do, with all of my heart. But there are so many obstacles. I cannot even begin to imagine a future with you when my past is so uncertain."

"Let me remind you that in the eyes of the law you are indeed a widow."

"That is so, but we both know that your friend Benjamin has proved otherwise," Angelique said.

Andrew took a deep breath. "I will not give you up to some phantom who may or may not ever appear."

"But like a true ghost, he will continue to haunt us, to cast a dark shadow on our happiness."

"My darling, I have thought long and hard about this. My work here on the island is almost finished. But I cannot, I will not, go back to Washington City without you. I am prepared to ask for a leave of absence. You and I will make the trip to New Orleans to find your worthless late husband. We will exhaust all of possibilities in the process. And we will persuade him to remain in his self-imposed grave, since you most certainly cannot divorce a dead man."

Angelique gasped. "Do you really think we can find him? That it would work?"

"We won't know if we don't try," Andrew said. "I am confident that the same benevolent God who brought us together will guide us during our quest. After all, as the Countess would say, love conquers all, right?"

Angelique smiled and turned up her face so that Andrew could kiss her. He put his arm around her, and they stood in silence for a long time, each lost in their own thoughts of what the future might hold.

Chapter Forty-five

Jean Paul entered the lobby of the Oceanview Hotel. It was impressive compared to the sparse reception room at Mrs. Pecot's, but he reminded himself that he was on the island to make money, not squander it, and he intended to devote his efforts into networking himself into a future card game. He looked around, unsure of where to go, but he followed the sound of the music and found himself at the door to the ballroom. The black masks were laid out on the table and after observing that the other revelers were wearing them, he followed suit. He certainly didn't want to stick out in the sea of unfamiliar faces.

He slowly walked over to where drinks were being served and ordered a whiskey. A group of men had gathered there, swapping jokes and slapping each other on the back as they laughed at the punch lines. Jean Paul waited for an opportunity to make his presence known. He leaned against the bar and took in the spectacle that the party provided. It had been a long time since he had been to a social gathering, and he found his mood lifted a bit as he watched the couples gaily swaying to the music. He thought of the night so long ago when he had spied Angelique on such a dance floor and smiled at the memory of how he had so boldly whisked her away from her suitor, determined to make her his. Certainly, he had lost more than money and property at the card tables he had frequented. He had lost his only chance at happiness and love. And he had no one to blame but himself, a grim reality he rarely allowed himself to ponder.

One of the men took off his mask, setting it on the bar top. It fell and Jean Paul bent to retrieve it. "You dropped this, sir," he said. "You might need it if you are to remain a mystery."

The man took the mask and replied. "Foolishness, if you ask me. All this hoopla so those darned women of ours can put on a fancy dress and force us to pretend like we are having a good time."

Jean Paul nodded his head in agreement. "I am a bachelor, so I wouldn't know, but I suppose that most men go to great lengths to please their ladies."

"Bah," the man said, "At least after suffering through this miserable night, the missus can't complain when I spend the next week engaged in a poker game."

Recognizing an opening, Jean Paul seized the opportunity. "I am new to the island, having just arrived yesterday. So is there a good card game to be had? I had hoped to find some diversion while here. I hope I am not being presumptuous by asking you to share the details."

"Not at all," the man said, extending his hand. "We are always looking to take a newcomer's money."

Jean Paul laughed. "John Smith, from Chicago," he said, introducing himself in his practiced accent.

"Far from home, Mr. Smith. My name is Gaston Cheramie. The wife and I have a little cottage here on the island."

"Pleased to make your acquaintance," Jean Paul said.

Mr. Cheramie turned to his companions. "This is Robert Hebert, Antoine Galloway, Bernard Gautreaux, and François Thibodaux. They are my partners in crime."

Jean Paul tried not to chuckle at the irony of that observation. He shook hands all around and called for the bartender to refill the men's glasses.

Half an hour later, Jean Paul had not only been given the location of the card game the following evening, but was urgently encouraged to join them. Deeming it a successful night, Jean Paul bid his goodbyes and turned to leave the ballroom. As he downed his last sip of whiskey, a woman caught his eye. Dressed in a royal blue gown and a peacock feathered mask, she gracefully moved around the room, stopping to exchange pleasantries with the other guests. Even with her face partially covered, he could tell that she was beautiful. And oddly familiar. Something stirred deep inside of him. She reminded him of Angelique, which he realized was utterly impossible, and he quickly shook it off as a combination of coincidence, nostalgia and alcohol. But he couldn't resist watching with rapt fascination as she embraced the tall blonde man who was soon by her side. "Lucky man," Jean Paul thought as he left the hotel and made his way to the boarding house. "*Sometimes,*" he thought, "*there is something more priceless than money.*" And then he laughed out loud at the absurdity of such wisdom.

Chapter Forty-six

The evening was drawing to a close and Angelique was tired. As the hostess, she felt obligated to remain until the last guest had left, but truth be told, she would have gladly crawled into her bed hours earlier.

"It was the most beautiful party," Madame Bienvenue said as she hugged Angelique. "Thank you so much for creating such a lovely evening for us."

"Well, Madame, I have you to thank for the prompting. But I am happy that you had a good time."

"The best," she said, waving goodbye.

Angelique sat in an empty chair and grimaced. "These shoes were better created for sitting than dancing," she said with a laugh. "I am certain that they were designed by a man."

Andrew kneeled in front of her and carefully unlaced her slippers. He slid them off one at a time and tenderly massaged her feet. "Andrew," Angelique whispered. "What will people say if they see you?"

"They will say that I am being a gallant gentlemen, trying to comfort my poor, tired sweetheart."

Angelique giggled. "I somehow doubt that. But now that they are off, I don't think that I will be able to get them back on."

"Then I shall carry them for you. Nobody cares if you walk around in your stocking feet. You have certainly earned that privilege."

The orchestra was packing away their instruments and Monsieur Muggah bid the last of the guests a good night. He made his way over to the couple, a broad grin on his face.

"My dear Angelique. What a triumph this night has been."

"Merci, Monsieur. I am so happy that you are pleased," she said.

"I am absolutely delighted! The guests had a wonderful time, and we had a most profitable evening, I might add."

"Then, I take it you don't regret giving me a chance on that fateful day at the St. Charles."

"On the contrary. It was one of the best business decisions I have ever made," he answered.

Angelique smiled. "Thank you, Monsieur. You are most kind."

He bowed. "And now, if you two will excuse me, I do believe I will call it a night. I suspect that most of the hotel guests will be sleeping late in the morning, so feel free to delay any activities you may have for the ladies. You deserve a bit of rest as well."

"I appreciate that. Goodnight, Monsieur."

The ballroom was deserted, and Angelique stifled a yawn.

"Let me walk you to your room," Andrew said, "better yet, let me carry you." And he swooped her up in his strong arms.

Angelique protested, but easily nestled her face into his neck and relaxed in the protective comfort of his warm embrace.

When they reached the door, he gently placed her on her feet. The hotel was quiet, and Angelique giggled as she turned the key in the lock.

"Goodnight, my darling," Andrew said. "I can barely stand being apart from you."

"I agree," Angelique said, slowly opening the door. "Perhaps we don't have to be."

She touched his hand and gently led him in. "Shhhh," she whispered.

The moonlight was streaming through the window, illuminating the room with a romantic glow. Angelique moved to light the lamp.

Andrew stood still. He was unsure of what to do and had hoped he had not misunderstood her intentions. "Angelique," he whispered. "I want nothing more than to be with you tonight and forever. But I would never do anything that would compromise your reputation or cause you regret later."

Angelique stifled a giggle. "Andrew, my love. You are always the gentleman. I would think nothing of seducing you right here and now if that's what I had in mind, but I am afraid that I simply need your help with my corset."

His face flushed, and then he had to laugh as well. "And to think I had hoped that you were set on having your way with me. Here, turn around."

Angelique turned as Andrew began to unfasten the many buttons down the back of her gown. It dropped to the floor. She placed her hands on her waist as he began to unhook the laces of her corset. He kissed her on the neck. Exhaling in relief, she turned to face him.

"Thank you," she whispered. "I can finally breathe again."

He looked at her. "Well, you have certainly taken mine away."

She considered his compliment and smiled. He bent to kiss her lightly on the lips and then felt her response. Locking her arms around him, she kissed him more urgently. He touched her and felt his pulse quicken. She softly moaned.

"I am afraid that if I don't leave now, I will be unable to do so," Andrew said. It was more of a question than a statement, and he held his breath as he anticipated her reply.

"Then, don't," she simply said.

As he removed his clothes, she watched him appreciatively. "Are you sure?" he whispered.

"I have never been surer of anything in my life," she said reassuringly.

He moved to her, gently stripping her of her undergarments. He lifted her onto the bed and caressed her face. "You are the most beautiful woman I have ever seen," he whispered. "How lucky am I that you are mine?"

"It is I who am lucky, Andrew. I was utterly lost, and then you walked into my life. You have awakened my heart to love once again, made me feel what I never thought I could. My soul honors yours, my darling."

Andrew tenderly kissed her. "I love you so," he whispered.

"I love you as well with all that I have to give."

And as the gentle Gulf breeze washed over them, they made love, consummating their union and solidifying their partnership. And when they were done, they slept in each other's arms, content and well-satisfied.

Chapter Forty-seven

The rising sun woke Angelique with a start. She reached for the blue and white clock. It was just past six. Looking over at her sleeping lover, her heart softened. They belonged to each other now, and she had never been happier.

"Andrew," she whispered.

He moaned. She reached over to caress his arm. "Andrew," she repeated.

Slowly, he opened his eyes. When he saw her, he smiled. "Good morning, my darling."

"Good morning," she whispered. "I hate to wake you, but I am afraid that I am going to have to send you on your way. It is still quite early, but the staff will be up and about soon. We can't have them see you sneaking out of my room now, can we?" She giggled.

"Of course not," he said sleepily. "I will guard your honor above all else."

Andrew rose and quickly dressed. He leaned over and kissed Angelique goodbye. "You go back to sleep for an hour or so. I know you are tired."

"That's because somebody kept me awake most of the night," she teased.

"And I would gladly do it again if given the chance," he said with a wink.

Carefully opening the door, he peered out into the hall. It was empty. He quickly made his escape and returned to his own room on the second floor. *The Countess was indeed clairvoyant*, he thought, stretching out on the bed, *it was a magical night*.

Angelique slept until eight. She had to splash water on her face several times before she felt fully awake, but her growling stomach gave her a sense of urgency. She dressed and set off for the dining room in search of food. The breakfast crowd was lighter than normal, a result no doubt of their late night of partying. Angelique was pleased to see Andrew sitting alone, nursing a cup of coffee.

"Well, good morning, Andrew," Angelique said with a smile. "May I join you?"

"I can think of nothing I'd like more."

"I trust you slept well," she said.

"Better than I ever have," he replied.

The waiter appeared with Andrew's breakfast and poured more coffee. Angelique ordered eggs, ham, biscuits, grits, and fried potatoes.

"Are you hungry?" Andrew teased.

"Starving," she said, taking a sip of coffee and stealing a piece of bacon from his plate. "You do realize that we didn't eat last night."

"How on earth did we miss that?"

"I was too nervous. Goodness, don't tell Mrs. Leblanc. She will be furious with me."

"Your secret is safe with me," he said with a wink.

Angelique blushed. "I am counting on it."

They finished their breakfast and parted for the morning. "I have work to do," Andrew said. "I will need to compile this data and prepare my report. Have to meet the boat to send it to the telegraph office in New Orleans. Might keep me busy for much of the day."

"You aren't avoiding me now that you have sullied my virtue, are you?" Angelique said, pouting.

"That would never happen, my darling. Besides, don't you have a job as well?"

"I do, although I think that ladies will simply want to sit around and gossip today."

"Then, it should be an easy day for you. I hope so, anyway. Dinner tonight?"

"It would be my pleasure," she said, hugging him goodbye.

He simply responded with a raised eyebrow and a knowing smile.

And just as she predicted, the ladies were abuzz with chatter as they recounted the events of the previous evening. They were too tired for games and simply wanted to sip tea and rest. Angelique basked in the afterglow of her success as the congratulations and good wishes poured in from the guests she encountered throughout the day. She was happy it all went well, but also glad it was over.

Later that afternoon, she went to the ballroom to oversee the cleanup. She carefully packed away the decorations and leftover masks, just in case the occasion for another masquerade ball presented itself. It might very well become an annual event for the hotel, and Angelique intended to be well-prepared.

As the sun began to set, the lobby was crowded with socializing guests. The hotel was busier than usual, no doubt because of the number of attendees at the ball. She knew that pleased Monsieur Muggah. Angelique mingled among them as she waited for Andrew to join her. There were many unfamiliar faces along with the regulars who were there on extended vacation. And Angelique hated to admit that she hoped for a lull in the activity once most of the visitors left in a few days. She welcomed a bit of peace and quiet.

A group of men sat together chatting excitedly about their post dinner plans. It was customary for a few games of chance and other entertainment to fill the evening hours. The billiards hall and men's lounge were often a place of activity where friendly and not-so friendly tournaments happened with regularity. Angelique had never understood the allure of gambling, especially after being the victim of Jean Paul's reckless behavior, but it was not her place to judge these men who were guests of the hotel.

"You gentlemen sound most enthusiastic about your evening," Angelique said to them, trying to sound gracious.

"We are, Madame, and we have you to thank for it," one replied.

"Me?" Angelique asked, confused.

"Yes, indeed," another offered, "our wives were so happy after the ball last night that they encouraged us to go and have some fun on our own tonight."

"Well, I am pleased that you were able to benefit from our little party," she said.

"Most certainly. Monsieur Muggah has arranged for a little supper for us, followed by a multi table card game. It should be quite interesting."

"And profitable, too," another added. The others laughed in response.

The gathering grew as some residents of the island joined the guests. Angelique smiled as she recognized that her employer had seized an opportunity to make some additional profit from their presence. He was crafty when it came to money. But his success was tied to hers, and she made a mental note to remind him of her contribution when she asked for a salary increase at the end of the season.

"Then I wish you all good luck," she said as she set off in search of her dinner date.

***

Jean Paul was pleased to see the assembly of men when he entered the lobby. He approached them and inquired about the card game. Gaston Cheramie recognized him and waved in recognition.

"I see that you found your way to our little gentlemen's group," he said, shaking Jean Paul's hand.

"I have," Jean Paul responded. "I am looking forward to the evening."

"And I am looking forward to taking your money," Monsieur Gaston replied, patting him on the shoulder.

As the men moved from the lobby into the gaming room reserved for the night, Jean Paul saw her. She was standing at the reception desk, her back to him, but he recognized her form as though he was looking at a piece of himself. Slowly, she turned in profile and confirmed what he knew in his heart to be true. It was his wife; it was Angelique.

Chapter Forty-eight

Jean Paul watched as the tall man approached Angelique. She smiled in response and they embraced. He felt the all-too-familiar pain in his heart, jealousy and despair welling up inside of his very soul. Forcing himself to look away, he followed the men into the venue. There were so many unanswered questions. He wondered if her presence at the very place he had chosen to seek his fortune was some kind of cruel irony. But then, he thought that perhaps it was opportunity in disguise. Should he make his presence known to her? Could he dare hope to win back her love? He was hopelessly confused, filled with trepidation and anxiety. Taking a deep breath, he tried to calm his frazzled nerves.

Seated at his assigned place at the table with six other players, Jean Paul willed himself not to think of Angelique. Distractions often proved to be costly, and he could not afford to make a mistake on this fateful night. He felt in his pocket, missing the lucky St. Christopher medal. As was his custom, he would play the cards he had been dealt and hope that his true mistress, the fickle Lady Luck would favor him.

The first hand was uneventful. The pot was lean and the player to Jean Paul's left won it with little resistance. The men sipped whiskey and watched as the dealer shuffled the cards. It took four rounds before the men loosened their purse strings and began betting more to Jean Paul's liking. By the time they had taken a break for supper, he had won close to four hundred dollars. He did the mental math. When he added this to what he had made at the tables in New Orleans, he was a thousand dollars away from his goal. If he calculated correctly, a few favorable nights at the Oceanview, and he would have what he needed to buy his freedom. Perhaps it would even be enough to persuade Angelique to leave for France with him. As a seasoned gambler, hope was his stock and trade, ever-present. But he knew not to count his money too prematurely as he joined the men to eat.

Monsieur Muggah made his rounds, greeting the patrons as he inquired about the quality of the food and asking who was ahead in the games. When he reached the table where Jean Paul sat, he introduced himself.

"Have we met, Monsieur?" he asked, shaking Jean Paul's hand. "You look oddly familiar."

Jean Paul subconsciously touched the scar on his face. He thought for a moment, unsure of how to respond and then made a quick decision to reveal that yes, they had met months earlier in Vicksburg in a similar card game. And, he added, that it was in fact at Monsieur Muggah's suggestion that he had come to Last Island to see what it had to offer. He went on to say that he was glad that he had done so since luck seemed to be squarely in his favor on this particular night. He thought it odd that Monsieur Muggah didn't respond but simply nodded his head and moved to the next group of men. But he shrugged it off as he thought of what the next round of cards might bring.

The men played well into the morning and although Jean Paul was tired, he was exhilarated. By the end of the night, as the group disbanded and were leaving for their rooms, he happily noted that he was eight hundred dollars richer and even closer to his financial objective.

"Tomorrow night," one of them called to Jean Paul. "Your fortuity can't hold out for very long, and you must give us a chance to get our revenge."

"Count on it," Jean Paul said as he donned his hat and walked out into the darkness.

Chapter Forty-nine

The knock on her door startled Angelique, waking her. She glanced at the clock. It was close to two a.m. Andrew was sound asleep in her bed, and she panicked at the thought of being caught in a compromising position. The knocking became more urgent, and he stirred.

"Shhhh," she whispered. "Do not speak."

She rose and donned her dressing gown. Slowly, she opened the door just enough to see who was there.

"Monsieur Muggah?" she asked. "Is there an emergency?"

"Angelique, I regret to wake you at this hour, but I must speak with you immediately. It is a matter of utmost importance."

"Of course, Moniseur," Angelique said. "Let me dress."

"I will be waiting for you in my office." His voice was somber.

She closed the door and moved to light the lamp.

"What is it?" Andrew asked sleepily.

"I don't know," she responded. "Monsieur Muggah wants to see me right away."

Angelique hoped that she was not about to be reprimanded for having a man, who was certainly not her husband, in her room. The rules of propriety were clear, and even a man of the world like the kind monsieur would frown on such affairs, especially from one of his employees. He prided himself on running a respectable establishment, and Angelique's conduct would reflect poorly on him. Her hands were shaking.

Andrew moved to put his arms around her. "Do you want me to go with you?"

"No, my darling. That would complicate matters, don't you think? Perhaps it would be best for you to return to your own room. I will find you in the morning."

"As you wish, my love."

The two of them dressed in silence, and Angelique made her way through the quiet halls to Monsieur Muggah's office. She knocked lightly.

"Come in," he said, "and please sit down." He walked to the table that held a crystal decanter and poured two glasses of sherry. "Here. Drink this."

Angelique took a sip, but her stomach was churning, and she found it hard to swallow.

"Monsieur?" she asked, hoping he would speak. Whatever was on his mind, she wanted it to be over with as soon as possible.

"My dear Angelique, you know how fond I am of you. I have come to view you as family, and I most certainly have your best interest at heart."

She nodded in understanding.

"That is why it is most difficult for me to tell you this. I have some unsettling news that I am afraid won't wait until morning."

"Go on," Angelique said.

"At the card game last night, one which is still in progress, I might add, I discovered among the players someone whom I least expected to meet."

Angelique swallowed hard. She was hopelessly confused, but fearful of what was to come.

"At first, I wasn't sure, but when he recounted our meeting, it erased any doubt. That and his distinguishing scar."

She felt faint. "Pardon, Monsieur. I don't understand."

"Your husband, Angelique. Jean Paul is here on the island. Presently, here in the hotel."

Her heart began to race as the panic rose from deep inside. "No, it is not possible. Surely there is some mistake. How could this happen?"

"If you recall, I had met him at a card game in Vicksburg. Well, at least based on the description and picture, I was pretty certain that it was he. We had a casual conversation, and I had told him about Oceanview with our lively card games. I offhandedly had invited him to visit if he ever felt so inclined. This was well before you came into my life, of course. But believe me when I tell you that I had no idea he would show up here so many months later. It is regrettable."

"It is more than that, Monsieur. It is a tragedy, a disaster. What am I to do?"

"I don't know if I am the one to offer you advice, but it seems to me that you have some rather unpleasant and unfinished business to handle. There is often no other way to solve difficult problems than to meet them head on. I will do whatever you need of me, of course, but I fear this situation is yours to handle. Sometimes, when you want peace, you must prepare for war. And I pray that, in the end, you will indeed find peace."

"Thank you, Monsieur," she whispered, shock and dismay overtaking any sense of reason.

Back in her room, Angelique threw herself on her bed and cried until no tears remained. And she lay there, unable to sleep as she tried to formulate a plan.

Chapter Fifty

A ndrew paced outside of the dining room, waiting for Angelique to join him. Whatever had transpired in the night, they would face together. But he hated to think of her alone and upset. He pulled out his pocket watch. It was half past eight. He had determined that if she didn't show by nine, he would send the chambermaid to check on her. Fifteen minutes later, she appeared. He could tell by looking at her that she had not slept, and it pained him to see her unhappiness. Dark circles ringed her lovely blue eyes. When she saw him, she attempted to smile. He took her hand in his, leading her into the dining room where he ordered coffee.

"I was so worried about you," he said.

She nodded her head in understanding, but did not speak.

"What is it, darling? Please tell me," he implored.

She swallowed hard, not knowing where to begin. Finally, she simply said, "It is Jean Paul. He is here on the island."

"Are you sure?" Andrew asked "How on earth did he find his way here?"

"It is ironic, isn't it, but through a casual encounter with Monsieur Muggah several months ago."

Andrew had already heard the story of their meeting in Vicksburg, but that was when there was only speculation about whether or not he lived. Of course, once his friend Benjamin had confirmed that he was not only alive, but too close for comfort, Andrew had worried about the possibilities. Now, his worst fears had been realized. He tried to control his anger. How he would have loved five minutes alone with Angelique's cad of a husband. Although not a violent man, he relished the thought of having an opportunity to give the scoundrel a thorough thrashing.

But revenge would have to wait. Angelique needed his support "I know it is hard to imagine it, but sometimes our blessings come to us in disguise," he said reassuringly. "Hadn't we already agreed that we were going to find him, to lay the issue of your marriage to rest once and for all? His appearance on the island just simplifies our search, my darling."

Angelique nodded her head. Intellectually, she knew that Andrew was right, but emotionally, she was distraught. "I just don't know if I can bear seeing him again."

"But you can and you will. You will stand before him and tell him that he is out of your life forever. You will threaten to expose him for the coward that he is. Your freedom is as at stake here, along with our future together."

"I know that you are right, of course. It is just so hard."

"But this is something that you won't have to deal with alone. I will be here at your side. And if he hurts you, I swear, I will kill him myself."

Tears formed in Angelique's eyes. "And I am so grateful for you," she said.

"I love you, my darling. And I will not only fight alongside you, but for you as well. Believe it."

"I do," Angelique whispered.

Angelique dried her tears and with a heavy heart went to conduct the activities for the day. She had responsibilities at the hotel and hoped, at the very least, that in keeping busy, she would have little time to think.

She was grateful when she found herself alone with the Countess at tea time. She needed the advice of her old friend. The old lady sat listening intently as Angelique relayed the events that had her life in utter turmoil. When she was done, the Countess reached over and took her hand.

"My dear Angelique," she said, "you can't run away from your problems because when you do, they have a way of catching up with you. Look at how brave you have been. You created a new life for yourself from the ashes of tragedy. You must believe that you are entitled to happiness and then, you must reach out and grab it with both hands. Jean Paul is dead to you and the rest of the world, for that matter. Now, take your shovel and bury him."

"But how?" Angelique wailed. "Where do I begin? Who will help me?"

"Sometimes, you can't wait for a knight to come along to rescue you. No, sometimes, a princess must take the sword and slay the dragon that holds her captive all by herself. That gives her the power to determine her own fate."

"I appreciate the fairy tale allusions," Angelique said, "but I am not sure what it all means."

"Go find him," the Countess said. "And make him set you free."

Chapter Fifty-one

The card players had once again assembled for their nightly game. Jean Paul took his seat at the table. He had hoped to get a glimpse of Angelique as he had made his way through the lobby, but she was nowhere to be found. It was probably just as well, he told himself. What on earth would he say to her? How could he possibly describe all that had transpired? If his luck held out, he could make some serious money tonight, maybe even enough to fund his trip to France, if he was careful with his spending. And if he could leave the island while he was ahead, Angelique would be none the wiser. Wouldn't it have been kinder to remain a dead man, to let her have her life? Did he love her enough to let her go? Certainly, he hadn't put her first for so many years of their marriage; maybe now, he should. He had no time to think of these questions as he held the cards in his hands. For now, the game was all that was on his mind.

Jean Paul lost the first two hands, along with a hundred dollars. His palms began to sweat and he took a deep breath. The third hand restored his luck, and he scooped up a two hundred dollar pot. This seemed to be the theme for the night as he lost two and won one, but it was much like taking one step forward and two steps back. Nevertheless, it was progress. He wasn't winning big, but at least he was winning.

Monsieur Muggah appeared at the door, holding a bottle of whiskey.

"I have brought out my private stock for my best customers," he announced, "Isn't it time for a break?"

The men rose from the table and presented their glasses. It was then that Jean Paul saw that the proprietor was not alone. Angelique took the bottle and began to pour for each man. When she reached him, he could see that her hands were shaking.

"Whiskey, Jean Paul?" she asked looking him squarely in the eye.

He swallowed hard and nodded, drinking it down in one gulp.

"More?" she asked, offering the bottle.

He shook his head, placing his glass on the table.

She looked at him with contempt. "I hate to interrupt your card game since I know how much it means to you, but I think perhaps we should talk. It is time, don't you think? Will you come with me, please?"

Still unable to speak, Jean Paul followed her out of the room and through the lobby to Monsieur Muggah's office. The proprietor followed, ushering them into the room. He closed the door and waited outside.

"Angelique," Jean Paul whispered.

"Do not speak my name," she snapped. "How dare you!"

He was caught off guard. Although Jean Paul was accustomed to being in control of every situation, he suddenly felt much like a man freefalling from the top of a mountain. He wondered how long it would take for him to hit the bottom.

"Please, let me explain."

Her anger bubbled over, filling the room. "Explain? What would you like to explain? How you left me a pauper as you gambled away every penny that I owned? That you not only mortgaged my home, but my future as well? That you humiliated me, broke me, hurt me? Can you explain why you faked your death, leaving me to left me to handle the aftermath, while I mourned the loss of my husband, a husband I thought I knew? What can you possibly say that will make me understand how you could do this to me while you escaped the consequences and went on with your life? I cannot fathom such cruelty. So yes, perhaps you can enlighten me."

"I am so sorry. I didn't mean…"

She cut him off. "Your apology is too little and far too late. Don't bother."

"I understand. There is no excuse for my actions."

"Well, there's something we agree on." She curled her fists. How she wanted to punch him in his ridiculous clean-shaven face.

"It is true that my gambling debts had gotten out of hand. I overextended myself, got in over my head until there was no way out. The creditors were bearing down on me. Yes, I had a problem, one that I couldn't admit to you or to myself."

Angelique laughed. "You HAD a problem?" she asked incredulously. "Didn't I just interrupt your card game in progress? Seems to me that you still have one."

Jean Paul hung his head, "I am afraid that you are probably correct in your observations. I kept my vices well hidden, I suppose. But I do regret that I put games of chance before anything else in my life, including you, the woman I loved. You must understand that the pressure for repayment was real. There was no way to settle, especially with all that I had borrowed. When I had exhausted all of our assets, the threats continued. They were going to kill us, Angelique. Both of us."

"So you conveniently pretended to be dead without a thought as to my welfare. Did you not even wonder if your debts might cost me my life? Did you not stop to think that your creditors might show up on my doorstep to exact their revenge? No, of course not. You put your own self-interests before mine, which was a recurring theme during our life together. I wonder what other misdeeds you have in your shady past, Jean Paul. I do believe that you are capable of anything."

"I didn't think about that at the time; I was unable to think clearly. But I had no choice. And I just acted in the best way I could to protect you. I thought it would save you. "

"Save me? Save me? To live in a debtor's prison?"

"I hoped it wouldn't come to that. I knew you had friends and that ultimately they would help you."

"That's rather presumptuous of you, don't you think?"

He nodded his head in agreement.

"So how did you orchestrate this farce?" She demanded. "I deserve to know the details of your underhanded plot."

"I had made a deal with the undertaker," he said quietly, "I gave him my grandfather's gold watch in exchange for a pauper's body which he presented as mine. It was all carefully planned: the men who would find me were chosen by him. I didn't think past that morning when I rode away from you with a broken heart and a shattered spirit."

"Do you want me to feel sorry for you?" Angelique asked contemptuously. "I have no sympathy to offer you, now or ever."

"I regret my actions. I regret it all. I wish I could go back and change the past, but I cannot."

"Nor can I, I'm afraid," she said. "You were selfish and weak, putting your own safety first. You are a scoundrel, a fraud, and I find you utterly despicable. I can't believe that I ever knew you, much less tied my life, my heart, to yours. I was a fool."

"I just need for you to understand why it happened. If you can't forgive me…"

She cut him off mid-sentence, unable to entertain the notion of forgiveness. "And I just need you out of my life forever."

He sat in silence. A few moments passed before he spoke, "I had no intention of ever seeing you again. Please believe me, I had no idea that you were here on the island."

"Well, I am sure that it was quite a surprise for you. It certainly was for me."

"Is there anything I can do for you now?" he asked, his eyes were pleading.

She laughed. "Some magnanimous gesture, you mean? Are you trying to be gallant? Yes, you can do something for me. You can leave this island on the next departing steamer. And I never want to hear from you again. You are a dead man, Jean Paul. I have the document to prove it. And since I can't divorce a dead man, I will simply leave you to your self-imposed exile. I hope that will be even more difficult and final than a grave might be."

Before he could reply, she turned and walked out of the room, leaving him there to ponder her words. Monsieur Muggah and Andrew were waiting for her outside the door. She fell into her lover's arms and began to sob uncontrollably. And although he wanted nothing more than to beat the man to a pulp, Andrew walked Angelique to the quiet of the library. Monsieur Muggah entered the office to escort Jean Paul to the door of the hotel.

"Please, Monsieur," he said, "do not ever return to these premises."

Chapter Fifty-two

The chambermaid knocked on Angelique's door. "This letter came for you early this morning, ma'am," she said.

Angelique was puzzled. She couldn't imagine who would be writing to her and thought perhaps it was the kindly Mr. Wilson, the manager of the St. Charles Hotel. She sat at her desk to examine the envelope. It bore no return address or distinguishing marks. She opened it and began to read.

My dear Angelique,

I am taking the liberty of writing to you. I will understand if you choose not to read past this first line, but I hope that you will allow me one last opportunity to communicate with you, even in this one-sided way. I do not expect for you to ever understand what motivated me to do what I did. It was the self-centered act of a desperate man. And ultimately, I had hoped to protect you, to spare you. I need for you to understand that. But in doing so, I only brought you sorrow and pain. It is inexcusable, and I must learn to live with the consequences of my actions.

I am sorry for my choices and beg for your forgiveness. We once had a love that was strong and true. And for me, that love did not die. In fact, seeing you again has only rekindled the emotions that I have tried to suppress and deny all of these months. I cannot imagine that another woman will ever fill my heart as you have.

It is my intention to leave the island as you have requested. The next steamer, I am told, will be in port tonight, but doesn't leave until tomorrow, but rest assured that I will be on it. Upon returning to New Orleans, I will then journey to France in an effort to begin a new life. Come with me, Angelique. Let us use this new place to erase the past and recapture what we have lost. Would you be willing to try?

I am at Mrs. Pecot's Boarding House if you wish to reach me. I am ever hopeful that you will remember that we were once happy together and that we can be again

With all my love,
Jean Paul

Angelique crumbled the letter and threw it across the room. *How dare he try to contact me?* She thought. *He is not only a fool and a criminal, but he is also completely insane. Did he honestly think that I would consider for even one moment the possibility of going away with him?* She began to shake uncontrollably. Fear and rage rose up deep inside of her. He had left her powerless once, but she would not allow that to happen again. Ever.

She quickly left her room in search of the Countess.

"I have come seeking your counsel once again," Angelique said.

"Of course, my child. I am here to help, always. But first, let me say how proud I am of the way that you stood up to Jean Paul. You were courageous and strong."

"Anger makes one brave, Countess," Angelique said.

"Well, from what you have told me, I think you have rightfully put him into his place and out of your life."

"I had thought so, too, but I received a letter from him today."

Angelique relayed in detail the words that Jean Paul had written. "It appears that he is a man who refuses to die quietly."

"And that makes him dangerous," the Countess said simply.

"Those were my feelings as well. I didn't want to alarm Andrew or Monsieur Muggah. Men have a way of charging off in an effort to fix things, often making them worse in the process," Angelique said.

The Countess laughed, "That's true, my dear, but if one of them killed him, it would be justified. Besides, it isn't like you can be charged with the death of a man who is already dead."

"While that is a tempting thought, I would prefer for him to just leave the island and go to France as he says he intends to do."

"And when will he leave?"

"Tomorrow."

"Then, we must do all that we can to insure your safety. Give me your arm. If you will accompany me to my room, I have a little gift for you."

Before Angelique could protest, the Countess was on her feet, holding her hand out to her younger friend for balance. They made their way to the suite on the first floor. Once inside, she pointed to an oversized chair. "Sit," she ordered. Angelique obeyed.

The Countess opened her dresser drawer and pulled out a small velvet pouch, placing it Angelique's hands. "Take this," she said.

"What is it?" she asked.

"Open and see for yourself," the Countess replied with a smile.

Angelique slowly drew open the drawstring and gasped. She pulled out the small pistol and held it in the palm of her hand.

"My dear Countess. Where on earth did you get such a thing?"

"Angelique, I have been a woman of the world for far too long not to have such a thing. Now slip it into your boot."

"My boot?" Angelique asked.

"Well where else can you put it where it is readily available should the need arise? I already know that you can shoot as well as any man."

Angelique chuckled and carefully slid the gun into her boot.

"Sometimes it takes something a little more powerful than a sword to slay a dragon, my dear girl," the Countess said, laughing at her own attempt at humor. "Now let's go meet your prince and have a bit of lunch."

Chapter Fifty-three

"The wind has picked up considerably today," Andrew observed from their table in the dining room. "I want to take some additional readings this afternoon." He reached into his satchel for his pad and took out pen and ink. "August 9, 1856," he said out loud as he wrote. "My work here is almost done."

Angelique tried to conceal her disappointment at the mere mention of their parting. She turned to address the Countess. "My sweetheart is the consummate scientist."

"His work is important," the Countess replied. "Think of how little we understand about the weather. Perhaps someday we will be able to prepare for storms well in advance thanks to his research. I think it is quite exciting."

"Well, I appreciate the vote of confidence," Andrew said.

"Not many swimmers out. Look at the waves. I heard a few guests grumbling about losing one of their days in the sand and sea. So many of them are leaving soon," Angelique commented.

"One guest on this island can't leave soon enough for me," Andrew grumbled. "I'd happily throw him out into the sea to swim or drown."

Angelique reached over to grab his hand. "Tomorrow," she said, "and then he will be out of our lives forever." She debated over whether or not to share the contents of Jean Paul's letter with him, but knew it would only add to his anxiety over her husband's presence. Above all else, she wanted to avoid a confrontation between them. Jean Paul, she feared, could be volatile and dangerous. She had witnessed his savage temper during their plantation days when animal or slave didn't respond to what he called his "training." She shuddered at those memories. If they could just avoid him until they were certain he was on the steamer and on his way to New Orleans, all would be well. And since Monsieur Muggah had made it clear that he was not welcomed at the Oceanview, she felt reasonably safe.

Andrew nodded. "You seem to be in deep thought, my darling," he said.

"I was just watching the birds," Angelique replied, anxious to change the subject, "so many of them flying so low and gathering on the beach."

Jean Paul stood for a better look. "Hmmm," he said, "I have heard that low pressure hurts their ears, and they do this to escape the distress."

"I don't understand," she said.

"Well, low pressure means rising air, which signifies storms," Andrew answered. "I'd say that we are in for some rather rough weather in the next day or two."

Angelique smiled. "I love that you know such things. And I love you."

He winked at her. "The feeling is mutual, my darling. Now, if you two lovely ladies will excuse me, I have some readings to take." He rose from the table and kissed Angelique on the top of the head.

"He is a wonderful man," the Countess observed once he was gone. "I am thrilled to see your happiness, my dear girl. I imagine that you two will have many joyful years together."

"Do you imagine it or see it in that crystal ball of yours?"

"Both," she said with a smile.

"Anything else you'd like to predict?" Angelique asked.

"Sometimes life is meant to unfold as it happens. We are not supposed to see into the future; it might scare us too much, although I must admit this humid weather had made me a little uneasy," the Countess said.

"Sounds like a rainstorm is coming. Might cool things off a bit, which I wouldn't mind. Besides, I love the smell of the air after a good summer shower."

"You are always the optimist, Angelique," the Countess said. "It is one of your more endearing qualities. And now, if you will excuse me, I think I will take a little nap."

"And I am going to collect some sea shells. With this increased surf, there should be lots of them on the beach. I have an idea of a little project for the ladies. We are going to cover boxes with them. I can remember doing it as a child with what I gathered from this very island. It will be fun."

"Be careful," the Countess admonished.

"Don't worry about me," Angelique said. "What could possibly happen?"

Chapter Fifty-four

Jean Paul paced around his small room at Madame Pecot's. Although he had spent years trying to control his explosive temper, he could feel the anger welling inside of his very soul. Angelique was his wife, his property. They had promised each other eternal love on their wedding day, and he had hoped that his note would remind her of that. But she had failed to come to him; she hadn't even responded. He thought of her in the arms of the man he had seen her with at the ball. It was his influence, no doubt, that kept her from resuming her rightful place with him, her husband. If he was out of the way, then perhaps he could make her see.

The room suddenly felt confining. He hated feeling like a prisoner on this godforsaken island. Soon, he would be on the steamer and far, far away. And he hoped Angelique would be with him. He grabbed his hat and made his way to the verandah of the boarding house. Once out the door, he took a left, walking the path to the cottages which faced the Gulf. He studied the architecture. There were so many varied styles among them from simple Acadian to mini plantations. He thought of his own two homes, and the one belonging to Angelique, which he had foolishly lost. They were among the finest, rivaling anything in the area. The memory filled him with pride, which soon gave way to despair. Is it any wonder that Angelique was upset with him for putting their assets in jeopardy, for leaving her life in ruins? He thought of how he could make it up to her. A few well played hands at a high stakes card game, could reinstate his fortune and give them the life they deserved together. He had heard that there was a grand casino in Germany. The idea of a place dedicated solely to games of chance made his pulse quicken. Yes, he could take Angelique to Germany for a bit before they settled in France. She might like that. He had promised her adventure on their wedding day, hadn't he? Satisfied that he had a strategy, he turned to walk along the beach.

The wind was blowing hard and Jean Paul held onto his hat. But he didn't mind. In fact, he welcomed the breeze, which was a relief from the oppressive heat of the previous days. He had walked only a short distance when he spotted her. She was alone, bending as she picked up something from the sand. He watched with rapt attention as she placed the objects in a bucket, and he wondered what she was finding. Angelique never failed to enchant him.

She didn't notice as he approached. "Angelique," he called, but his voice was carried away by the wind. He moved closer. "Angelique," he said.

Suddenly, she turned to face him. The fear on her face pained him. "What do you want?"

"Just to talk," he said, reaching out to her.

"I have said all that I need to say to you," she replied, moving to leave.

He grabbed her arm. "Please, hear me out."

She tried to wrestle free, but he tightened his grip. "Let me go," she yelled.

"Not until you listen to me. Please, Angelique. I love you. You are my wife. Your place is with me."

"I am not your wife. My husband is dead."

"But look at me. I am alive. This is our second chance."

His eyes were pleading, but she was unmoved. "There will be no second chances, Jean Paul, now let me go."

"It is because of your lover, isn't it? That man I have seen you with has stolen your heart, hasn't he? Well, he can't have you because you belong to me." He was becoming agitated.

Angelique tried not to show her fear as she struggled against him. "I most certainly do not belong to you, and I never will. That much I know."

"You will always belong to me," Jean Paul sneered.

Looking up from his weather instruments, Andrew could see the form of two people in the distance. *Foolish people. They have no business out here in this blustering wind. I hope they don't plan to wade into the surf,* he thought, noting the strong current. He began to walk toward them to issue a warning. As he got closer, he realized that it was Angelique, and Jean Paul had her firmly in his grasp. He began to run, the adrenalin and anger fueling his every step.

"Let her go," he yelled.

"Andrew," Angelique called.

When he reached Jean Paul, he knocked him down full force. Angelique lost her balance in the scuffle and fell into the sand.

Within seconds, the two men were fighting, the sound of fists making contact with flesh drowned out by the roar of the sea.

Angelique saw the shiny object in Jean Paul's hand almost immediately. She yelled in warning as the knife made contact with Andrew, piercing him in his shoulder. He reeled from the attack and fell. Blood was seeping from the wound. He fought to get up, but staggered. After that, she reacted on instinct, the fury swelling in her Creole blood. Reaching into her boot, she pulled out the gun and in one swift move, pointed it at her husband.

The expression of alarm on Jean Paul's face seemed a stark contrast to the rage he had shown only moments earlier. He spun around. She was a crack shot, especially at close range, and she had a split second decision to make. Lowering her aim, she squeezed the trigger. The gun fired, and the bullet lodged in his thigh.

"You shot me, Angelique," he screamed. "Would you kill your husband?"

"I can't kill a dead man, Jean Paul," she said coldly.

Andrew struggled to stand, holding his shoulder.

Before he was able to move to her defense, Angelique cocked the gun again and centered it on Jean Paul. He staggered, moved toward her, and then reconsidered. "Please, Angelique, no. I beg of you. I will leave. I promise. And you will never hear from me again." He collapsed into the sand and then, with some effort rose to his feet. She watched as he turned, limping away.

She stood for a minute with the gun in hand. It was tempting to shoot her worthless husband in the back, to have him out of her life forever, but Angelique had her limits and a murder, even a justified one, was not in her nature. Above all else, she remembered to protect her immortal soul. She returned the gun to its hiding place.

"Andrew," she said, rushing to his side, "I'm here." She tore away the bottom of her petticoat and began to apply pressure to the wound.

"Angelique," he said, shaking his head in wonder. "You never cease to amaze me."

Chapter Fifty-five

Angelique and Andrew stumbled into the lobby. Monsieur Muggah, who had been stationed at the reception desk moved to their aid immediately. He helped them into his office and placed Andrew in a chair. "I'll go and fetch Dr. Hansen," he said. "You two can explain this later."

The bleeding had temporarily stopped thanks to Angelique's quick thinking, and when the doctor appeared, Andrew seemed to be doing better.

"It's not very deep, thank goodness, but my main concern is blood loss," the doctor pronounced. "Do you feel weak, sir?"

Andrew shook his head. "No," he affirmed.

"Then, I will clean the wound and bandage it. I must warn you, this is going to hurt."

Angelique held his hand.

Monsieur Muggah appeared with a glass of whiskey. "Drink this," he ordered Andrew, handing the bottle to the doctor, who poured it on the injury and bandaged it tightly.

"Now, you want to tell me what happened?" he asked.

"It was Jean Paul. I happened upon him at the beach. He wanted me to leave with him tomorrow, using his own unique manner of persuasion," Angelique said.

"He assailed her. And he would have probably taken her against her will," Andrew corrected.

"But you came to my rescue," Angelique added.

"Getting stabbed in the process," he said, "some help I was."

"Jean Paul played dirty. Don't underestimate yourself. You saved me," Angelique said, squeezing his hand.

"No, darling, you saved us both," Andrew said.

"And how did our little lady manage that?" Moniseur Muggah asked.

"She shot him in the leg," Andrew said.

"What?" Monsieur Muggah asked incredulously.

"Jean Paul is out there somewhere with a bullet in his leg, and I am not the least bit sorry," she said. "I sure hope that Madame Pecot doesn't mind a little blood on her rugs."

Monsieur Muggah stood up. "This is no joking matter, Angelique. We must put together a party to find him. I see this as attempted kidnapping, assault and battery. He must be brought to justice."

Angelique grew somber. "I suppose that you are right. Perhaps if he is locked away, I will finally feel safe."

Andrew looked out the window. "Weather still looks threatening and the sun will be setting soon. Do you want to do this now?"

"Absolutely," Monsieur Muggah said. "I will get some men together, and we will begin our search. And if we don't find him tonight, then, by golly, by morning light, we will begin again."

***

Jean Paul had managed to limp to a deserted area behind one of the cottages. The wind was blowing harder, and he shuddered in response. His leg ached; it hurt like the dickens, but he was grateful that his occasional cigar habit meant he had matches to start a fire. It was difficult and risky, but necessary, to cauterize the wound. The red-hot knife had sent him reeling, his senses heightened, but when it was over the bleeding had stopped, much to his relief. Thankfully, he had learned how to handle such situations back home at the plantation. And many soldiers live for decades with bullets in various parts of their bodies; he could, too, he reasoned. Besides, once he reached New Orleans, he could seek out a doctor. It wouldn't be long; he would be fine. *It could have been much worse,* he thought. Angelique had spared his life. How easily she could have pulled the trigger and ended it all for him. And he wondered if a part of her still loved him. He willed himself not to think of her or what might have been.

He knew that he had to make it back to his room without detection; he needed to get his money and the bottle of whiskey had had there. Then, he would lie low until the steamboat arrived. The past eight months had taught him survival skills, and he had become an expert at slipping out of dicey situations. But he was on the lam again, and he hated it.

He entered the great room of the boardinghouse, which was blessedly quiet. Climbing the stairs was painful, and he was grateful when he reached his room, carefully opening the door. He wanted nothing more than to down the bottle of whiskey and climb into bed, but he couldn't afford that luxury. Hastily, he tore a shirt into strips, winding them tightly around his leg, and washed the blood from his hands. He changed his trousers and stuffed the remainder of his belongings into his satchel as he searched for the pistol hidden among his clothes, placing it in the inside pocket of his waistcoat. He was sorry that he had not had it with him earlier; the outcome might have been quite different. Taking a long pull on the whiskey bottle, he threw it in as well. After retrieving the money pouch from under the mattress and stashing it alongside the gun, he was ready.

Slowly, he made his way to the dining room where Mrs. Pecot was setting the table for supper. She looked surprised to see him.

"Are you going somewhere, Monsieur?" she asked. "I had just set a place for you. Shrimp gumbo tonight."

"Yes, ma'am," he said, "And I do regret having to miss your fine meal, but I have been extended a kind invitation to stay with Mr. Gautreaux and his family tonight. They are having a dinner party. Since it will be a late evening, and with the weather unsettling as it is, they offered me their guest room for the night. And as my time here on the island has come to an end, I will be leaving tomorrow morning on the *Star*."

Mrs. Pecot's expression suddenly changed as she eyed him suspiciously. She was a smart woman, intuitive when it came to people. He hoped he was being convincing. He couldn't chance arousing her mistrust.

He grimaced in pain and then rubbed his shoulder as a way to deflect the attention. He prayed that his leg would not start bleeding again.

"Did you hurt yourself?" she asked, raising an eyebrow.

"I am afraid that I clumsily fell off the horse I was riding this afternoon. I am going to have a nasty bruise."

Her face softened, and she shook her head sympathetically. "Well, it has been nice having you stay with us, Mr. Smith. I hope that you will find your way back to the island someday in the future."

"And I thank you for your hospitality," he replied, anxious to make his exit. "I'll be going now."

Mrs. Pecot went to the window and watched as the man she knew as John Smith limped away into the twilight. *There is something quite curious about him,* she thought, *quite curious indeed.*

Chapter Fifty-six

Jean Paul had not thought past leaving the front door of the boarding house. It was foolish of him not to have a plan, but he couldn't wait around to see what the consequences of the altercation with Angelique and her beau might be. They would be looking for him, no doubt, and he wouldn't be caught like a sitting duck. His leg ached, and he reached into his bag for the whiskey. He took a big gulp from the bottle. The warmth spread down into his stomach, helping to soothe the pain. He headed for the far end of the island where there were fewer cottages. Nightfall was imminent, and he didn't want to be stumbling around in the dark. Relief washed over him when he spied a ramshackle shed, possibly an abandoned smoke house, set apart from the other structures. Once safely inside, he peered through the broken wooden slats, hoping to catch a glimpse of The *Star* as she made her way to port. It would take a miracle to get him onboard without detection in the morning. And he tried not to think about his leg. He would get medical help soon enough. Taking another swig of whiskey, he thought of his lost medal, praying to St. Christopher, patron of travelers. He had a long journey ahead and needed all of the protection he could get.

The guests at Mrs. Pecot's had just sat down to supper when the men appeared at the door. She rushed to greet them, hoping not to disturb her patrons.

She walked out onto the porch, rather than inviting them in. "Monsieur Muggah," she said, "What on earth are you doing out in this blustery evening?"

"I am here on a matter of grave importance, concerning one of your boarders."

Concern registered on her face. "To whom are you referring, Monsieur?"

"I think you know him as John Smith, but his real name is Jean Paul LaTour. Is he here?"

Mrs. Pecot gasped. "Latour? Isn't that Angelique's last name? Are they related?" It was a small island and everyone certainly knew the hostess at the Oceanview.

"He is her husband. And while it is a long, complicated story, you need only know that he is dangerous, and we must find him," Monsieur Muggah said. "Is he here?" he repeated.

"Her husband?" she asked. "No, Monsieur, he left a little over an hour ago. Said he was going to the Gautreaux's for a party. You might try there. He mentioned staying with them overnight and that he would be leaving on the *Star* in the morning."

"Thank you, Madame. We will. And if, for any reason, he should happen to show up here, please send word to us immediately."

Mrs. Pecot nodded, "And I don't know if this is important, but when he left here, he was limping."

"I imagine that he was," Monsieur Muggah said with a laugh, "his wife shot him."

The men left as Mrs. Pecot stood speechless, watching them walk off into the darkness.

With torches in hand, the group made their way to the home of Monsieur Gautreaux. They were not surprised to find that there was no party in progress and that he had not seen the notorious Mr. Smith since the card game the night before. They searched in vain for another hour until deciding it was best to suspend the hunt until they had the morning light in their favor.

Less than two hundred yards away, Jean Paul slept fitfully in an alcohol induced slumber, dreaming of sweet freedom and the beautiful Angelique.

Chapter Fifty-seven

"Red sky at morning, sailor take warning," Andrew said, peering out the window at the multi-colored sky. He studied the raging waters of the Gulf.

"I am surprised that there is any sun for us to see at all," Angelique remarked.

"It's the calm before the deluge. See the clouds off in the distance?"

Angelique followed his gaze.

"Looks threatening," he said. "Now listen."

"What is that?" she asked.

"Brontide," he said.

"I've never heard that word," she said.

"The low rumble that sounds like distant thunder from an undefined source," he said, a serious expression on his face. "Hear it?"

She closed her eyes to listen, then nodded. "Seems like storms threaten us from all sides, Andrew."

"One named Jean Paul and the other from Mother Nature," he agreed.

"And I don't know which is more dangerous," she replied.

He reached over to take her hand. "Not to worry, darling. Life is often turbulent. It might be stormy now, but it won't rain forever. And whatever comes, we will face it together."

Angelique smiled. "Yes, we will."

Andrew returned his attention to the sky.

"I can tell that you are itching to get out in it," she said with a laugh, "the weather does fascinate you, doesn't it?"

"It is unpredictable. Like you," he said bending over to kiss her cheek.

"But Andrew, you do realize that you must rest, don't you? Your shoulder is hurt, and you can't take that lightly."

"I am fine. You worry far too much," he said.

"And I have earned the right to worry," she replied, "Besides, do I need to remind you that my unstable husband is dangerous and somewhere at large on the island? I won't rest easy until he has been apprehended."

"Monsieur Muggah has that firmly under control. He knows this island better than anyone. There is no place for Jean Paul to hide where he can't be found," he said, wanting to reassure her. "I know that the *Star* was due last night. There was some concern when it didn't show, probably due to some hazard they encountered, so we can only assume that it is safely anchored somewhere. I suspect that she will be making her way to the island this morning, and Jean Paul will be anxious to get on board. He will be readily captured when that happens."

"I hope that you are right, but I would still feel better if you spent the morning lounging around like a gentleman of leisure."

"And I would prefer to spend the morning in your bed."

Angelique blushed. "You are incorrigible."

"Don't blame me. I am just a man hopelessly in love with a beautiful woman."

She reached for his hand, squeezing it tightly. "And I love you right back. Now, if you will excuse me, I need to get ready for the day. The ladies will need a little extra care this morning with all of this talk of storms."

"I think I will check the wind speed. Then, I am going to see if I can pay The Schlatres a visit. I won't be long, but I want to be sure that they are prepared for what might come. There should be some advantage to having a meteorologist in the family."

"Please don't go alone, Andrew. You are not cautious enough; it could be risky. There is more peril than a storm lurking outside."

"And I reiterate, you worry far too much," he said.

"With good reason," she replied, turning on her heels.

***

The hunger gnawed at Jean Paul's empty stomach. He was tired, thirsty, and hung over, a dangerous combination for a fugitive. The pain in his thigh had dulled to an ache, and he was relieved to see that it hadn't started bleeding again as he slept. He was tempted to down the rest of the whiskey but considered the folly of that and decided against it. Instead, he determined he needed a different course of action.

It was barely daylight, and he hoped to have a few minutes before the posse he assumed was after him would begin to search again in earnest. Peering through the wooden slats of the shed, he saw that the beach was mercifully empty. The waves crashed to the shore, breaking with a violent force, and he wondered about the recklessness of what he was about to do. But like most of his recent decisions, he had no alternative. Removing all of his clothes, he poured the whiskey over his head and was pleased to see that it had the desired effect. The henna started to release its color and the burnt orange liquid began to run down his shoulders and onto the ground. Slowly, he opened the door and made his way to the Gulf. He worried about wetting the wound, but found that the salt of the sea soothed it, washing away much of the lingering pain. It was hard to fight the waves as he submerged his head over and over again until none of the tint remained. Satisfied that he had restored his hair to its original jet black, he returned to the shed and quickly redressed. He stuffed the useless spectacles into his satchel and removed his handkerchief. Carefully, he folded it, covering his nose and mouth. It was a feeble disguise, but with the sand blowing wildly along the beach, it would be useful as well.

Jean Paul returned to the vantage point he had discovered earlier and surveyed the landscape. Still no sign of anyone. The pending storm had, no doubt, kept everyone indoors. Perhaps he could break into one of the nearby cottages, he thought. He might find a bit of food left by some of the inhabitants. But he considered the chances of discovery, especially if he miscalculated and found someone home, and decided against it. Out of the corner of his eye, he saw a slave carrying a basket. He was hastily walking, struggling against the powerful wind. Following the black man's path with his eyes, he saw him throw the contents of the basket into a corral surrounded by a low fence. He turned and quickly made his way back to his master's house.

In one swift move, Jean Paul ran to the pen and scrambled over the fence. The pigs squealed at the intrusion, but he shooed them away, grabbing the food from the muddy ground. He spied the water trough and bent over it to drink. Clutching the bits and pieces of the dinner their owners had enjoyed the previous night, he hurriedly made his way back to the safety of the shed. He ate ravenously, his hunger overtaking his sense of reason. *I am no better than the swine,* he thought and then laughed at the absurdity of his predicament. Soon, he hoped, he would be back in New Orleans, and he promised himself a hearty meal at the finest restaurant in the city as a reward for what he had endured. He was, after all, a fighter, a survivor. History had proved that, above all else, to be true.

Chapter Fifty-eight

Angelique entered the crowded lobby. The guests chattered among themselves, nervously discussing the black clouds forming in the sky. The ferocity of the waves had grown, and there was some concern that the tide would rise and reach the hotel.

"Appears that a bad summer squall is brewing," one of them commented.

"It will pass," another said, "happens all the time out here."

"But this one looks quite dangerous," a woman said loudly, "I am afraid."

Angelique moved to comfort her. "No need to worry. Our resident weatherman says it will merely be strong wind with lots of rain."

"Well, you may have faith in your beau's weather predictions," she said curtly, "but nobody can know for sure what could be heading toward us."

Smiling in response, Angelique simply said, "We will be fine."

But it was hard to conceal her worry as well. She was sorry that Monsieur Muggah and the men were out looking for Jean Paul. It was her fault that he was away from the hotel and his duties. He needed to be here, reassuring everyone. His absence was noticeable.

"And where is Monsieur Muggah?" one of the guests demanded. "What does he know, and what plans does he have for our safety?"

"He will be with us shortly," Angelique said in an effort to stall them.

"And what about the *Star*? It is our only way off of this island. It should have been here by now," another man asked.

Angelique felt the burden of being responsible for their welfare. Clearly, this was out of the realm of her duties as a hostess, and she was ill prepared to field the questions. She had no answers. In an effort to divert the guests, she suggested that they move to the dining room for a bite to eat or perhaps use the time for reading or games.

"Are you daft, woman?" one of the men yelled.

Her distress over the storm was quickly replaced by a fear of the angry group. She knew that she could not charm her way out of this and hoped that someone would come to her aid.

Suddenly, Andrew appeared by her side, and Angelique smiled, relieved to see that he had safely returned.

"Please remain calm. We are inclined to believe this is no more than a bad windstorm with accompanying rain. There is no reason to panic," he said.

"With all due respect, you are not in charge here. Where is Monsieur Muggah?" the man repeated.

"I am certain that he will be here shortly. Your safety and welfare are his top priority."

The grumbling continued as no one moved from the lobby.

Angelique breathed a sigh of relief when the front door opened and Monsieur Muggah and the men entered the hotel. He had barely walked three feet, when he was surrounded by the irate guests.

"What do you know of this bad weather?" one of them demanded.

"How are we going to get off of this island?" another asked.

"Please, please," Monsieur Muggah said in his calm demeanor. "I have spoken to several old timers as well as some of the fisherman. They assure me that there is no call for concern. Just a summer storm. I have been through many of these in my years here. And so have they."

"Well, unless one of these old timers is God Almighty, he has no way of knowing," another said, as several of the guests agreed.

"And what about the *Star*? When will it get here? And better yet, when can we expect to be onboard?"

Monsieur Muggah's face grew somber. "I am afraid that there has been an incident with the vessel."

"Incident? What kind of incident?" a man demanded.

The proprietor of the hotel took a deep breath. "Captain Smith waged a valiant effort to fight his way to the island, but as it grew close, the swelling sea, along with a sudden wind from the northeast blew it ashore near the entrance of the bayou. The *Star* has run aground, I am afraid,"

There was a hush among the crowd and then the chatter began in earnest.

"A wind strong enough to divert a ship the size of the *Star*?" a man asked.

"What is to become of us here at the hotel?" another inquired.

Monsieur Muggah raised his arms to get everyone's attention. "We are in the process of securing the premises. Most of the people in residence are doing the same. Let me assure you that I have built this place to withstand even the strongest of winds. In fact, we will be welcoming anyone on the island wishing to join us as we ride this out. I suspect that our numbers will grow over the course of the afternoon.

We have plenty of food and fresh water. And I happen to know that there are several cases of champagne in the store room that I intend to bring out tonight. Shall we turn this little adventure into a celebration of sorts?"

Angelique could see that he was trying to be cheerful and optimistic, but he was unable to hide the uneasiness on his face.

"Champagne, sir? Shall we dance as well?" one of the guests said mockingly.

"We might better spend our evening in prayer for our survival," a lady offered.

"You sound much like Nero, who played his fiddle while Rome burned to the ground," another said. And several simply nodded in agreement.

Chapter Fifty-nine

Once the crowd had dispersed, Monsieur Muggah entered his office and sat behind his desk. He was bone tired, but knew that he didn't have the luxury of time to rest. Taking out a pen, ink, and paper, he began to make a list of pressing details that would have to be accomplished to protect the hotel and its occupants. When he was finished, he called in the front desk clerk to dispatch his orders to the housekeeping and kitchen staff as well as the groundskeepers.

"Monsieur," the clerk said, "there is a group of people who would like to speak with you."

"Send them in," he replied.

Soon, his office was filled with men. "We understand that the *Star* is unable to leave the island. However, we wish to board now. If the water were to rise, then the steamer would be free, and we could sail to safety." the spokesman for the group said.

"Your theory is not plausible, I am afraid. My brother is the owner of the vessel, and he would agree with me if he were here on the island. Even a skilled seaman like Captain Smith would not sail into these waters, right into the storm. It would capsize, for sure," Monsieur Muggah said. "Besides, you are safer here. I hope that you see it to be true."

"We have weighed those probabilities and are willing to chance it, along with our wives and children," one of the men replied, speaking for the rest.

"I do think it is unwise. Besides, with the way the steamer is positioned, how would we even get you onboard? It is a question of logistics, sir," Monsieur Muggah said.

"Can you not build a gangway?" the man asked.

Monsieur Muggah laughed. "Do you think I have a staff of carpenters at the ready for such an undertaking? I don't see how it is possible."

"It is indeed possible. And I want you to make it happen, sir," the man demanded.

Monsieur Muggah rose from his chair. "And how would you suggest I accomplish it, gentlemen?"

"Accompany us to the ship. Do you have rope? Boards?"

"I do," Monsieur Muggah replied.

"Then bring it along. We will be hoisted to the deck, if need be. We are determined, as you can see. And as our host, it is your responsibility to see that we are safely aboard."

Monsieur Muggah protested once again, concern registering on his face as he followed the men out into the lobby where a dozen women and children stood in their traveling clothes.

"I ask you to reconsider," he implored, considering the vulnerability of the youngest guests.

"I am afraid that we have made up our minds, sir," the spokesman for the group said. "We will take our chances."

Monsieur Muggah shook his head. Fear had made them irrational, he reasoned: they would not be persuaded.

"Come then," he said, "but I must warn you, the wind is quite strong. It will be quite a feat to get to where she rests. And we must do what you require before the rains come." He summoned several members of his staff and slaves to help as they walked out of the hotel and into the turbulence of the storm.

Chapter Sixty

The wind shook the rickety shack and the boards rattled in response. Jean Paul tried to control his anxiety, taking deep breaths to keep the fear at bay. The storm, he knew, was imminent, and he couldn't ride it out there. But his mother used to say that every cloud had a silver lining, and this one did, for sure. Certainly, no one would be out hunting for him; they wouldn't chance it. He couldn't help but marvel at the irony. The very thing that currently threatened his safety had provided him with a chance to escape from another looming danger, being apprehended.

He adjusted the handkerchief around his nose and mouth and ventured out onto the beach. The wind was blowing harder, and he squinted his eyes to keep the sand from blinding him. It was a mile to the dock, where he hoped to see the *Star* moored and loading passengers. He dreaded the walk on his injured leg, but knew he had no recourse. Unfortunately, it would take him dangerously close to the hotel, but if he could blend in with the crowd making their way onboard, he would be safe. And he hoped that his jet black hair would be a diversion. Even if they were looking, the manhunt would be for a redhead who wore glasses. He no longer fit that description.

As he approached the steamer, Jean Paul was shocked to discover that instead of being anchored at the marina, it was resting at the mouth of the bayou and about ten feet inland. He marveled at such a powerful wind that could have had that kind of an effect, but having just walked through it, he fully understood its strength. Relieved to see that a crowd had gathered on the port side, he assumed that they had figured out a way to board, although it was obvious from the ship's position that it wouldn't be sailing soon. He considered his options and determined that if he was able to get onto the vessel, he could readily find a place to hide as he blended in with the rest of the passengers. At any rate, there would be food and water. The rains would be coming soon, he reasoned, and at least he would be dry.

He made his way to the line of people, surprised to see so many women and children among them. As he got closer, he noticed that they were following along, holding tightly to a guide rope. There was a makeshift ramp of weathered boards, which reached only part of the way up the side of the ship. A rope was being lowered from the railing and one-by-one passengers were hoisted aboard, much like cargo. There was chatter among the group, but the fierce breeze drowned out their words, and Jean Paul wondered what they knew that he didn't. He inched his way forward. When he was six feet or so away from the point of entry, he spotted Monsieur Muggah, who was clearly in charge of the loading process. Panic rose in his heart. He adjusted his handkerchief in an attempt to cover his face. Perhaps the man would be so distracted by the task at hand that he wouldn't recognize him. After all, his luck had held out so far, hadn't it?

The loading was slow. Women and children screamed in fear as they were pulled onto the vessel. Jean Paul tried to curb his impatience as the wind howled around them. When he was next in line, he averted his gaze in an effort to avoid eye contact with Monsieur Muggah. Just as he was about to set foot on the board, a firm hand gripped his wrist.

"Jean Paul!"

Unable to hear, he could only see the proprietor mouth the words, but he understood that he had been recognized. He struggled to wrestle his arm free and with the other hand, swung his satchel at Monsieur Muggah, landing a firm blow to his chest. He loosened his hold in response. Jean Paul turned and ran, the searing pain in his leg growing with every step.

One of the men attempted to give chase, but when Jean Paul looked over his shoulder, he was relieved to see that he had turned back to the steamer. Panic and despair engulfed him. Passing the hotel, he slid around the side of the billiard hall, pausing to catch his breath as he tried to formulate another strategy. It was then that he saw the weatherman, his adversary. Laughing at the folly of the man, who stood in the merciless wind, instruments in hand, Jean Paul could feel his fear give rise to anger. It was he who had taken Angelique from him and dashed any possibility for them to reunite; it was he who had caused the fight on the beach. He had a bullet in his leg because of him. Yes, this man was the cause of all of his troubles, the reason he was being hunted like an animal, the obstacle that stood between safety and peril. The hatred he felt toward Andrew Slater was palpable. He wanted him dead, even more than he wanted to save himself.

Jean Paul reached into the pocket of his waistcoat and pulled out the pistol. He was sorry that he hadn't remembered it was there. It would have been a better way to convince Monsieur Muggah to let him board the *Star*. It is hard to argue with the barrel of a gun. He shook his head, thinking of his hindsight.

Spinning the chamber, Jean Paul aimed the pistol at his foe. He pulled the trigger, but missed. As the wind howled around him, he pointed it for a second time just as Andrew staggered in the sand, shielding his eyes. He cursed, realizing once again that he had not hit him. Debris began to fly around the beach. He tried to steady the revolver to counteract the fierce gale and fired three shots in rapid succession, each one failing to make contact with his target. The rage within him grew. When he was finally able to balance the gun, he smiled, his rival firmly locked in the sight. Suddenly, the weatherman turned to adjust the apparatuses and the two men locked eyes.

There was alarm on Andrew's face, which quickly gave way to terror when he saw the weapon pointed squarely at him. Jean Paul took a moment to savor the power position that he was in as it was obvious to both men who was in control of the situation. Andrew swallowed hard, taking a step back as his assailant took a step forward. It was a delicate dance, and there was no doubt who was leading. Andrew placed his hands in the air, a gesture of surrender.

"Coward," Jean Paul said. "I wonder what Angelique would think if she could see you trembling with fear?"

Andrew stood stone still with his eyes locked on the gun.

Jean Paul took several steps forward, putting him at close range. He squeezed the trigger. The gun clicked. He tried again. Nothing. Confusion crept over his face. Had he miscalculated the number of shots?

Andrew seized the opportunity and charged, knocking Jean Paul from his feet. His fist made contact, and he angrily pounded him about the head, rendering him unconscious.

Grabbing the gun, he looked around for something to use to tie up his attacker, but finding nothing, he opted to seek help. The wind was blowing even harder. Andrew saw that his shoulder was bleeding again as he made his way to the *Star*, a minor inconvenience in light of what had just transpired. To his relief, Monsieur Muggah was helping the last two passengers board as he approached.

"Monsieur Muggah," he said breathlessly, "It's Jean Paul. I have him on the other side of the hotel by the billiard hall."

"What?" he asked, unable to hear over the roar of the gale.

"Come with me," Andrew yelled. "I've captured him."

The men followed Andrew to the spot where he had left Jean Paul. But no one was there.

"Where is he?" one of the men shouted.

Andrew looked around, bewildered. He pointed behind the building to the marina. "Let's look there."

The men rushed to the harbor. Pleasure craft and fishing vessels carefully tied to the dock in preparation for the storm, were bobbing like miniature toys in their resistance to the fury of the wind. They scanned the scene, looking for a trace of Jean Paul, but he was nowhere to be found.

"Look, there," one of the men pointed. A small boat began to move away from the wharf as a man rowed feverishly. "It's him."

Andrew raised the gun. He set his aim and pulled the trigger, but it didn't discharge. It was clearly out of ammunition, a fact which had saved his life only moments earlier. How he wished it had simply been a misfire and that one bullet would have remained for Jean Paul.

Monsieur Muggah began to laugh as the men looked at him incredulously.

"Do you find this humorous, sir?" Andrew asked.

"I do," he replied. "The fool will most certainly drown. Clearly, we can leave the punishment to Mother Nature, whom we can count on to release her fury on her overconfident and imprudent son."

And with that, the men quickly returned to the shelter of the hotel.

Chapter Sixty-one

Angelique tried to control her irritation. "You did what?" she asked, glaring at Andrew.

"These weather conditions are unique, like nothing I have ever experienced. Few men have. It was a rare opportunity, darling, one that I just couldn't let pass."

"It sounds like it was a rare opportunity to get yourself killed," she said.

"But I am very much alive, aren't I?" Andrew said. "Really, there is no need to fret."

"No need? There is a massive storm out there, and you could have gotten hurt, or worse. And then, Jean Paul pointed a gun at you, did he not? You do realize, don't you, that it would have only taken one bullet to end your life. And your shoulder," she said, looking at his blood-stained shirt, "you have opened the wound."

"It's fine. Besides, you have forgotten one very important thing," Andrew said with a grin.

"And what is that?" she asked.

"I am incredibly lucky."

"Oh, and what makes you so sure of that?"

"Because the most beautiful, fascinating woman in the world loves me."

Angelique's face softened. "Your flattery is lovely, but I am still angry that you put yourself in jeopardy like that. Promise me that you won't be so foolish in the future."

"I promise," Andrew said, putting his arms around her. "I never want to cause you unnecessary distress."

"Then, you are forgiven," she said. "Now, tell me again. Is Jean Paul really gone?

"He is," Andrew replied.

"How can you be so sure?"

"We watched as he fought his way from shore. It was almost comical as he frantically maneuvered the oars in an effort to get as far away from the island as fast as he possibly could. The wind will most likely be in charge of his itinerary. He may well end up in Mexico," Andrew said, laughing. "And at the very least, if he tries to return, theft as well as attempted murder charges would be added to those he already has pending."

"From stealing the boat, you mean?"

"Well, yes. I am certain that the owner of the water craft will not take too kindly to discovering that it is missing."

Angelique thought on it for a minute. "He is unstable, completely out of his mind, not just for what he has done, but to think that he can possibly survive out there in this storm when a massive vessel like the *Star* could not navigate those waters."

"Well, some people create their own storms, Angelique. Jean Paul certainly has. Whatever happens to him is simply a law of nature. Truly wicked people don't just intentionally hurt others, they take great pride and satisfaction in the pain they cause, while never accepting any responsibility for inflicting it. But eventually, that malevolence comes back to haunt them. We attract what we show to the world."

She held out her hand as Andrew took it in his, "Hmmm… That's certainly true, especially in Jean Paul's case. You are a wise, man. And I am incredibly lucky myself. Now, let's join the others. I think perhaps we have a reason to celebrate in spite of this tempest raging around us."

The pair entered the ballroom, where most of the guests had gathered. They were surprised to see that the atmosphere was somber. Monsieur Muggah had produced champagne, as promised, but no one appeared to be drinking it. The rain pounded on the tin roof and the wind howled as the windows rattled in response. Debris crashed against the exterior of the hotel and people jumped in reaction to the noise.

"It's getting worse, much worse," one of the guests said and the others concurred.

"I'll see if I can assess things," Monsieur Muggah said, leaving the room.

Andrew went to the window to observe the conditions. I fear it is a North American cyclone," he said, trying to conceal his concern.

"What does that mean?" someone asked.

"You may have heard the term hurricane. Strong wind, rising tides, and the chance of tornadoes," Andrew said. "It is a frightening possibility."

"It sounds more serious than we might have realized," one of the men commented.

"It is," Andrew whispered, more to himself than the group.

Angelique moved to his side. "How bad is it?"

"Bad," he said solemnly.

"And your cousin and his family? Are they safe?"

"I am afraid that we have a difference of opinion on that. He thinks it will be rather benign. And he insists that his house is strong enough to withstand whatever might come along."

"I hope he is right." She squeezed his hand in response. "I am glad that we are facing this together."

"Together," he said, kissing the top of her head.

One of the women among them pulled out a rosary and began to pray loudly. "Glory be to the Father, the Son, and the Holy Ghost," she said. "Lord, Jesus, please protect us."

Monsieur Muggah returned, his face expressionless and pale. "There is water everywhere. The tide has reached the front verandah, I'm afraid. Visibility is incredibly low, but it looks like several cottages have been blown down, along with trees. It is dangerous out there with roof tiles and fence parts flying about. But let me assure you that we are safe here. The hotel is very well-built."

"Should we move to the lower level," someone asked. "What if we lose the roof here?"

Andrew stepped in to answer. "There is a chance of that, of course, but if the water rises, we are safer on the second floor."

The crowd nodded in agreement.

"All we can do is sit tight and hope it passes soon," Andrew said.

"And pray," the woman with the rosary added.

Angelique thought of Jean Paul out in the maelstrom. He had brought her heartache and sorrow. He was despicable, cruel, and selfish. But even he didn't deserve to be met with such a brutal, frightening death. "Mon Dieu," she prayed. "Please make it quick and painless for him."

Chapter Sixty-two

Andrew looked at his pocket watch. It seemed like hours had passed as they sat huddled in the dim light of the afternoon storm. Some prayed to their God, some whispered words of love, some told stories of days gone by, some sat in quiet reverie, lost in their own thoughts. All knew that what they had viewed as a minor inconvenience the previous day, now threatened their very existence.

Angelique rose and walked over to where the Countess was sitting. "Are you alright?" she asked, reaching out to touch the old woman's hand.

"I am fine, my dear. I have lived a long life, filled with excitement. My journey has been a happy one. If this is my time, I am ready. I have a very handsome

Count waiting for me in heaven. I think I may be long overdue to be reunited with him."

Tears welled in Angelique's eyes. "Please, don't speak that way. We are not going to die this night."

"That is not for us to decide," the Countess said, matter-of-factly. "Only God knows the appointed hour when He calls us home."

Angelique nodded, "I understand your faith, but it pains me to hear you speak this way. You must know that if need be, Andrew and I will do whatever we must to protect you."

The Countess looked at Angelique squarely in the eye. "You must promise me that you will not. I cannot having you risk your life to save mine. The two of you have managed to find each other in spite of the overwhelming obstacles. You have a future to embrace. My wish for you is a lifetime of love, happiness and babies."

Wiping away a tear, Angelique shook her head. "I will not agree to such a thing, although I do appreciate your good wishes. My hope is that the storm will pass and tomorrow will find us safe and sound, laughing about this adventure."

"If it is meant to be, then so it shall be," the Countess simply replied.

Their conversation was interrupted by one of the guests, "the wind has died down," he said.

"A blessed respite," another replied.

Andrew walked to the second floor verandah, surveying the landscape. He swallowed hard at the sight. The water was still dangerously high with waves lapping at the steps of the hotel. Wreckage floated everywhere. There were bodies of the unfortunate, who had drowned in the turbulence. It was a gruesome sight. A few people huddled on the only high spot that remained of the beach. Strangely, the sun eerily peeked out from behind the clouds, setting in the greenish-colored sky.

He was soon joined by others. "My God, how could this be? It is impossible to fathom," one of them said, looking out at the carnage.

"The worst is over! We have been spared!" a woman exclaimed.

"I'll take that champagne now," another said with a laugh. "Perhaps we should have some music and dance?"

"How could you even think of such a thing when so many have perished? Are you that cruel and insensitive?" A man directed an icy stare toward his fellow guest.

The excited chatter continued. "When will the water recede?"

"Shall we make plans to leave tomorrow or stay through the week? When will we be able to leave?"

"How many others do you think have survived?"

"Can you see the *Star*? Is it still aground?"

"Thanks be to God."

But Andrew remained still. Darkness was approaching. He quickly went inside to retrieve his barometer and began to take readings. His brow furrowed.

"What's wrong?" Angelique asked. "You seem worried. Look, the sky has cleared. The danger has passed, hasn't it? We are safe."

He turned to her, enveloping her in his arms. "No, my darling. It is not over. Not by a long shot."

Chapter Sixty-three

A simple dinner of cold meat, bread and cheese was served in the dining room. The guests ate and then milled about the hotel, their mood subdued, but hopeful.

Unable to eat, Andrew sat quietly with Angelique and the Countess. Monsieur Muggah soon joined them.

"So explain what you mean by the eye of a storm," he said.

"I need a visual," Andrew replied and then he dumped the contents of the salt cellar into the middle of the table. Using his index finger, he moved it around into a circle and made a concentric pattern. Then, pushing the grains aside from the middle of the pile, he cleared the center. "A hurricane is a wall of wind that moves in a counter clockwise, circular pattern. Think of it like water flowing down a lavatory. There is this space of calm in the middle, which is called the eye."

"That means it is simply a lull, correct?"

Andrew nodded his head.

"How long do you think we have?" Monsieur Muggah asked, apprehension written on his face.

"We have no way of knowing. Could be a couple of hours, but it could be imminent," Andrew replied.

"Then, I must warn the guests," the proprietor said.

"As soon as possible," Andrew agreed.

Monsieur Muggah rose from the table and addressed those in the dining room. "Please, may I have your attention? I have it on good authority that we have yet to see the worst of this storm. The wind and rains will commence again very soon, and I ask that you prepare accordingly. I urge you to return to the ballroom. Bring pillows and blankets from your room as I suspect that we will spend most of the night there. As you make your way through the hotel, please help me spread word to the others. Time is of the essence."

There was grumbling amongst the crowd, who slowly began to move.

"Tout suite," Monsieur Muggah called. "Quickly, please. Your safety is at stake." He set out to find the others in the residence to warn them on what was to come.

An hour later, the wind began to blow with a mighty force from the opposite direction, even stronger this time. The water rose at an alarming rate. As the remaining cottages on the island broke apart, it washed them out to sea. Carriages toppled into the raging waters, and stables collapsed as the horses fought to keep their heads afloat. Livestock were tossed into the deep, sinking within minutes. Master and slave alike faced the horrors of the night, as the rubble heaved in every direction, impaling and injuring some, rendering others unconscious, their bodies floating out with the uncontrolled fury of the powerful waves.

Gale force gusts hurled the wreckage into the air, breaking several windows of the ballroom. As the huge waves crashed to the shore, it battered the hotel, which creaked and shuttered in response. The guests, unaware of the massive destruction occurring outside, cowered in fear, praying that the terror would soon end.

A woman began to sing "Amazing Grace," her voice soft and melancholy.

Angelique and Andrew huddled together closely, locked in an embrace. The Countess sat close by, her eyes closed.

"What will become of us?" Angelique asked.

The alarm in her eyes pained Andrew, who wanted nothing more than to spare his beloved the anguish and uncertainty that awaited them in the darkness.

"I don't know," he said, hating that he was unable to lie to her.

"If we are to die tonight, I can do so knowing that the last weeks of my life, although challenging, have been filled with wonder and love, because of you."

Andrew tightened his hold on her. "Please, my darling, do not speak of dying. The universe is not that cruel. Truly. We have not found each other only to be lost in a storm."

Angelique swallowed hard, trying not to cry, "I hope that you are right."

"Look!" someone among the group shouted. Water poured onto the ballroom floor. Panic erupted as people scrambled on top of tables and chairs, pushing and shoving each other in the process.

A woman began to loudly pray The Act of Contrition as others made of the sign of the cross in response.

Suddenly, there was a loud noise, like unbroken thunder, followed by the low murmur similar to the sound of a distant train. Windows shattered, shards of broken glass fell down on them like a rainstorm orchestrated by Satan himself. In a swift explosion of force, the hotel broke apart, disintegrating into the churning Gulf, hurling everything and everyone with it. People were knocked unconscious by falling timbers and quickly swept out with the current. Furniture tumbled across the broken ballroom floor.

Angelique could feel herself sliding into the abyss.

"Andrew!" she screamed above the clamor.

"I've got you," he said, firmly gripping her arms.

"I can't swim," she screamed as they reached the water.

"But I can," he yelled, although he seriously doubted his ability to navigate the savage sea.

Angelique began to sink, and he struggled to keep her afloat. Reaching down, he tore away her long skirt and layers of petticoat. It seemed to help as she bobbed to the surface, gasping for air in the process. She flailed her arms, trying to stay afloat.

"The Countess!" she cried, frantically trying to find her friend in the darkness. But she was nowhere to be seen.

Andrew reached out to grab hold of a nearby timber piling, possibly part of the foundation of the hotel. He pulled Angelique to his side, wrapping her arms around the structure. Removing his belt, he lashed her to it.

"Hold on tight to this and don't let go," he ordered.

"Where are you going?" Angelique yelled.

"To find the Countess," he said as he swam away.

Angelique cried. Terror gripped at her heart as she imagined the two most important people in her life fighting for their lives against the unrelenting tide. "Please, God," she prayed.

Ten yards away, Andrew found the old woman, caught between a tree and a window frame. She was barely breathing. He released her, and she looked deep into his eyes.

"Countess," he said, "let me help you. Grasp onto me, and I will pull you to safety."

"No," she whispered, her voice inaudible over the surrounding sounds.

He grabbed her arm, placing it around his neck, but she refused to take hold. Instead, using the last of her strength, she pushed away from him, and as he tried to find her in the darkness, she slowly slipped away, sinking into the murky waters which enveloped them.

Reaching out once more, frantically grabbing in the darkness, his attempts to save her failed as she eluded him. With sad resignation, he finally turned and with great effort swam against the raging current to where Angelique waited, still clutching to the piling. Relief washed over him when he saw that she was safe. She looked at him expectantly. He simply shook his head. She wailed, her cries of sorrow drowned out by the relentless rain.

The thunder crashed and lightening illuminated the sky. As Andrew surveyed the scene, his alarm grew. The noise that surrounded them was deafening. "Angelique," he yelled, taking her face in his hands, "we must move to safety."

"But where? There is no place to go," she cried.

"The *Star*. It is our only hope," he shouted.

"How?"

"You trust me, don't you?" Andrew yelled.

She nodded her head emphatically. "Then believe that I will get us there."

Chapter Sixty-four

Captain Abraham Smith prided himself on having a sixth sense when it came to the weather, but it had woefully failed him. He had navigated vessels through many a stormy sea in his career, and this one was the worst he had ever encountered. In hindsight, it would have been more prudent to have turned the *Star* back when the wind and waves had issued a dire warning the day before. But now, with the ship firmly stuck after running aground, he shifted his focus to riding out the storm and keeping his passengers safe.

He walked to the wheelhouse and, using his nautical telescope, surveyed the landscape. The water had risen at an alarming rate as rain pounded the island. The steamboat rocked in response as the unrelenting wind began to tear at the structure.

Darkness would soon be upon them, and the experienced captain knew with some certainty that the worst was yet to come. He called in the first and second mate.

"Get block and tackle, chains, crowbars, axes and hammers. Gather all available hands. I want this ship stripped of everything above deck level. Smokestack, Gallery cabins. Even the pilot house. Nothing that can be pressed by the wind should remain. We cannot risk capsizing in this storm."

The men stood, rooted to their position. "Captain?" the first mate asked, waiting for clarification.

"Are you deaf? That's an order. Now, move. Post haste. Time is of the essence here."

Captain Smith scrambled about the area, grabbing navigation maps and instruments, which he placed in a leather bag. He donned his rain gear and went out to supervise the dismantling.

His right hand man, Thomas Ellis was out on the main deck, taking periodical measurements of the depth of the water below. He observed that the *Star* was inching closer to the deep water that lay beyond and reported his findings.

"Order the setting of the additional anchor," the Captain responded. "And let's hope that it holds."

Ellis nodded in agreement, and then added an additional warning of the danger that the passengers faced on the cabin deck. "It will most certainly go, too. We must move everyone into the cargo hold."

"Then, see to it," the Captain yelled.

Panic ensued as the people made their way through the formidable wind and blinding rain to the hatch which led to the space below. Men aided women and children as they descended the ladder into the confines of the cramped quarters. Darkness enveloped them until someone lit a lantern, which cast eerie shadows along the walls. There was quiet among the group as fear gripped their souls.

An hour later, the ship was a shell of its former self. The process, aided by the ongoing wind had gone swiftly. And now, only the hull remained.

The Captain went to address the passengers.

"This is a major storm system," he said in his calm, authoritative voice. "I suspect that we are experiencing a hurricane and with conditions as they currently are, it would be impossible to sail to calmer waters, even if we were not aground. We will ride it out here. The *Star* is an old ship, but she is a fine seaworthy vessel, equipped to handle turbulent seas. You have probably heard the noise above you. We have dismantled anything that might put us in peril. Rest assured, there is no danger of us sinking or keeling over. You are to remain here for your safety. I ask for you to find a place on the floor and brace yourself for the intense motion that will inevitably come. And if you are so inclined, pray that it will be over soon."

He left the assembly and took his place at the top of the stairs. It was hard to see in the darkness, the salt and sand blowing about with such massive force, but the sounds of enormous destruction and muffled screams of anguish confirmed his worst fears. If he had been a believing man, he might have considered that he was in the midst of the end of the world as God released His righteous anger upon the earth. Suddenly, a deafening noise, much like that of a cannon, startled him. He moved to the main deck, shielding his eyes and holding tightly to the rail as he fought against the wind just in time to see the nearby Oceanview Hotel collapse in response. Staring in disbelief, he gave himself a few moments to contemplate what he had just witnessed and then, he sprang into action.

"How many swimming belts do we have readily available?" he called to the first mate.

"We have fifteen, sir," the seaman responded.

"Bring them here, along with all the rope you can find. We must try to save those in the water." The captain ordered.

"Aye, sir."

The forceful wind and pounding rain were merciless. Captain Smith tied himself to the deck railing and positioned the navigation lantern so that it illuminated the water below. Among the floating remnants of buildings that littered the sea, he could see people, some of them gravely injured, clutching to whatever they could to stay afloat. Many flailed their arms in a desperate attempt to save themselves from drowning. The bodies of the ill-fated floated along the surface. He could feel the emotion welling up inside, but refused to allow himself to be distracted from the formidable task ahead.

"Hold the lantern," he ordered the crewman.

"Tie the swimming belt to a rope and then to the railing. Lower it down," he said to another who complied, although with some difficulty.

Almost immediately, there was a pull and the men struggled to hoist a man to the deck as he dangled and swung like a pendulum in the wind.

In an act of sheer heroism, Thomas Ellis slipped into the turbulent waters below, stretching a length of rope to the small sand bar where several people stood huddled together. He secured it to a nearby fence post and, using it as a guide, led the group, one by one, back to the steamer.

Throughout the night, the commander and his crew waged a courageous battle, a vigorous tug of war against Mother Nature, who held the victims in her tight grasp. She had already claimed the lives of many, but the daring Captain Smith refused to let her have them all.

Chapter Sixty-five

Andrew reached out to grab a timber as it whisked by where he and Angelique remained, clutching to the piling. He missed it. "Damn it," he cursed.

"I don't know how much longer I can hold on," she said, shivering in the wind. The belt had slipped below her knees, rendering it useless.

"For as long as it takes," he said impatiently. And then his voice softened, "I'm sorry, darling. Please be strong. We just need something substantial to keep us afloat. I'll keep trying."

Suddenly the voice came to Angelique as clearly as if the speaker was right beside her. "You is strong, chile. Remember that. The Lawd has big plans for your life."

"Hannah," she whispered. She doubled her resolve and tightened her grip.

Chaos reigned. Flotsam was being hurled in all directions by the strong current, and debris was tossed about like mere feathers in the savage wind. The dead and injured surrounded them. He feared that they, too, might be hit by some random piece of wreckage, the force striking them like a westbound train. They had to move to higher ground, out of the water and closer to the steamboat, if they ever hoped to survive.

Andrew squinted in the darkness, wiping away the onslaught of the stinging rain and salt water. Sand blew from every direction, pelting his face, obscuring his vision even further. He struggled to see, but through the blinding haze he spotted a door, possibly part of a wardrobe, moving in their direction. He weighed the odds, and in a sheer act of fortitude, steadied himself, stretching his arm as far as he could. His shoulder ached, and the wound began to bleed again, a matter of insignificance, considering that their very lives were at stake. It took all of his strength to fight the resisting waves, but he reached out as it passed within inches of where they clung.

"Got it!" he yelled in triumph. "Grab on and get as close to the middle as you can," he told Angelique.

"I don't think I can," she shouted.

"Yes, you can. I am right here. I will not let you fall." He held firmly to the board as she flung herself onto it and gripped tightly.

"There you go," he said encouragingly. And he followed her. They immediately began to float with the furious current as Andrew tried to get his bearings.

"The *Star* is in that direction," he said, pointing to a place east of where the hotel had once stood. "To get there, we must kick with all of our strength to keep from being washed out to sea. You do understand, don't you?" He looked at her imploringly.

She nodded her head.

"Can you do it?" he asked.

She nodded again.

He pushed against the board and the two of them struggled to guide it. Salt water splashed into their faces, and Angelique coughed in response to swallowing some of the vile liquid.

"Imagine yourself to be a beautiful mermaid," he said encouragingly. "Kick that lovely tail of yours toward freedom and safety."

She furrowed her brow and flexed her legs in response.

Slowly, the door began to move as they had hoped it would and the lovers kicked in a synchronous rhythm.

Andrew sensed that Angelique was becoming weary, so to keep her distracted, he sang silly little songs, their words lost in the wind. The rain pounded incessantly; the forceful air howled around them. And although it was difficult, the constant motion of their legs never ceased.

Bodies and rubble floated past them. The turmoil of the churning waters was unfathomable. But the door managed to divert much of it, and miraculously, they escaped injury as they continued on their arduous journey.

Staring into the darkness, Andrew spotted a light in relatively near proximity. He hoped that his eyes weren't deceiving him.

"Do you see that?" he yelled.

"A light!" She answered. "Yes!"

The closer it appeared, the more rapidly they thrashed about, fighting against the swift current.

"It's the *Star*," Andrew shouted, doubling his resolve.

Time seemed to stand still as the pair fought their way to the hapless vessel. When they were several yards away, they could see the captain standing at the rail and the crew valiantly pulling person after person from the water onto the ship.

They pushed with all their might, narrowing the space between them and the rescuers. "Here," they called, waving their arms, hoping to be spotted.

As they grew near to the hull of the ship, Andrew breathed a sigh of relief. He imagined the swimmer's belt around Angelique's waist, and in his mind's eye, she ascended, much like an angel on her way to heaven's gate. She would be rescued, which was all that was important to him.

"Almost there," he said to her.

Suddenly, a wall of water appeared out of nowhere, taking them by surprise. The door jerked in response as Neptune unleashed his fury, pushing them back out into the sea.

"Nooooo," Andrew screamed in disbelief, placing a protective arm around Angelique. The force of the storm surge propelled them once more into the raging current and at least a hundred feet from shore. Soon, they were lost in the darkness that surrounded them.

"Hold on tight," he yelled, barely able to see her in the blackness that enveloped them.

She stared straight ahead, expressionless.

Andrew fought against the fear and weariness that overcame him, but knowing that Angelique was fighting her own physical and emotional battle was even greater cause for concern to him. He clung to the hope that the storm would soon end, knowing that otherwise, they would easily be desperately lost in the wide expanse of the Gulf. He tried not to think of what might become of them. But as a man of science, he clearly understood the peril of their situation.

"It will be over soon," he yelled to her.

She turned her head to face him, and he could see the look of defeat and resignation in her eyes. His heart clinched in response. It was a though she had emptied the well of strength and determination that had defined her, the resolve gone. More than anything, he wanted to save her, protect her. He had failed dismally.

"I love you," she said, her voice barely audible over the unrelenting wind.

"And I love you," he responded, wondering if these would be the last words they might ever utter to each other.

Into the night, they rode the merciless tide, clutching to the door until they had little strength left. The exhaustion was overwhelming as the line between life and death became more tenuous with each passing moment.

Although not a religious man, Andrew began to pray. "Dear God, please spare my beloved. If one of us is to perish, let it be me. I humbly offer my life in exchange for hers. Let her be safe."

He wiped the caked salt from his face and wondered if he was simply imagining that the wind seemed to calm ever so slightly. The rain had stopped. And he listening intently as the howling slowed to a less intense roar, the seas becoming less turbulent. Certain that he was hallucinating, he waited and watched and listened.

"*Is this possible*?" he thought. But an hour later, his observations had been confirmed. The storm had subsided, and although they still clung to the board, surrounded by water, they were alive.

His hope renewed, he turned to Angelique, "I think it has almost ended."

"Do you reason it to be so?" She asked.

"I do. At least, I pray it is," he said.

"And did you pray?" she asked, searching his face.

"I did," he replied.

"Then a merciful God heard both of our cries."

"I'll keep watch. If you can pull yourself further onto the door, perhaps you can rest," he said. He hoisted her up, and although she protested, she dozed, completely overcome by fatigue. Andrew remained on alert for dangers, which lurked in the still unsettled waters, as they bobbed helplessly.

When dawn broke the horizon, it brought with it the morning tide. The wreckage to which they clung moved with it, slowly, at first, and then, ever so urgently. Andrew spotted the *Star*, its battered hull resting like a beacon on the beach. And people, it appeared, stood nearby.

He reached over to touch Angelique on the shoulder. "Darling," he whispered, suddenly aware of the quietness around them. She stirred slightly, and then struggled to open her eyes.

"Yes," she said, her voice hoarse.

"Look there," he said pointing to the shore.

Angelique gasped. "Is it possible?" she asked. "Is it truly over?"

He nodded. Having kept his promise, he took her hand. Yes, they would live to see another day, and he was grateful. But most certainly, difficulty lay ahead. In fact, he feared that the nightmare of the storm was far from over.

Chapter Sixty-six

The water seemed to have receded as quickly as it had risen, as though Mother Nature had simply grown tired of her cruel game and moved on to other diversions. The gloomy grey of the early morning light matched the mood of those who had survived the terrors of the night. Dense humidity clung to the air like a velvet curtain. Some emerged from the *Star* to survey the damage. Most shuffled about aimlessly, calling for loved ones in the carnage that littered the landscape. Sounds of the wind had been replaced by the piteous moans of those who lay injured, their battered bodies bleeding, broken legs and arms protruding at awkward angles. And the heartbreaking keening of those in mourning added to the chorus of voices that filled the air.

Andrew and Angelique stumbled half-naked to the beach, falling upon the sand as they wept from exhaustion laced with gratitude. Weak and weary, they struggled to get to their feet as they tried to make sense of the scene before them. No structure remained; only the vastness of debris and bodies, which littered the landscape. The beautiful island, once a place for fun and frolic, romance and adventure, had become a death zone, a battle ground littered with the casualties of the war its inhabitants had raged against the elements. It was difficult to comprehend.

Angelique cried out in despair, "How can this be? Has God forsaken us?"

Andrew wrapped her in his arms as she sobbed uncontrollably, her grief inconsolable. "I know that this is unimaginable," he said, "but we are very much alive, my darling, thankfully uninjured, and spared by that same God. We will do what we can to aid the others until help arrives."

Wiping away her tears, Angelique nodded in agreement as she and Andrew waded through the sand and wreckage to where a group had assembled.

Thomas Ellis stood among them, directing the efforts. "We must divide ourselves into search parties. I am certain that there are other survivors, who must be found. Bring them here. It is best if we all gather in one place. See if you can find any fresh water. There may be containers filled with rain that are unpolluted by the salt from the sea. And food. Any living creature spared by the storm can provide us with sustenance. We will attend to the injured. Is there a doctor among us?"

Dr. Hansen raised his hand. "You can assess the wounded. We will move them to the *Star* as soon as possible. Is there a lady among us who can accompany him?"

Angelique moved forward. "I will," she said, grateful to see the kindly physician who had treated Andrew's shoulder only two days earlier.

"The rest of us are left with the gruesome task of burying the dead. Dispatch any remaining slaves to help. Look around for anything that can be used to dig a grave. I need not remind any of you that it is imperative that we do this not only for the dignity of those who were lost, but also for our own safety."

And slowly, as though mocking those who had survived the ungodly events of the previous day and night, the sun peeked out from behind the clouds, its cheerful glow an affront to their plight. The air was still, in stark contrast to the howling wind that had wreaked havoc only hours earlier. Immediately, the heat became oppressive.

Ellis shielded his eyes. "Let me remind you that the August sun is brutal. Those of you who have lost your clothing would be well advised to find some protection," his unspoken suggestion to remove what was needed from the bodies of the dead made Angelique shudder in response.

"Now, let's tackle the tasks at hand," he said, "And may God be with you all."

Slowly, the group disbursed to attend to their melancholy assignments.

Angelique followed the doctor, unsure of how she could be of service beyond trying to comfort those in pain, but she was willing to try. They attended to the injured, one by one, as he sent her out to find narrow timbers to be fashioned into makeshift splints and discarded cloth for tourniquets. The board that had saved her and Andrew was pressed into service as a stretcher and used to transport those who were hurt to the ship. Mounds of sand had packed firmly around the hull, providing access to the main deck, and Angelique momentarily thought of it as a gift among the devastation.

"Your help has been invaluable," Dr. Hansen said as he saw the last of his patients loaded onto the *Star*. I will stay with them if you will direct any new casualties to our makeshift hospital.

Angelique nodded as she made her way down the beach in search for others in need of help. And Andrew. She found him, digging a shallow grave for a small child, no more than two or three years old. Tears ran down his cheeks as he scooped sand with a piece of a wine cask.

"This sweet innocent babe," he said solemnly. "His life had just begun. The unfairness of it all is hard for me to understand."

"I know," she said, as she began to cry as well. "It is not our place to question, although it is hard not to do so. So much pain and anguish surrounds us."

He placed the tiny body in the hole and tenderly crossed the little boy's arms over his chest. Slowly, he covered him with sand as the two said a prayer for his immortal soul.

"Rest in peace, chèr," Angelique whispered, making the sign of the cross, "may God welcome you into His loving arms."

She hugged Andrew and reluctantly parted from him as they both had tasks to fulfill. A quarter of a mile away, she found a dazed and confused woman, babbling incoherently to the infant she held tightly in her arms. Her leg was firmly trapped by a large timber. Angelique tried in vain to free her, signaling to a pair of men nearby for help. She took the baby from the injured woman, and tried to console the wailing child, thinking back to her sweet Josephina. She choked back the tears as she accompanied the men, who carried the woman to Dr. Hansen.

"One is taken, another is spared," she observed, grateful that she had happened upon them.

Angelique was relentless in her search as she managed to discover several others who had been hurt, some pinned by the wreckage, some partially buried in the wet sand. She held the hand of an old woman as she took her last breath, praying with her in those final moments. It caused her to think of the

Countess. Oh, how she longed for just one more moment in the comforting presence of her dear friend. But such wishes were futile, and she knew it, not allowing her mind to take her to that place of sadness.

But there were also moments of joy that day. Angelique found Monsieur Muggah sitting against a felled tree. He was in shock, no doubt, with a cut to his head dripping blood into the sand. At first, he looked at her blankly as she spoke softly to him, but in a sudden moment of clarity and recognition, he reached for her hand.

"Angelique," he said, "you are here."

"I am, Monsieur. And happy to see you as well."

"We made it," he whispered.

"Indeed we did," she agreed. "Now, let's get you some help for that wound."

He nodded absentmindedly as she helped him to his feet and slowly led him to Dr. Hansen.

"I will be there to check on you soon," she said, embracing him as they parted.

Racked with heat, hunger, and weariness, she sat in the small patch of shade the hull of the *Star* provided.

When Andrew appeared with a small cracked bowl of water and a dirty tattered petticoat he had found among the rubble, she welcomed the gifts as though they were diamonds and gold.

"Drink," he said, and she obliged, swallowing the water in huge gulps. "And I brought you the latest fashion, too," holding out the garment.

Angelique smiled. "You do take care of me."

"I try," he said, kissing the top of her head. He sat beside her.

"What is to become of us?" she asked.

"We will be rescued, in due time," he answered matter-of-factly. "Look around you, darling, we are the lucky ones."

She nodded her head. "I understand. And I will be strong."

"I know you will," she said, reaching for her hand. "You have shown me that over and over again."

As morning gave way to afternoon, more and more survivors emerged from the sand and marsh. There were tearful reunions among loved ones, who only hours earlier had been presumed lost or worse. And there were stories to be told from those who had lived through the chaos by holding on to tree limbs and broken furniture. An entire family had scrambled into an empty cistern to ride through the waves in the giant barrel, all the while praying that it wouldn't come apart in the current, dumping them into the raging sea. One brave group had managed to find shelter in a corral for terrapins, fighting for survival alongside the big turtles, while another grabbed onto the arms of a whirligig as the apparatus, designed for the amusement of the children on the island, spun around and around in the unrelenting wind. People spoke of the terror when their cottages fell apart, hurling wreckage in every direction, of heroic deeds carried out by slaves, who risked their own lives to save their masters. And they talked in reverent tones of their losses, of friends and relatives, the grief and sadness gripping their hearts with painful sorrow. Although most were battered and bruised, they were grateful that they lived to tell the tale of the night from hell, trying not to think of what might have been.

"I wonder how many more might still be out there?" someone asked. There were countless unaccounted for among those who had been in residence.

"There is no way of knowing," another offered. "But we must cling to the hope that there are others."

"Yes," they all agreed.

Angelique looked at Andrew who wore a somber look on his face. "Thinking about Captain Schlatre and his family?" she asked, reading his mind.

"Yes," he said. "I inquired of Mr. Ellis and Captain Smith. They are not aboard the *Star*. No one I have spoken to has seen them either."

"Then, we will pray that they are yet to be found. They could have been swept beyond the island onto land."

He nodded in agreement, although she could tell that he didn't share in her optimism. His cousin's kindness had brought him to the island and to her. They both owed him a debt of gratitude. She whispered a prayer for their safe return.

Angelique thought of Jean Paul who had foolishly escaped in a small boat just as the storm was brewing. Her hope that he had drowned at sea was a stark contrast to the expectation that others had survived. She felt a pang of guilt as she tried to find some compassion for him, but after their troubled past, there was none. In a terrible twist of fate, the storm had possibly given her what she needed most to be happy, freedom and peace of mind. *But Jean Paul was much like a cat with nine lives*, she thought. And she would not rest easy until she gazed upon his dead body or saw his name on an official list of those who had perished.

"Do you think he is dead?" she asked of Andrew.

"Who?" he questioned.

"Jean Paul."

"We may never know," he simply said. "And we must be prepared to live with that uncertainty."

Angelique nodded her head in agreement, although the prospect was unsettling.

As the sun began to set in the west, Thomas Ellis addressed those on the beach. "Night is approaching and the mosquitoes will make staying out here unbearable. Please, make your way to the *Star*. We have some remaining food that we will gladly share. It will be cramped quarters, but after all we have endured, we should spend this evening together, survivors one and all."

The group boarded the stricken vessel and huddled wherever they were able to find an empty place. The sick and injured had been moved to the back of the hull, where Dr. Hansen tended to them. Food was distributed throughout the starving crowd, as all were thankful for the bit of sustenance. Once everyone settled down, there were quiet whispers among them. Angelique settled into Andrew's arms.

A voice broke the darkness. "Does anyone know we are here? Is there even a way for us to send word? How will we get off of the island?"

And the questions hung in the air for all to ponder as one-by-one they drifted off to sleep.

Chapter Sixty-seven

The morning light brought more challenges for the survivors. The stores of food and water had been quickly depleted the previous day as the rations were distributed among the many. One of the women prayed out loud for a miracle like the one Jesus had performed when he fed the multitudes with a few fishes and several loaves of bread.

"The only fishes around here are unfit for consumption," a man replied, pointing to the carcass of one that had washed ashore, rotted and bloated in the searing sun.

"We will most surely die of starvation and thirst," she wailed.

"Surrounded by water unfit to drink," he said, "in a sea brimming with food that we cannot catch. It is a harsh reality."

His words only caused the woman to cry more loudly. "What kind of cruel fate is this?"

The man shrugged his shoulders as he walked down the beach, bending down to retrieve a random piece of cloth that he tied around his head as protection from the burning heat. Far off in the distance, he could see a man leading a cow. They were headed in the direction of the *Star*. He rubbed his eyes in disbelief. "I have heard of men seeing mirages in the desert," he said out loud to no one, "perhaps all of this sand and heat has turned this godforsaken place into one." He stood riveted to the spot as the man and the heifer grew closer. When he was convinced that it was not a figment of his imagination, he ran to greet them. He was quickly joined by others.

"A cow!" one exclaimed. "Where on earth did you find a cow?"

"On the other end of the island. I suppose she managed to survive by hunkering down in the tall reeds, which is where she was when I spotted her."

"Milk is a good substitute for water," someone said.

"And the meat will keep us from starvation," another added.

Suddenly, the somber mood was lifted, as they patted the cow on the head, cheering for the man who had found her.

They were joined by the woman who only moments earlier had been in the depths of despair.

"It is a miracle!" she exclaimed, falling to her knees. "God has sent this to us, just as surely as the hands of Jesus broke that bread. Thank you, Lord!"

The men chuckled among themselves, but they bowed their heads reverently in gratitude for the wonder that stood before them in the form of a cow.

Chapter Sixty-eight

John Davis was a savvy businessman, accustomed to tackling problems with the intention of solving them. He hated feeling helpless, and he intended to do something about it. The first day following the disaster called for quick response to save the injured and bury the dead. The collective trauma that came with the aftermath of the storm was the most pressing issue. But with that firmly underway, it was time to think about survival and rescue. Close to two hundred people's lives hung in the balance, and he paced the beach as he went through the possible solutions in his mind. When he was satisfied that he had a plan, he returned to the *Star* to find Captain Smith and Thomas Ellis.

The three men stood on the main deck looking out at the adjacent harbor. "There were several boats in that marina before the storm. There must be one, perhaps buried in the sand or pushed down the island that we can find. Even if it was damaged, if repairable, it would be seaworthy."

"It is possible, although highly unlikely," Captain Smith said.

"I am willing to take my chances with possibilities, Captain," Davis replied.

"What are you proposing?" Ellis asked.

"Help me find a boat, and I will sail it to mainland to get help."

"Alone?" Smith asked.

"I am certain I can convince someone to come along. My friend John Miller might agree. We have both taken this route hundreds of times on our way to and from the island, although I must admit, neither of us were at the helm. Nevertheless, I am confident that we can do it, given the proper vessel."

Ellis pondered the idea. "It is worth a try if you are willing to chance it."

"I most certainly am," Davis replied.

Within the hour, a group of ten men, including Andrew, were scouring the island in search of a shipwrecked boat, capable of navigating the treacherous waters that lie between them and civilization. When a small sailboat with minimal damage was located in a forgotten cove, shouts of victory went up from the men as they set about the task of making the necessary repairs.

The two Johns excitedly made plans that evening to set sail at dawn the next morning. They had carefully mapped out the route with Captain Smith's guidance. He warned them of the debris that they would encounter and advised them how to set the sails to take full advantage of the wind.

"It won't be as easy as you might think," Smith cautioned.

"Nonsense," David said. "We will get through, and we will succeed."

"We will return as quickly as possible with rescuers," Davis announced to the survivors.

"How long do you think it will take?" someone asked.

"Two days, at most," Davis replied. "Prepare to be saved day after tomorrow."

The crowd cheered in response.

Angelique looked at Andrew expectantly. "What do you think?" she whispered.

"I think we may be staring at the face of overconfidence," he said. "But Godspeed them on their way. Right now, they are our only hope."

***

The spirited pair left at daybreak, calculating that it would take eight hours to traverse the sixty miles of treacherous waters that lay between them and the closest mainland. Twenty hours later, they navigated their sailboat into Bayou Leboeuf, tied to the dock, and stepped onto land. Miller kissed the ground as they made their way into town to solicit help for those they had left behind. And within hours, a large group had gathered at a nearby hotel to hear the men describe the horror that had befallen those who were fated to be on Last Island on August 10th.

Miller and David looked at each other with satisfaction. The rescue operation was about to begin.

***

In a strange coincidence, most likely guided by the hand of providence, Desire Comeau had spent the previous twenty four hours trying to hire a steamer to take him to Last Island. His parents were vacationing there, along with his five siblings, and when the storm had hit the Louisiana coast, he became concerned for their welfare, given their remote location. Regardless of what it cost him, he would go to them to see for himself, if for nothing more than to calm his fears. The arrangements had been made, and he met with Captain Atkinson of the *Major F.X. Aubrey* to finalize the plans at the same hotel where Davis and Smith spoke of the plight of the stranded survivors. He listened with rapt attention and overwhelming concern as he heard the stories the pair told. Finally, he could bear to hear no more and moved to address the group.

"Monsieurs," he said, raising his arms to get their attention. "My family is on that dismal island. I pray to God that they are alive and well, I must go to them, to provide assistance." He turned to the Captain, who stood nearby. "Many of you know Captain Atkinson. I have hired him to take me there tomorrow morning. We will gladly transport your relief supplies. And Monsieurs Miller and Davis, you are welcomed to join us, along with anyone else who can render aid once we are there."

There was talk among the men, who rose and then broke off into smaller groups to organize the relief efforts. They had only a few hours to gather what was needed for the journey and to determine who had the needed skills to make the trip. Emergency medical supplies as well as food, water, and clothing were assembled for dispatch.

And indeed, early the next morning, as the sun broke the horizon, the Captain ordered his crew to stoke the boilers and untie the moors as the rescuers set off for Last Island. Finally, help was on the way.

Word traveled quickly through the bayou country into New Orleans. Newspapers, which had originally reported the storm as a mere nuisance to the plantation owners, who focused on crop damage, recounted the harrowing stories of overwhelming devastation and a tragic loss of life. Friends and family waited for a survivor lists to be posted. The events of August 10, 1856, would most certainly go down in Louisiana history.

Chapter Sixty-nine

Angelique could not sleep. The heat was oppressive in the confined quarters of the *Star* and the smell of the unwashed survivors was unbearable. Hunger and thirst gnawed at her insides. It was difficult not to give in to the utter wretchedness, which was ever-present. She quietly tiptoed out of the cramped space, careful not to rouse anyone as she made her way to the deck.

The moon illuminated the predawn sky as Angelique gazed up at the stars, trying to remember the names of the constellations that Andrew had so carefully pointed out to her weeks earlier. Those moments of joy they had shared when their romance was just beginning were among the sweetest she had ever known, and she locked away those memories deep within her womanly heart.

Clouds slowly drifted by, their clean white puffiness in stark contrast to the filth and muck which surrounded her. She questioned if God lived there, high above the haze, in His heavenly home. More importantly, she wondered if He heard their petitions, their pleas for mercy and pity, as the desolation and misery grew stronger with each passing hour. With child-like faith, she began to pray, begging to be released from another night of uncertainty and anguish, asking for guidance and protection for her beloved, and finally, thanking the Lord for sparing their lives. There is always something for which to be grateful, she reminded herself; so many were not as fortunate to have survived as they had.

The morning sun appeared just below the horizon, casting a red and orange glow as it slowly moved into view, ushering in a new day. Angelique surveyed the landscape; buzzards flew overhead, diving into the rotting animal corpses that still littered the beach and beyond. She shuttered, wondering if she would ever be able to wipe the images of death and destruction from her mind's eye, the pictures so firmly implanted in her brain. Would they return to her in her dreams, the nightmare appearing over and over again?

Far off in the distance, she saw a group of men bending as they dashed from place to place. She studied them. Were they survivors on an early morning hunt for food? Focusing her gaze, she watched as they grew closer. To her horror, she observed a man dig in the sand to uncover a body. He pulled out a knife and swiftly cut off the swollen finger of a woman, pocketing the ring she had worn in death. Another rummaged through the waistcoat of a man, searching for money and his watch.

She ran to rouse the Captain. "Looters," she said urgently. "They are everywhere."

He and Thomas Ellis quickly sprang into action, their pistols at the ready. The others, suddenly aware of the commotion, wiped the sleep from their eyes as they shuffled to the main deck.

"What is it?" Andrew asked as he appeared at Angelique's side.

"The bandits," she replied. "They have come to steal, to desecrate the bodies, to rob us of anything that we may have managed to save."

Andrew looked around, the anger rising in his heart. "What kind of man would do this?" he asked.

"No man," Angelique replied. "You are seeing nothing more than mere animals, savage beasts."

Several of the pirates, brazenly approached the *Star;* their intention to board was clear. Ellis and the captain moved to the bow, and in unison, cocked their guns and fired. Two of the men, fell into the sand. They had joined the dead. "I send you to hell," Ellis yelled, firing again, mortally wounding another.

The remaining brigands, who heard the shots ringing out, made a hasty retreat, jumping into their skiffs as they frantically paddled away.

"Is there no end to our torment?" a woman in the crowd wailed.

"Today," another replied. "This is the day our Lord will set us free."

"I pray that you are right," Angelique whispered.

Chapter Seventy

Throughout the morning and into the afternoon, the weary survivors stood along the deck of the *Star* and positioned themselves at various vantage points along the beach, scouring the infinite stretch of water for a rescue boat.

"I see smoke," one of them exclaimed, pointing out into the distance.

Several people rushed to his side in breathless anticipation. "No," someone said, "it is merely a low lying cloud."

The dejected group resumed their watch as the sun beat down on them relentlessly, their skin scorched and burned from so many days of exposure.

Suddenly, Thomas Ellis cried out. "A steamer!"

"Is it truly so?" a man questioned, afraid to once again have his hopes dashed.

"It is!" Ellis replied as the ship grew closer.

It began to sprinkle, a light summer shower, as the crowd gathered in the demolished harbor. There were no cheers, no sounds of triumph, only the quiet hush of relief and gratitude as the rain washed over them.

The *Archer* slowly made its way into port and with some difficulty the vessel was secured to the few remaining moorings.

Desire Comeau was the first to disembark, scanning the crowd for his family. He wept with joy as he found his father, their joyous reunion witnessed by the group. But the others knew, as Comeau was soon to learn, that his mother and all of his siblings had perished in the terror that was the great hurricane of Last Island. Some are spared; others are taken. It was a lesson they had all sadly learned.

The captain and rescuers soon followed, carrying food and water, which they quickly distributed. They handed out clothes and blankets. The skies cleared.

"We made it," Andrew said, giving Angelique a piece of bread. "Today, we begin to live again."

She nodded her head. But the words would not come as tears filled her eyes.

One by one the passengers were loaded, starting with the sick and injured. The exhausted Dr. Hansen boarded with them. Then, the elderly, too weak to walk were carried onto the ship. Finally, the rest were escorted aboard, and as they stood in silent reverie, each lost in their own thoughts of home, the *Archer* pulled away from the island and headed out to sea. They were accompanied by a rainbow, which stretched across the sky, God's assurance that He had heard every prayer, every cry, and every plea, even those that went unanswered.

Chapter Seventy-one

Three days later, the carriage pulled in front of the St. Charles Hotel. The driver opened the door, and Angelique extended her sunburned hand. It was shaking as he took it, but he pretended not to notice.

"Thank you, Robert," she whispered, her voice hoarse. "It was kind of you to meet us at the train."

"Madame Latour. It is the very least I could offer, after all you have done for me. I will never forget your kindness," he said.

She simply smiled, turning to take Andrew's arm.

The door of the hotel opened and George Wilson rushed out to greet them.

"My dear Madame Latour. I am so happy to see that you have safely returned. When we received the dreadful news of the peril you all faced at the island, we were stunned and worried, of course. But seeing you now is indeed an answer to a prayer," he said.

"To all of our prayers," Angelique said.

"Please, please. Come inside. I know that you are tired from your journey. I have already prepared your room and moved your things from storage. I hope that you will be able to rest and recuperate here."

"As always, you are most kind, Monsieur," she said.

Mr. Wilson extended his hand to Andrew before Angelique could introduce him. "I'm George Wilson. Will you be staying with us as well, sir?"

"This is Andrew Slater, Monsieur. He is my fiancé. And yes, he will require a room."

"Then, it will be my pleasure to see to it. And if I may be so bold, let me congratulate you on your upcoming marriage. I am so happy to see that you were able to find some joy among the tragedy that has befallen you."

Angelique smiled. "Great joy, Monsieur."

"And I have arranged for dinner tonight," Mr. Wilson added. "It is my treat. You have much to celebrate."

"We do," Angelique said, reaching for Andrew's hand. "We most certainly do."

Chapter Seventy-two

Over the next few days, which stretched into weeks, the rescue operations continued as steamships and fishing boats combed the surrounding marsh looking for survivors. There were miraculous stories which surfaced of people blown as far as twenty miles from the island, who managed to sustain themselves on raw fish and brackish water, fighting the elements and relentless insects.

Lists of survivors as well as those who had perished in the storm were published in *The Picayune* as Angelique and Andrew gathered each morning to read through the names. They were joyful to discover that many they thought were lost had indeed been saved and mourned when they recognized some of the names among the casualties whose bodies had been recovered.

"And Jean Paul?" Angelique asked. The question hung in the air between them.

Andrew shook his head. "No John Smith either."

Angelique stared off into the distance. "I suppose his fate will remain a mystery forever."

Andrew nodded. "Unfortunately so," he said, turning his attention back to the paper. He shouted with glee when he saw that Michael Schlatre was among the living and much to his relief, received a hand delivered note from him several days later.

My Dear Cousin,

I have received word that you and Angelique made it through the storm and were rescued by the Archer. News of your safe return has filled me with great happiness as I spent many moments wondering what had befallen you. I prayed for your protection and well-being as I am confident that you prayed for mine.

I am certain that hell itself could hold no greater terror than those days we endured in the tempest. Tragically, my family has perished, a shocking reality that I am still yet to comprehend. I don't know if I will ever be able to forget the moments when I watched my children drown. It is a horror and sadness that no man should ever have to live to tell. Lodowiska, the love of my life, was swept out to sea. She was rescued by a passing boat, only to die the next day. They buried her in the water, I am told, which compounds my pain. Grief, I am told, stays with us forever; a fact that I don't doubt as I live in unbearable anguish.

As for me, I survived in the marsh after spending a harrowing five days, the details of which I shall share later. I saw ship after ship passing by, including ironically, The Blue Hammock, which I was unable to signal. Fate is a fickle woman, is she not?

Soon, we will meet again to raise a glass in memory of those we have loved and lost as they would want us to do. And we must continue to live in gratitude to God that our lives were saved. I can only assume that we have endured for a reason that we are yet to discover. Such things are part of a bigger plan.

With my kindest regards,
Michael

"What bittersweet news," Angelique said, reaching over to touch his hand. "How terrible for your cousin, and yet how happy you must be to know that he is alive."

"I can't imagine his sorrow," Andrew said solemnly.

"I am a woman well-acquainted with grief, Andrew. Losing people is the price we pay for loving them so much while they were with us on this earth. But it also teaches us about worth, reminding us of the importance to value every person, every experience, every precious instance of our lives."

Andrew smiled, "I am grateful for every day that I am with you."

"I am too," Angelique said, squeezing his hand. "But, you know, your cousin is right about something else,"

"And what's that?"

"We were spared, Andrew, when so many others perished. Surely, there is a reason, perhaps one even larger than we can presently comprehend. There is no denying that our lives have been forever changed, that we will always view moments in contrast, marking them as time before and after the storm."

Andrew smiled. "I agree. So let's look ahead. We must think of our future together. It is time for us to plan, darling. I wanted to surprise you over dinner tonight with the news. Just this morning, I received the telegraph that I have been waiting for from my employers, offering me a promotion, a challenging position at the Smithsonian that will enable me to use what I have learned about hurricanes, feasibly, to warn others in the future."

"Your purpose, perhaps?" Angelique asked.

"I hope so. Think of it. Imagine the lives that could have been saved had we known what was coming?"

"Ah, yes," Angelique said, "What a gift to the world that would be."

"But that aside, my purpose is to love you, to protect you, to bring you joy every day of your life."

"And you do,"

"Shall we consider a wedding in Washington City then? Our train departs day after tomorrow. Autumn is upon us. How about next month, among the splendor of the changing leaves?" he asked, "October is quite breathtaking in the North."

Angelique smiled knowingly. "How about tomorrow, here in New Orleans?" she answered. "I'm afraid that we can't wait," touching her belly.

Andrew moved to her side as he looked lovingly into her eyes. "Really? Yes, tomorrow, then. You will become my wife, and you shall make me the luckiest man in the world. For indeed, I most certainly am."

Author's Notes

Growing up in South Louisiana, specifically Terrebonne Parish, provided me with a rich cultural heritage. Weekends were spent at "the camp," which almost always included a boat ride out to Last Island. And as a child, I thought it was the most magical place on earth, a pristine sandy beach to explore with wild abandon, while the grown-ups fished in the surf. I can't remember the first time I heard the story of when it was a lively resort more than a century earlier, the holiday destination of choice for the well-heeled, the bourgeoisie, as the French liked to call them.. But those tales always ended with a vivid description of the devastating hurricane that whipped through the island, destroying everything in its path. The tragedy seemed to cast a somber shadow over the beauty of the place, but in my mind, it was all so dreamy and exciting and terrible.

My interest in the last barrier island never waned as I grew into adulthood and sadly watched it slowly erode into the Gulf, its vulnerable position causing it to grow smaller and smaller with each passing decade. I happily brought my own children there to collect seashells and catch blue crabs, to build sand castles and swim in the salty water. And I shared the history with them as well, a legacy passed on to the next generation. When I moved to Georgia, I had to visit one last time, just to say goodbye.

It seemed appropriate, then, that I chose this mystical place as the setting of my debut novel. And while I certainly felt a kinship with the island, researching the stories of those who lived, played, and died there renewed my enthusiasm for writing a story about what might have happened. My imagination took it from there with the creation of Angelique, a unique Creole heroine, unlike her compliant contemporaries. The story is of her journey, which led her from the plantation to New Orleans and finally, to Last Island.

We never see history directly. Because it is in the past, we can only envision what happened, based upon the tales handed down to us. But that is also what makes it so captivating. We study the documents and fragments left behind by those who lived it and attempt to piece together a puzzle, until we have created a picture of a moment in time. This is what I tried to do with the characters of Angelique, Jean Paul, Andrew and the Countess.

So yes, *Angelique's Storm* combines much of the conflicting accounts of what happened on that fateful day and night of August 10, 1856. It has been interesting to merge the real with the make-believe, to weave a tapestry of a period and place that existed so long ago. The Muggah brothers and Schlatre family did indeed exist at the time of the storm, their backgrounds gleaned from historical literature; the heroic rescue by the two Johns is accurate. And the *Star*, commandeered by Smith and Ellis, was indeed a hapless vessel caught in the crosswinds. But this is, most certainly, a work of fiction, a romantic tale of love and betrayal. Set against the horror of nature's fury, it is a saga of triumph of the human spirit through seemingly insurmountable odds. History is not only inspiring and fascinating, but it also gives us hope, doesn't it?

Connect with me on Facebook (Paula W. Millet) or visit my website. www.paulamillet.com. I'd love to hear from you!

Other books in the series:
Angelique's War
Angelique's Peace

Bibliography
Suggested reading on the history of the Last Island
Storm

Dixon, Bill. *The Last Days of Last Island*. Lafayette:
University of Louisiana at Lafayette Press: 2009.

Sothern, James. *Last Island*. Houma, Louisiana:
Cheri Publications, Inc., 1980.

Other books by Paula Millet:

Cosigning a Lie
Ovacoming: The First Teal Year

Made in the USA
Middletown, DE
23 April 2024